D1505172

THE AMBER EFFECT

RICHARD S. PRATHER

A SHELL SCOTT NOVEL

THE AMBER EFFECT

TOR

A TOM DOHERTY ASSOCIATES BOOK

THE AMBER EFFECT

Copyright © 1986 by Richard S. Prather

First printing: November 1986

A TOR Book

Published by Tom Doherty Associates, Inc.
49 West 24 Street
New York, N.Y. 10010

ISBN: 0-312-93024-0

Library of Congress Catalog Card Number: 86-50320

Printed in the United States

0 9 8 7 6 5 4 3 2 1

FOR TINA—again, and always

CHAPTER ONE

WOULD you believe me if I told you that when I opened the door that Thursday afternoon in September an absolutely stunning and stupendously shaped strawberry-tressed lovely was standing there naked? Right there in the second-floor hallway? Of the Spartan Apartment Hotel in Hollywood? Wherein I, Sheldon Scott, reside? And that this magnificent nude beauty was calling my name and pleading with me to let her inside?

You wouldn't.

Well, in that case, you probably won't believe the other wonderful things that happened either. But I think you ought to try. Because I would lay upon you—for your own good, of course—a truth known to the old wise men for billions of years. According to them: If you don't *believe* good things are going to happen to you, there's only a fat chance that they will.

Fortunately, I have believed in gorgeous naked babes for

1

half—actually, more than half—of my thirty years. That's how long it took—thirty years—before I managed to open a door and find a stupendously gorgeous and stunningly shapely lass standing there with no clothes on, burbling:

"Oh! Let me in! Are you Mr. Scott? The detective? Oh, of *course* you are. Let me in *quick*! Please?"

It was late afternoon, but there was still bright-enough daylight outside. And I knew I had never seen this eye-cooking creature before, because I would have had no difficulty in remembering the occasion. So where had she come from? Where were her clothes? How did she know my name? Why had she been hammering so frantically on my door while letting out little yelps?

All these questions occurred to me a bit later.

But it did occur to me almost immediately that because during my years as a private investigator in the L.A.-Hollywood-San Andreas Fault area I had sent a large number of hoods to the joint, and several much farther away than that, there were dozens of local slobs who sincerely believed a lot of very bad things were going to happen to me if they could manage it. And the more perceptive among them must have realized that the best way to catch me off guard would be by attacking me at my weakest point. Which, in case this is not instantly clear, is the same as yours. Consequently, the thought brushed my mind that this could be some kind of trick. A way to trick me into one of the local graveyards. A wonderful way to.

So I had my guard up. But not *way* up.

"Is this a trick?" I asked her.

But by then she was inside, and had slammed the door shut.

She leaned back against it, her head—covered by masses of hair the color of crushed strawberries mixed with a little cream and a lot of brandy—pressed against the wood, eyes the bright blue of those little flames in gas ovens open very wide and fixed on my face, tender-looking lips parted, magnificent heavy but high breasts rising and falling quickly as she breathed through the provocative "O" of her mouth.

After a moment she said in a rush, "You've got to help me, Mr. Scott, you've just *got* to. I didn't know what else to do, and I knew you lived here, so I just came here first thing, the very *instant* I could. You will help me . . . won't you?"

It was some kind of plot, all right.

Her last sentence was spoken more slowly, more softly, in a warm low lilting voice smooth as honey ice cream but several hundred degrees warmer, and the heavy lids blinked over those blue eyes, sweep-sweep of long curving lashes a guy could comb his hair with—my hair, anyhow, which is white like my peaked eyebrows and militarily erect, sticking straight up into the air for a mere inch.

Her last ". . . won't you?" came out like an invitation to an orgy with a hundred other people. She could not have made that sound and that question more seductively attractive, more half-growlingly appealing if she'd practiced it for hours in a bubble bath with Tarzan of the Apes.

"Sure," I said. "Of course."

"Oh, good! I just *knew*, as soon as I *thought* of you, you were the one."

"Uh-huh. What's the problem?"

3

"Well, there's this man."

"It figures."

"He just tried to kill me."

"He did? Ah . . ." I looked her over again, trying not to be obvious about it. "How?"

"Well, when I found out he was there, he had a *gun* in his hand."

"About that, miss. Where's this there? I mean, where in the world did you—"

"But he said he didn't want to shoot me because it would make so much noise. And it was supposed to look like an accident, anyway. Then he decided to rape me, and made this awful—"

"Wait a minute. You're making this up, aren't you? Ah, I'd hate to believe that. A man's got to have *something* to believe in—"

"I don't know how to describe it, but it was awful. He made this funny little sound, sort of like *ssscck*. And then he just fell over. So that's how he is now. He's dead, I think."

"I'm pretty sure I missed something along the way. Where is this guy?"

"In my apartment. Just down the hall."

"You mean here in the Spartan? Down *this* hall?"

"Of course. How do you think I got here dressed like . . . Oh, goodness! I forgot I was—you must think I'm some kind of freak!"

"No, no. I wouldn't say that. Now, about this stiff—"

"Have you got a—a robe or anything? Something I could put around me?"

"Sure. This guy's dead, huh?"

4

"I think so. He looked awfully dead, but I don't know much about things like that. You'd know, though, wouldn't you?"

"Yeah, I sure would. So he's lying there now, dead or alive, on the floor of your apartment, right?"

"Yes, but I'm almost certain he died when he fell over. He didn't wiggle or flop around or anything, just lay there naked."

"Naked? You didn't mention that."

"Didn't I?"

"If you did, I must not have been listening closely."

"Well, he is. That's partly what made it such a mess. I didn't know *what* to do. Until I thought of you, Mr. Scott."

"Good thinking. Call me Shell, huh? Well, I suppose I could go check this chap, see if there are any wiggles left in him—"

"Weren't you going to get me a robe, Mr. Scott?"

"Yes, of course. Call me Shell. Incidentally, I'm not a policeman, you know, just private fuzz, but if I were a cop, I'd think it was a *little* strange that this gentleman in your apartment appears not to have any clothes on, and you yourself are, ah, um . . ."

"Well, the way it was, Mr.—Shell, I'd been soaking in the tub, and when I came out of the bath—I just had a towel wrapped around me—there he was! In the living room, I mean. I told you what he said, he was going to kill me and all, and he really meant it! I got—frightened, excited, and that's when my towel fell off. And that's when he decided to rape me."

5

"That's when it was, huh?"

"He said if I was going to get killed anyway, what was the difference, and if I was cooperative—imagine, cooperative—I'd live that much longer. Anyway, that's when he took his clothes off, and for a little bit he just stood there, staring at me. With his mouth open. Like yours."

"Ah . . . mmm. Yes. Go on, please."

"That's all. That's when he made the funny little *ssscck* noise, and keeled over. Please get me a robe or something, Mr. Sc—Shell. I keep thinking of that man standing there, just before he died, with his eyes bugging and his mou—"

"Yeah. Right away. No sooner said than done."

I turned and stomped into the room farthest from the front door of my three rooms and bath, the bedroom. But once there I did not immediately seek a robe for my unexpected guest. Instead, I walked over the black carpet to the king-size bed and sat for a moment on its edge, and while sitting there shook my head back and forth like a silent, solid bell.

Damnedest story I'd ever heard. Dead guy, indeed. Naked, indeed. Made a funny little *ssscck* noise and just keeled over.

Well, I'd do what the lady wanted. I would check her apartment and look all about for the late rapist. Probably nobody there at all—nobody dead, that is. Maybe three guys with clubs and guns, and not *quite* enough keen psychological know-how about my weak points.

But, wow, I thought, they, whoever they turned out to be, had sure picked a marvelous weapon to employ in their attack upon my foible. That girl in my living room was truly one of the most ravishing, one of the most blisteringly lovely and

6

miraculously fashioned women I'd ever seen, and I've seen a bunch. Perhaps in my time I had lamped a few approximately her equal, but none measurably superior, none with a more harmonious and sweetly unique combination of face and form, bright glance and wanton lips, torches in her voice and sparks in her eyes.

Wouldn't it be great, I asked myself, if she's really telling me the truth, and I can dash to her aid and win her sincere gratitude and things? But even discounting the various little doubts I'd been experiencing, I would have dashed with some caution today, because this, already, had been an unusual day.

The reason I was home on a Thursday afternoon instead of at work on the streets or in my office—*Sheldon Scott, Investigations,* up one flight in the Hamilton Building on Broadway in downtown L.A.—was that I had only recently departed from the L.A. Police Building, wherein I had been thunderously chewed out by the captain of Homicide.

My best friend in Los Angeles is Phil Samson, who is also the captain of Central Homicide. Good friend that he is, Sam is also a very good cop, and a stickler for the letter of the law, with reference to which he often feels I do not stickle sufficiently. Indeed, that was what he had been colorfully informing me about once again, earlier this afternoon.

Even the passing thought made vivid before my eyes the ferocious picture of Phil Samson sinking strong teeth into an unlighted black cigar, burning holes in me with sharp brown eyes, hurling at me words that should have been considered individual felonies.

I am a six-foot-two ex-Marine, and weigh two hundred and

six solid pounds, but when I left Sam's office in the LAPD I felt—for a minute or two, anyhow—as if he'd sliced an inch and twenty pounds off me.

But it was merely a warning—final warning, he'd told me—and all I had to do was stay out of trouble for a while. And not annoy any more citizens, especially innocent ones. And make Captain Samson very happy. Which, even on normal days, wasn't the easiest thing in the world for me to do. Besides which, I knew Sam was trying to clean up work on his desk in preparation for a long-delayed vacation, commencing on this upcoming weekend, and therefore fervently desired that I not present him with any little calamities that might require his personal attention, certainly not for at least the next fortnight.

I shook the appalling image of Samson out of my head and let the much lovelier view of my unexpected visitor enter, then got up and walked to my bedroom closet. I'd been wearing canary-yellow slacks and soft-soled shoes, with a white knit short-sleeved sport shirt, so I grabbed a white loafer jacket and slipped it on, then stepped to the dresser.

My gun harness was there, where I'd left it earlier. I slipped my Colt .38 Special from its clamshell holster, dropped the revolver into the right-hand pocket of my jacket, moved back to the closet. A few seconds later I walked out of the bedroom carrying a blue robe for my guest. A thin blue robe. For which I'd lost the belt somewhere.

As I strolled back into the living room, my guest was sitting with her back to me on a big leather hassock before the chocolate-brown divan to my left. She was not, I was pleased to note, staring with a dubious expression at "Amelia" on the wall above my fake fireplace.

Amelia is a large and colorful nude done in bright oils, perhaps a bit fleshy, even a mite bawdy, and some babes appear to become less than thrilled upon lamping her. This one, however, was gazing with apparent interest in the other direction, at my two tanks of tropical fish in the corner of the living room.

That gave her a few more points in my book, as did her reaction when I stopped before her and handed her the blue robe. She merely said, "Thank you, Shell," and stood up, shrugging into the robe like a gal slipping a coat on over her sweater and blouse and overalls.

"Well," I said when that was done, "well. Well, I guess we're ready to go. By the way, miss, what's your name?"

"Aralia. Aralia Fields."

"Splendid. Which apartment is yours?"

"Two-eighteen."

Since I am in two-twelve, that made it only three doors away. "I'll find it," I said, smiling, as if I had not a care in the world.

She smiled, too.

So, smiling together, we went out of my apartment and down the hall a few paces to 218.

The door was unlocked, slightly ajar. We went inside, me first, hand in coat pocket, gripping the butt of my gun.

Inside, I glanced around. Setup the same as my own apartment: living room here, small kitchenette ahead on the left, bath beyond it, bedroom all the way back, its door open. Large, fluffy-cushioned purple couch placed at an angle on our right, about where the chocolate-brown divan is in my living room.

But here, a few feet from the couch, approximately where my big leather hassock rested down the hall in 212, a blob of white. A bath towel, crumpled. And a yard from it . . .

"How about that?" I said. "It sure looks like there's a dead guy in here."

CHAPTER TWO

"WELL, of *course* there is," Aralia said from behind me. "I told you—"

"Yeah. Hold it a shake."

I gave the apartment a quick prowl, then came back into the living room and looked down at the brawny, thick-muscled, hairy-chested guy motionless on the floor. I knelt by him, felt for the pulse in his neck, then stood up again.

So far, Aralia Fields was batting a thousand.

There was, indeed, a man sprawled on the carpet, and he was naked, absolutely without a stitch. He was still fairly warm, but he would never get any warmer.

"Who is the guy?" I asked Aralia. "You know him?"

"No. I don't have any idea, I never saw him before. Doesn't he look awful, lying there all sort of waxy?"

"Aralia, that's no way to talk about . . . Yeah, he does look pretty pasty at that. Must not have got out in the sun much. I guess those are his clothes." I pointed toward some garments scattered on the carpet near the wall.

11

"Yes. He just threw them away. Like they were hot or something."

"Probably were. Well, maybe he's got a wallet in his coat—there. Or his pants—there. Pink shorts, why would a big husky guy like this cat wear pink shorts? You don't need to answer that. Yeah, here it is."

I'd found a billfold in his inside coat pocket by then. A thin job, shiny-new, expensive, made of tough alligator hide. The coat itself was lightweight, a rich brown, very soft fuzzy fabric. "Our boy must have had a little money—yeah, bunch of hundred-dollar bills in his wallet, along with some small stuff. Like twenties, fifties."

The dead man's trousers were gold-tinted beige, woven brown leather belt still in the loops. A hip holster was on the belt. Not in the holster, but on the carpet near one alligator-leather shoe, was a .357 Magnum, well worn, not new.

Squatted on the floor, I said, "Looks like this guy was serious, all right."

"He *was* serious." Aralia's bright blue eyes widened again, flashed a spark or two. "You should have seen him. I *did* see him, you know. And, believe me, Shell, he was . . . serious. A girl can tell."

"Yes, I, ah, was thinking about this here gun here."

"That was the last thing he got rid of. First his clothes, even his shoes and socks—why would he take off his socks?"

"Beats me. I suppose he . . . is it important?"

"Anyway, when he had everything off, but still had that ugly thing in his hand, that awful gun, he just threw the gun away, too. And then he stared at me, you know, and sort of advanced upon me, his intent unmistakably clear."

"Well put. Then what?"

"That's all. Then he got all rigid, I mean all over, and fell down. Right where he is now."

"O.K. Now, we're up the point where he conked out. Did he say anything significant just before that?"

"Like what?"

"Like . . . help? I'd like a glass of water? *Ack?*"

"Are you all right, Shell?"

"Of *course*—I am pretending I'm *him*. I'm probing for clues."

"Oh, did he say anything—intelligible, just before he died? No. Just toppled over, and all the air went out of him in a whoosh. And didn't come back."

"Uh-huh. Before he keeled over, did his face get horribly contorted, or purple, anything like that, as if he was having a heart attack, or was painfully constipated, or—"

"A little. But I didn't think he was dying then. I thought he was just . . . well, sometimes when men see me without anything on, like I was—for the first time, I mean—they make funny little faces. And, oh, sort of gurgle or make noises I can't translate in words."

"Well, let's say he died of a heart attack then, so he wasn't poisoned or bludgeoned—"

"Poisoned? How would he die from poison—or bludgeon—here in my—"

I didn't hear the rest of it. I'd been poking carefully through the wallet and was looking at the dead man's driver's license: Edward Brett, 1428 West Hyacinth Drive, Hollywood, California. He was—had been—thirty-eight years old, five feet, eleven inches tall, weight one-eighty, eyes brown, hair brown, complexion pale. . . .

I straightened up off my haunches, thumped the heel of one hand against my forehead.

"What's the matter?" Aralia asked me.

"If this guy came here to kill you, we may assume with some confidence that he didn't walk over. So his car should be around here somewhere. There's also good chance he wasn't alone."

She was nodding. "Of course. I didn't think of that."

I walked past her, stopped with my hand on the doorknob. "Lock this until I get back."

I trotted down to the lobby. The Spartan Apartment Hotel faces North Rossmore and the Wilshire Country Club's green acreage across the street, but I didn't go out that way. Instead, I went through the rear exit, moved at a brisk walk past enclosed parking spaces and garage, on up to the alley's end at Rosewood Avenue, and then turned left, walked the few yards to Rossmore.

Standing at the intersection and looking back toward the hotel, I could see only two cars, both parked at the curb on this side of the street. And there was only one person in view, a man, tall and thin, about fifty feet away, walking up the sidewalk toward me.

It was that quiet predusk hour, with plenty of light to see by but a softness in the air, much cooler than it had been an hour before. The nearer of the two cars was a blue Mercury with paint scraped from one front fender. As I walked toward it, the man stopped on the sidewalk, fumbled in his pocket, and pulled out a pack of cigarettes.

I checked the Mercury's registration. It belonged to a woman, Mrs. Eleanor Wessen, address nearby on North Rossmore. It smelled of leaking oil, perfume, and powder. When I stepped back onto the walk the man was puffing on his smoke, strolling this way again, long legs swinging, shoes scuffing against the cement, making a wispy scraping sound.

When we were a yard apart I stopped and asked, "I beg your pardon, but is that your car?" I nodded toward the year-old but polished and gleaming gray Lincoln Continental ahead, twenty yards this side of the Spartan's entrance.

He stopped, blinked at me from small dark eyes. Then he glanced at the sedan, back to me. "Wish it was." He smiled a thin, not overly joyous smile. But that was all he said.

"Do you live around here, sir?"

The straight black brows twitched down over his eyes, rose slowly. "Yes. At the Canterbury." He paused, gazing steadily at me. "My wife and I . . ."

The Canterbury was a new condominium complex little more than a block from Rossmore on Beverly Boulevard. Could be. Possibly the man was a ladies' underwear salesman, getting a few breaths of pollution while his wife took dinner out of the freezer and started melting it. But there was something odd about this guy.

He was around forty, maybe a year or two older, and even taller than I, probably six-three or -four. But his eyes were level with mine because he slumped, sagged, as if the little flesh he had was loose on thin bones. And his neck stayed bent forward slightly, lowering his head even more, much as a vulture's neck curves and lets its head slope forward.

15

All things together, the guy wasn't exactly standing there in a snappily erect military posture; it was more as if most of his muscles were at ease, and a few of them possibly even AWOL. The left side of his face was slightly larger than the right, or appeared so. Not much, only a little, and it probably wasn't, really. He was just . . . odd.

He sucked on his cigarette, held in the smoke so long that when he exhaled, very little of it came back out.

"Why do you ask?" he said softly.

"I expected to meet a guy here. Thought maybe it was you."

"What was his name?"

"I don't know yet."

Apparently he failed to find that curious. At least, he didn't make any comment.

I said, "Would you mind telling me where you were going?"

If someone had asked me that, I very likely would have said I minded. But this one merely replied, "I'm walking my dog."

I actually started to look around for the mutt, then noticed, again, that thin juiceless smile. A smart-ass.

"Why, of course," I said jovially. "Taking a leak on your pants leg, isn't he?"

It was my most rewarding moment of the day—with him, that is—when he started to look down, caught himself, stared back at me again. But what then happened to his chops, his eyes, his expression, might best have been characterized as ominous. The eyes, small to begin with, got about the size of dried black-eyed peas, the lips thinned still more, and his entire face seemed to get—cold. Very cold. As if, should you wet a finger and touch him with it anywhere in that area, even on the tip of his nose, it would stick there until it thawed.

While he was presumably off balance, I threw a last quick one at him. He wore a dark suit, loose-fitting coat, but I got the impression it was—somewhat like the barely perceptible lopsidedness of his face—not so loose on the left. Filled out a bit more there at the armpit, where a man might carry a gun, if he ever carried a gun.

So as he said gently, "Good evening," and started to walk past me, I stabbed a finger at the left side of his chest, not touching him, and said quickly, "By the way, is that bulge a heat?"

There was no delay, no hesitation. Just "What's a bulge?" as he moved past me, long legs swinging, shoes scraping the cement.

So he sold ladies' underwear, did he?

I let him go. Felt a small chilliness behind my ears. But let him go. The Lincoln was registered to one Gunnar Lindstrom, of West L.A. My smart-ass acquaintance didn't look like a Lindstrom. I checked the plates, made a note of the number.

The door of Apartment 218 swung open mere seconds after I knocked. Aralia smiled out at me, looking even more radiantly gorgeous than when I'd left, if that was possible, and I decided it was possible.

"I'm the dead guy's partner," I said cheerfully, aiming my finger at her and wiggling my thumb. "And I came here to

kill you. Bang. Thanks for opening the door like the sweet
trusting soul you are. Bang.''

She blinked, then put the smile back on. "Thank God,"
she said. "I was afraid you came here to rape me."

What the hell was going on around here? Did everybody
have to top me? "Don't be a smart-a—don't be stupid," I
grumbled sourly. "I just came here to bang you."

"Well, you might as well come in then," she said. But
after a moment she sobered. "I do see what you mean, Shell.
I just didn't think. I can't get used to the idea that anybody
would really want to *kill* me."

I nodded, silently, as I went inside. Recent events had
been unique enough in my experience that I hadn't gotten
around to wondering much about that myself. I noticed that
while I was gone Aralia had draped a blanket over the body.

I said to her, "We'd better start at the beginning and go
over this whole thing again, but first things first. Which
means I call the cops." I spotted the phone on a small table
in the corner, dialed the complaint board, told the answering
officer who and where I was, and filled him in. I told him
about the man I'd briefly spoken to, gave him the description
of both cars parked on Rossmore, and hung up.

Aralia was sitting on the purple couch by then, and when I
joined her there she asked me, "Did you see somebody down
on the street?"

"Yeah, a weird character. But just because he looks like a
guy who picnics in cemeteries doesn't mean there's anything
wrong with him. I probably annoyed him as much as I could
afford to—especially if he's a run-of-the-mill taxpayer. Any
more, and word of my terrorizing innocent citizens might

have reached my old buddy, Samson, who already today has chewed—warned me about bugging the populace, in a convincing way he has.''

"Samson?''

"Captain of Central Homicide, downtown. Good friend, but he's become a mite annoyed with me lately, and with Sam a mite is more than plenty.''

"What did you do?''

"A muscle-bound hood, ex-pug and ex-con, beat up a client of mine. Smashed him around pretty good, put him in the hospital. I tailed the mug to a house on the corner of Fletcher Drive and Vista Street. At least, that's where he disappeared. So I crashed into the place, gun in hand, gnashing my teeth and all. Turns out he was in the house next door, *not* the one on the corner.''

"Golly, what did you do then?''

"Well, since the nice old couple who lived there were entertaining four invalid friends of theirs, all recovering from severe heart attacks, and I made a bit of racket kicking the door in, and my appearance, especially when I am not expected to appear at all, is apparently not such as to spread peace and joy unalloyed over six octogenarians having a vegetarian dinner after lots of elderberry wine, I had some small difficulty in convincing them I was not from another planet.''

"You must be exaggerating.''

"Yeah, I must be. Sometimes I do that. But, this time, not much. Would you believe that they, collectively and individually, reported me to the police, the district attorney's office, the humane society, and NASA?''

"No."

"Well, they sure called the cops. I have this on good authority. Namely, the cops they called."

"Golly," she said again, those bright blue eyes widening. "What did they say to you?"

"The police officers? Right at first, nothing, because by the time they showed up, I was next door. You will be pleased to hear that I kicked in the right door this time, and there found, and formally placed under arrest, the culprit."

"Well, you did that part right anyway. . . . You didn't?"

"Not exactly. I am allowed to make a citizen's arrest, true. But when one arrests an individual these days, one is supposed to do certain things. I did all these things. I advised the subject of his rights, apologized for the inconvenience, promised him a pension at sixty-five, and offered to give him a rubdown. Unfortunately, he was unconscious at the time."

"Oh, oh."

"Well put. More, the suspect displayed upon his person numerous suspicious-looking bruises. Besides which, there was his broken leg."

"He broke his leg?"

"I broke it. See, he knocked me down, and that griped the hell out of me, and then he tried to kick me in the head—forget it."

"I see. And all that made your friend mad at you?"

"Oh, boy."

"I guess that means yes."

"I guess. You can take my word for it, during the next few days, perhaps even years, if I unduly annoy any innocent citizens—or even hugely guilty citizens—I will be in much deeper trouble than they.''

I shut up, shook my head a bit, then said to Aralia, "It might be a good idea for you to slip into something more . . . adequate. Since you'll be spending a little time at the police station.''

"Oh? Will I have to go there?''

"Yep. Me, too. Dictate statements, sign them, answer lots of questions, that sort of thing.''

"All right.'' She got to her feet, looked down at me. "I'll hurry.''

"Do. We should talk a bit more before the police arrive, anyhow. And it would be better if you were then clad very sedately, preferably in something hideous. You see, some of my friends downtown, and also from the Hollywood Division here, are uncouth types who delight in—joshing me, shall we say? About matters we need not go into at the moment. And that gets a bit thick at times, it really does. Especially, should the first officer to arrive be someone like Sergeant Kowaski—''

There was a loud, solid, authoritative crash of knuckles against the door.

"Why, who would that be?'' Aralia asked curiously.

"Who do you suppose?'' I looked at the door, still vibrating from the blows upon it. "Is that you, Sergeant Kowaski?'' I called.

I shouldn't have called. The door wasn't locked, and Sergeant Kowaski, hearing and recognizing my voice, naturally took my query as an invitation to come in and see the corpse. So in he came, followed by his partner, also in uniform.

Aralia reached up to fluff her ripe-strawberry hair, which

21

was already in place, into place. Why do women do that? Don't ask me. Don't ask them, either. Nobody knows.

But women seem always to do it when about to see—or be seen by—a stranger. It doesn't make any difference who; it could be the Boston Strangler; they'd still do it. Needless to say, since that blue robe of mine still had no belt holding it together, and Aralia's hands while performing the absolutely necessary nonfunction of patting her hair could not hold it together either, nothing held it together.

Kowaski, all two hundred and thirty pounds of him, thudded into the room, thick face splitting in a muscular grin as he saw me and said, "What are you up to now, Shell?"

Actually, he didn't quite get all of that out. He failed to include the "ell" of my name. Right after ". . . to now, Sh— " his very large dark eyes fell upon Aralia, standing there patting, and those eyes I will swear upon a stack of solid-gold Bibles got perhaps larger than they had ever been before, and he just stood there stuck on the start of my name, going "SHHHHHH."

"Nothing much," I said. "Where were you when you got the call, Sergeant? Downstairs in the lobby? Could you stop making that noise, Sergeant?"

Aralia turned, started to step past me, saying, "I'll go slip into something . . ."

"Swell," I said. My voice was dull, very flat.

She went out of the room.

Kowaski—after Aralia was out of sight—looked at me, still showing visible effects of sudden shock. "How do you do it?" he asked me.

22

"Do what? In case you're interested, the dead guy is under the blanket there."

"All I got is, there's a nekkid stiff here. Did she bump him off?"

"Don't be vulgar. He merely had a sudden seizure and fell down dead. Possibly checked out from heart stoppage. Probably. Name's Edward Brett."

"Brett? You recognized him?"

"He's new to me. I peeked at his driver's license—"

"Scott, you're not supposed to—"

"Knock it off. I was careful, no prints or smudges. Hell, I was curious."

He shook his big head, then stepped toward the blanket saying, "Brett . . . Edward. Would that be a mean, lumpy, strong-arm lad, pimp, ex-con, two-time loser name of Buddy Brett?"

"Beats me. You know a Buddy Brett?"

Kowaski had pulled back the blanket, was looking down. "Yeah," he said. "This is him."

CHAPTER THREE

I got up and walked over next to Kowaski. "He's got a record?"

"That he does. Half a dozen arrests locally, mostly strong-arm stuff, if I remember. Have to check it. Did time at Q in the last year or two, I think."

"See if this rings any bells." I described the man I'd so recently spoken to down on the street.

Kowaski shook his head. "Nobody in sight when we pulled up. And only one car parked in this block on Rossmore. We were cruising on Beverly, got here pretty quick."

"You sure did. Eight to five it's the Lincoln that's gone."

He nodded.

Aralia came back in wearing a simple white dress with fine red and blue stripes—looking, needless to say, at least twice as good as sensational—then a team of detectives arrived, closely followed by men from the Scientific Investigations Division downtown, the Central Division. Initial statements were taken, then Aralia and I, and the two detectives, left for the Police Building.

I drove my own Cadillac, a new sky-blue coupe, but Aralia rode with the detectives in their plainclothes car. I had noticed, during those last minutes in her apartment, that she was becoming more and more subdued, quiet, features getting a little drawn, a small frown-wrinkle between those bright blue eyes.

I was standing on the sidewalk before the Spartan when they drove away. Aralia sat in back, not relaxed, perched on the edge of the seat, her lovely face turned toward me. Lovely, but a bit different now—frightened now. She stared at me for long seconds as they pulled out from the curb.

So, it was getting to her. Understandably.

She would be remembering that body sprawled on the floor of her apartment, remembering sudden, unexpected death. And if she'd told me the truth about what had happened, and I had no reason to suppose she had not, Aralia was thinking that it could have been, almost had been, her own body sprawled there. She was, surely, thinking a lot about that.

So was I.

By seven P.M., with the routine behind me, I was checking the notes I'd made. I had spent twenty minutes examining some of the record-filled envelopes down in Records and Identification—or the "packages" in R and I—and had talked with men in the Intelligence Division. I'd also spent a few minutes with a couple of officers working out of Homicide. I hadn't seen Samson yet, but he knew I was in the building, and word had been gently conveyed to me that the captain

26

"hoped" I would drop in and say hello if I had nothing better to do. It wasn't likely I would have anything better to do this year.

So, after picking up copies of three mug shots I'd asked for—these being unappetizing police photos of individuals who had run afoul of the law—I strolled down the third-floor corridor to Room 314, Homicide.

This happened to be one of those rare times when the squadroom was, briefly, empty. There were no officers drinking bitter coffee from paper cups, not even one tired-looking cop filling out his final report of a long day. But the door to Sam's inner office was open, so I said loudly, "Still goofing off on the taxpayer's time, eh, fuzz? Well, how is our leader, the Beast of Belsen, this evening, men?"

"Shell, goddammit, I told you—"

For a big man, Samson moved pretty fast. He was filling the doorway, looming there, the gathering storm beginning to darken his usually pink, smoothly shaved face. Just a flick of his sharp brown eyes made him aware that the squadroom was empty, and with only a brief pause he went right on. "—your goddamn mouth was under arrest. Get in here."

He was out of sight, back at his desk again, before I got my chops shut. But when I walked into his office he was smiling. As usual, one of his unlighted black cigars was clamped between his strong teeth, so it appeared that at least half of the smile was snarling.

I grinned, and said hello for the second time this day to Sam. To Detective Captain Phil Samson, big, burly—but solid, as more than one hood who mistook coiled muscle for flab learned the hard way—with iron-gray hair screening his

27

pink scalp, wide mouth over a jaw like the front end of a small diesel rig.

I grabbed my usual wooden chair, placed it near Sam's desk, and sat down straddling it, arms resting on its back.

"I've been filled in by everybody else," Sam said, "including a statement from Kowaski. So give me your self-serving version of what happened. And make it fast. I see the chief in ten minutes." He paused, shifting the cigar from one side of his wide mouth to the other. "Not about you, fortunately. Not *this* time."

"Isn't a whole lot to tell, Sam." I gave him the story, then, checking my notes, laid out for him the info I'd gathered since arriving at the LAPD.

"This Edward 'Buddy' Brett, the dead guy, was a dandy. Dozen or more arrests—burglary, assault and battery, procuring, you name it. Fell from here for ADW two years back and put in eighteen months at San Quentin, got out earlier this year."

"February," Sam said quietly, leaning back in his swivel chair, eyeing a long yellow legal pad held in a big-knuckled hand. "Seven months ago."

"Right. Known close associates, both before and after his jolt in Q, Alvin 'Al the Clam' Hauk, Elroy 'Puffer' Werzen, Wally 'The Nose' Wilson—recently deceased, due to a small gunshot wound in the back of his head, accompanied by a comparatively enormous hole in the front of it, where formerly his famous nose—"

"You can leave out the dead ones. *And* your usual gratuitous, and exceedingly annoying, embellishments."

"You've got to quit looking things up in the dictionary,

Sam. Also, one Virgil Kovick, former all-pro lineman—tackle with the Rams, I think—now pro heavy man, sometime wheelman. Hasn't been much on him, though, last couple of years. Finally, one Charles E. Ellisohn, engraver, forger, paper hanger, possible counterfeiter. Nice bunch, what?''

"Beautiful.''

"While in the joint this last trip, Brett's cellmates during the first few months were a first-timer named Norman Amber—probably not important, no prior convictions, a scientist, physicist, and inventor it says here—and two-timer named Fred Luntz. But, locked up with Brett for more than a year—our item of current interest—was the aforementioned Elroy 'Puffer' Werzen.'' I paused. "Little goof there, putting the two pals in together? Or special privilege maybe?''

Sam ignored my last comment, slid his yellow pad back onto the desk. "Go ahead and finish it. I recognize that dumb look on your face.''

I fished in my pocket, pulled out the three mug shots, spread them on Sam's desktop. "I checked the packages on Brett, Hauk, and Puffer Werzen. Seems those last two have been almost as close since Puffer got out of stir—four months ago, middle of May—as they were while locked up. First picture there, Alvin Hauk, that's the guy I braced on North Rossmore, right after eyeballing Brett's corpse.''

Samson blinked, showing more than mild interest at last. "You're sure?'' But he was already picking up his phone, growling into it. He passed on the info, gave orders to check Hauk's last known address, then hung up and said to me, "I hope you just found this out.''

"Just did. Came straight here from R and I, Sam. That's

29

where I found out he's called The Clam, or sometimes Clammy. Looked pretty clammy to me, I'll tell you. Some kind of cold fish for sure.''

"That's not where he gets the handle. We've had him in here five, six times, suspicion of one thing or another. Never got a word out of him.''

"Not very cooperative?''

"Not very. What I mean, he doesn't say word one. Just clams. Won't even say hello. Attorney always showed up to spring him, but Al the Clam never asked for one. How could he? Never opened his goddamned mouth.''

"One of those, huh? And you can't coax the chaps very much these days.''

"Doubt it would do any good with Hauk, Shell. Some very hard boys grabbed him a half-dozen years back, wanted him to tell them something they greatly desired to know. These hoods pounded on him, strung him up by his thumbs, beat his bare feet—you know?''

"Yeah, bastinado—a little like walking on broken glass with your bare stumps. Some sweeties tried it with me once. If there hadn't been an interruption, I might have spilled.''

"Not him. So, all over Southern California he's known— respected—as Al the Clam. He may look a little spindly, but that one's tough. Or else he's got a very low pain threshold.'' Sam chewed on his cigar. "O.K., what do you propose to do in the hours and days ahead? About Buddy Brett, I mean.''

"I suppose I'll nose around a little, try to dig up—''

"Let me put it this way. Is the lady, Miss Fields, your client?''

"Sure. We haven't settled my fees and such yet, but—yeah, she's my client. Why?"

"I am painfully aware, Sheldon, that you seem often to lose your acquaintance with caution, even reason, when blundering pell-mell to the aid of a damsel in distress. Especially if she's got a big pair of—"

"Sam, I thought you had to see the chief a couple of minutes ago. And what do you mean, blundering—"

"How long have you known this girl? Does she have a criminal record? Was she, or was she not, acquainted with the late Edward Brett before this afternoon? Is it possible, or is it not possible, that Buddy Brett did not in fact fall in a lifeless heap on her living room floor but instead passed away after strenuous exertions in Miss Fields's bedroom—indeed, in her bed itself—and was thereafter carried or pulled or rolled from there by Miss Fields herself to the spot where you first observed the deceased? How long has this girl resided at the Spartan Apartment Hotel, in which establishment you—"

"Sam, you make me nauseous when you talk like that. But I'll confess, I have not yet explored all of those fascinating areas. If I ever get out of here, perhaps I may. But, Sam, why? What's the use? Why not concentrate on the important things?"

"The items I've mentioned, they're not important?"

"Well, to a cop, sure—but where's the fun in that? Watch it, Sam, I was only kidding. . . . Ah, I mean, Aralia—Miss Fields—has told me her tale, and I believe her to be reliable. For one thing, she has an honest face. Among other reliable things. Hey." I stopped. "You *were* just tossing some wild

31

possibilities at me, weren't you? I mean, she didn't really know Brett before, did she?''

Samson shrugged. "I don't have any idea. She might have. But if someone failed to mention such obvious possibilities, Shell, I fear they might not occur to you in this century.''

"You'll make a cop of me yet, won't you?''

"Dear God.'' He rolled his eyes toward the ceiling, then glanced at his watch. "Get out of here. You might be interested in these items.'' He slid some folded sheets of the yellow paper over the desk to me. "I won't repeat what I said to you this morning. But you will keep it all in mind, won't you?''

"You can count on it.'' I stood up, put the wooden chair back where I'd gotten it. "How did Miss Fields make out? The boys take her home yet?''

"She completed her statement, and was through answering questions, half an hour ago. But, no, she hasn't been taken home. She is waiting, presumably biting her nails to the bone, in the lobby below.''

"Waiting?''

"For you. As reported to me, she couldn't bear to leave without seeing Mr. Scott again. And thanking him. For being so wonderfully helpful. So dear. So sweet.''

It sounded odd, coming around Sam's black cigar like that. But I grinned and said, "I know you, you old codger, you're just making all this up to make me feel good.''

He was growling into his phone again as I left.

Aralia was indeed waiting for me in the lobby.

I drove her home. We chatted a bit, and even had a drink

32

in my apartment. But that was all we had in my apartment. Didn't have anything in her apartment, either.

During our chat, however, I did elicit from her several important facts I either had not known or had only guessed at. For example, she was five feet six inches tall; thirty-eight, twenty-three, thirty-six; weighed one-hundred and twenty-seven pounds; and was twenty-five years old.

That was convincing enough. But she also vehemently denied that she'd ever seen, or heard of, Edward "Buddy" Brett before this afternoon. Nor did she have the least idea why he might have wanted to kill her.

We were sitting on the chocolate-brown divan in my front room, and I said, "Any chance he made a mistake? Thought you were somebody else, maybe?"

She shook her head. "He called me by name. Aralia. He knew who I was. That's what makes it so . . . It's just crazy."

"How long have you been living here at the Spartan?"

"Only three weeks. I just got my phone connected yesterday. And I need a phone, for modeling calls."

"You're a model? I never got around to asking what you do."

"Part of the time."

Aralia explained that she'd had secretarial training, and convinced me she was a whiz at typing and taking dictation and "everything around the office"—"whiz" was her word, too—but had held only one secretarial job in her life, and lost that one six months back when the small advertising agency where she'd been whizzing went bankrupt. Possibly the demise of the firm had nothing to do with the fact that the agency's number-one account at the time was paying big bucks for a crash campaign to create catchy advertising slogans to be printed on Loving Touch toilet paper. On the other hand, possibly it did.

Since then, Aralia had lived on her small savings, income from some modeling jobs that apparently paid quite well, plus cash from a "prize" she'd very recently won. I hinted, but she didn't say what the prize was or what it was for. I hinted quite a lot, but she never explained to my satisfaction. More accurately, she didn't explain it at all.

She hoped to continue with her modeling, perhaps apply for another secretarial job but "not with a dumb ad agency" this time, and might even win another prize before long if she was "awfully lucky." In addition, like approximately ninety-four percent of all babes under forty-nine years of age, she was an aspiring actress. So far, in that area, all she'd done was aspire.

"Well," I said, finishing my bourbon and water, "that's fascinating. Like another drink, Aralia?"

"Not tonight, Shell. I'm pretty tired."

"After this day, I can understand that. You get along O.K. with the officers downtown?"

"Oh, yes. It's just that I was never *in* a police station before, and it was, oh, kind of scary. But the policemen were awfully sweet."

"Huh. Cops are sweet, too, huh?"

"What?"

"Never mind. You're living here alone, Aralia? I mean, is your family in Los Angeles?"

"I don't know, really. And I don't much care."

Maybe she saw me blink. Anyway, she continued. "I suppose that sounds strange, Shell. But my father died before I was born, my real father, I mean. Ma got married again, to a man named Charles Fields, but he ran off somewhere after two or three years, so I never knew him, either. And, finally, I ran off, too, at least I left home nine years ago. When I was sixteen. All the time I was growing up it was just Ma and me and my brother Petey, a year older than me, and it wasn't the happiest home I ever heard of. I haven't even been in touch with either of them for years, since I was about eighteen."

She spoke without bitterness or self-pity, almost as if she were reciting mildly unpleasant facts about somebody else. After a moment's silence she said, "Last I knew, Ma and Petey were living in Burbank, but I don't know if they still are or not. Well . . ." She stood up.

I didn't try very hard to talk her out of leaving; she did look more than a bit tired. But my offer to look for and overpower any suspicious characters lurking in her apartment was accepted; and there, after grumbling about not finding any, even under the bed, I went back to my own apartment again.

Showered and between the sheets, I glanced once more over the typed pages Captain Samson had given me, essentially info about associates of the late Buddy Brett. There was also a statement that the Lincoln Continental I'd checked on Rossmore had been reported stolen a couple of minutes before six P.M. At least that was the time when the owner had phoned the report in. The owner was, of course, the man whose name—Gunnar Lindstrom—I'd noted on the car's registration slip.

Lindstrom himself, judging from all available info, was not merely "clean" but a very accomplished and respected citizen, not only from the official police point of view, but in the estimation of the scientific community, of which he was a well-known and several-times-honored member. It seemed he was some kind of super-scientist, mathematician, engineer, inventor with more than eighty patents in a number of different fields. That was interesting. Second scientist-inventor I'd run across today. Who was the other one? Amber? Yeah, Norman Amber.

I glanced sleepily at the additional paragraph about Lindstrom—head of the prestigious Lindstrom Laboratories on Olympic Boulevard here in L.A., recipient of this award and that award during the past twenty years, and other highly soporific intelligence—then I turned out the light.

I thought briefly about Buddy Brett, the somewhat ghoulish smart-mouthed Al Hauk, hoods, Samson, even the crook whose leg I'd cracked, and then about Aralia.

Not so briefly, more leisurely, about Aralia. About the eye-bruising beauty of her face and the gland-cooking curves of her remarkable body, her bright eyes, warm lips, gentle smile. She moved in my mind . . . lingered in thought . . . and deliciously dissolved into dream. . . .

CHAPTER FOUR

IN the morning I came to, then slowly awakened, and not long thereafter opened my eyes a crack, which is the way I usually spring forth from slumber to greet the glorious dawn.

I smacked my lips, uncracked my eyes, opened them a slit again, bubbled air between my lips. Undoubtedly, there was a glorious dawn out there somewhere, but not where I was at; no matter the time of day or season, I wake up at midnight on Halloween. Later in the day, any day, I am full of beans, yes; I am possessed of almost obnoxious vitality; but that condition is not something I arrive at instantly, or even close to it.

So I sort of wallowed over and got all set on the edge of the bed, planted my feet on the black carpet, scratched the hair on my chest, stuck out my tongue and slowly hauled it back in again. With the morning's calisthenics thus completed, I got to my feet and trekked toward the shower, not forgetting to plug in the coffeepot on the way.

Soon life would be once more a thing of considerable virtue. Not quite yet, but soon.

There was a bit of gloom in the Southern California air, thin gray clouds overhead accenting soft blueness beyond them while briefly dimming the sun, but all was bright and warm inside me as I rolled up Wilshire Boulevard, the Cad's windows open and the slightly chill nip of September air scrubbing my chops. I felt great. Clearly, I had come a long way. Despite my five minutes with Bernie Hooten.

After three cups of coffee, two bites of lumpy oatmeal mush—I have not yet discovered how to keep those little lumps out of the stuff—and four cigarettes, I had managed to depart from the Spartan without forgetting to put my pants on. There followed a couple of hours during which I talked to a few of my less savory acquaintances, doing what I generally do at the commencement of a case, putting my lines out, letting a handful of my best informants know what I'm looking for.

Usually, if those lines hook anything at all, I don't get the word until hours or days later, since ordinarily you can expect to fish quite a while before catching anything. But this time I picked up, from a retired box man named Hooten, an item worth filing away—mainly because of the timing—even though there was only a chance in ten, if that, of its having anything to do with Aralia, or Buddy Brett and his lethal chums.

I found Hooten in a dark, damp, sour-smelling bar on Sixth Street, where the whiskery clientele ordered mostly beer and wine, and drank it alone at small round tables covered with cracked and peeling linoleum. And where Hooten spent most of his mornings. He was the only man I knew who actually dumped a shot of booze into his beer and then drank the mixture, which struck me as even less appetizing than little lumps in mush.

I'd bought him a shot of Early Times while telling him my tale, and he said, "I dunno. Funny. Maybe."

"Maybe what, Bernie?"

He steadied the shot glass on the rim of his beer mug, tilted it, watched with interest as a thin stream of brown bourbon dribbled into his beer. "I don't know who it was done it, Scott. Or for who—I mean, to hit who. But somebody here in L.A. called a pro back east to come here and kill somebody. Late last night or early this ayem, it was. Looks like pee, don't it?"

"What?" He finished trickling the bourbon into his beer. "Oh, yeah. I guess," I said. "A pro?"

"One of the best, way I get it. It's outa my field, you know, Scott. I never run with no wipers, even when I was openin' a can a week. Didn't pack no heat myself, never. And I don't know nothin' about on this end, because I got it from a friend who I know on the other end."

"Where was that? Other end where?"

He didn't answer. I sighed.

"But this guy I mention to you, the pro," he went on, "is maybe here already by now. It was like special delivery, he's suppose to get his ass here fast so the business can be over with quick. Wish I had more for you, Scott, but that's all I know. That and his handle. And where he come from."

He gulped down half the beer-and-booze drink. Smacked his lips.

39

I sighed again. It always depressed me when I talked to Hooten. The name, "his handle," that was one. "Where he come from," that was number two. Extortion at very close to its lowest level. But, still, extortion. I caught the bartender's eye, held up two fingers.

The bartender nodded, patted his bulging stomach, burped a couple of times, coughed wheezily, and ran an index finger swiftly under his nose before wiping it on his pants.

"O.K.," I said to Hooten. "What's the guy's name?"

"All I got's the monicker, how they tag him." He glanced around, saw the bartender pouring, and only then went on. "One-Shot."

I didn't know if that was a question or not, so I said, "Fat Mike's bringing a couple over, Bernie."

"Knew I could count on you, Scott. Ain't what I meant, though. That's his handle, One-Shot. And I guess, since he is in the business of hitting people in the head, and he's s'pose to be like about the best there is, it means he don't use a machine-gun."

"O.K. You got this from the other end, wherever it is this guy's coming in from?"

He nodded. And waited. And I waited. The sweet-sour air in there was beginning to make my nostrils feel greasy.

After Fat Mike brought the new mug of beer and placed it, plus two shot glasses brimming with Early Times, on the linoleum-topped table, Hooten finished his other drink, carefully shoved it aside, then picked up both shot glasses and balanced them opposite each other on the fresh mug's rim.

"Jersey," he said.

And that was the last word from either of us. As I shoved

back my chair, got up, started walking out, Hooten was dribbling booze slowly into his beer from both sides of the mug, staring with apparent fascination and possibly mild pleasure. I could still hear the faint trickling sound as I went out the door. Into the clean smog, and the brightness of cloud-dimmed sunlight.

It took a while after that for me to get all my bounce back, but after dropping in again briefly at the LAPD, a real steak-and-eggs breakfast with more coffee and smokes had fully restored all my beans and then some.

Consequently, bright of twenty-twenty eye, when about two P.M. I passed the Weir Building on the corner of Wilshire Boulevard and Whicherly Drive, I made the guy even though his back was to me and I caught him—at first—only from the edge of one eyeball.

It was merely a ripple at the rim of sight and memory for a second or two, but when I cranked my head around and took a good look at the Weir Building's entrance on my right, the tall but sagging figure, and the face seen in profile, head sort of slumping down and out on the bent-forward neck, tagged him in that moment: Hauk. Alvin Hauk, or Al the Clam, the charmer who'd been walking his bulge on North Rossmore last night.

He wasn't alone.

He stood a few feet outside the massive glass-and-stainless-steel doors of the building's entrance with three other men. One of them, short and chunky, was turning to go into the Weir Building—and Hauk followed him immediately, close

41

behind and with his long torso blocking my view—so I never did get a look at the chunky guy's face.

I knew one of the other two, though. We hadn't met, I'd never seen him in the flesh, but in my coat was his mug shot. Tall, nearly bald, red-faced Elroy Werzen, monicker Puffer. The con who'd spent more than a year sharing a cell at San Quentin with the late Edward "Buddy" Brett.

As Hauk followed the chunky guy through the Weir Building's entrance, Puffer Werzen and the other man stepped briskly toward the street, where I was rolling along in moving traffic. That fourth man was a stranger to me, about fifty years old, six feet tall, weight maybe two hundred pounds, with a lot of it crowded into his midsection.

I had to pull my eyes briefly from him and Puffer, but then braked the Cad, slowed, eased to a stop several yards farther up Wilshire, parallel to the solid line of parked cars on my right. I considered trying to catch up with Hauk and whomever he was with, but only for a moment. The building was twelve stories; there were probably a hundred offices and suites in it. Besides, at the moment I was more interested in keeping a tail on Buddy Brett's former cellmate.

Two cars swung out and around me, but the last guy gave me a blast from the horn and gunned me with mean eyes as he went by. Both of my men climbed into a black Mercedes parked at the curb twenty-five yards to my rear. Three cars were stacked up behind me now, apparently not planning to swing around my Cad.

So I took my foot off the brake, eased forward, waving an arm to encourage the people behind me to pass. A couple of them did. I waited long enough to see that black Mercedes edge from the curb into the traffic stream, then drove ahead.

With any luck, I could tail the men from in front until there was a chance for me to fall in behind them. Sure—I lost them at the next stop light. When the light turned green I drove ahead, checking the rearview mirror, and caught the flash of black as the Mercedes swung left. I hit the brakes, stuck my head out the window, got a glimpse of the license plate. But that was all, just a glimpse, then the black sedan was out of sight.

I turned left, sliding, at the first cross street, took another fast left a block farther on. I'd missed part of that plate but was pretty sure the last three letters were KDG. Either KDG or KDC. And the middle letter might have been an O. Not enough; but it was all I was going to get.

Ten minutes later I quit trying to spot the Mercedes, parked, and phoned the LAPD. Because I'm not a member of the department, instead of dialing Communications direct I placed the call to a friend of mine in the Auto Theft Division, a Sergeant Gageron, and asked him for a make on the partial registration.

"Could take some time," he said. "The little you've got."

"That's O.K., Gage, I'll check back later. But another reason I called you, I'd like to know when this guy Lindstrom phoned in last night about his stolen Continental, when exactly. I think it was a couple minutes before six, but I'd also like the time I asked for the check on it. I'm not certain when I called in."

"Sure, hold on a minute," he said. "By the way, that

Continental was found abandoned a mile from your place last night, half a block off Beverly. Latent Prints checked it out, didn't find anything important. Owner's already been notified.''

"Speedy. Must have made Lindstrom happy."

"Don't ask me, I wasn't there. O.K., hold on." Then, a few moments later, "You're right, Scott. Lindstrom phoned in just before six P.M., five fifty-eight it was. Got your call at five-fifty."

"Uh-huh. Thanks."

"Mean anything, Scott?"

"I'm not sure."

The stolen vehicle report had been logged by the police eight minutes after I'd called in. Add four or five minutes while I checked the Lincoln, trotted back up to Aralia's apartment, jawed briefly with her.

"The way it figures, Gage, the owner called about his stolen heap not more than fifteen minutes after I braced Al Hauk there near the Spartan. Kind of close, but it doesn't have to mean anything."

"Well, you never know. Here's one other bit you might want, Scott, since you're interested in this guy. Four, maybe five years back—Lieutenant French was mentioning it to me this morning, so if you want more you can get it from him—was the only other time we heard anything about this Lindstrom. He reported his kid missing, afraid the boy had been kidnaped or maybe run over by a truck. Called back next day to report the boy home again. Kid just ran away, pooped around for maybe twenty-four hours, got hungry, and came home for dinner. So Lindstrom informed Missing Persons, anyhow, with some small embarrassment."

All Gage could add was that Lindstrom had been a widower for a couple of years at that time and his only child, Sven, was then twelve years old. I thanked Gage for the info and filed it away, next to the mental wastebasket. Maybe it would come up during my conversation with Gunnar Lindstrom himself, which would commence in about twenty minutes, I estimated, since Lindstrom Laboratories was on Olympic Boulevard, only ten minutes driving time from where I'd parked my Cad.

I used the extra ten minutes to visit the Weir Building, where I easily restrained myself from spending a day and a half visiting all twelve floors of offices. Instead, I contented myself with reading the board, listing occupants of those offices, on a wall inside the building's entrance. Doctors, lawyers, merchants; no names that meant anything to me. But I read them all a couple of times, then headed for Olympic.

CHAPTER FIVE

LINDSTROM Laboratories was a solid-looking two-story building filling half of a city block, its entrance facing Olympic Boulevard. The walls were of off-white cement bricks, their surfaces smooth, equally smooth lines of gray mortar forming a checkerboard pattern of neat and perfectly straight parallel lines across the building's face—its solid face: the walls were unbroken, windowless.

I parked at the curb, walked toward heavy wooden doors. Above them was the street number, that was all. No name there, or on the solid-looking doors themselves. I knew without looking that there wouldn't be any mat at my feet with "Welcome" crocheted on it.

There was, at least, a bell to the right of the entrance, with a small sign saying RING BELL. I rang bell, waited. A minute passed. Another. Then one of the two doors opened halfway and a short evil-looking guy about forty years old looked up at me.

I told him who I was and that I wanted to see Mr. Lindstrom. He said I couldn't see Lindstrom without an appointment. I said I wished to discuss the matter of Mr. Lindstrom's stolen automobile. He scowled fiercely, closed the door again. I waited some more. After another couple of minutes the short man opened the door again and said simply, "Follow me."

I walked behind him down a softly lighted corridor, my feet silent on slightly spongy gray plastic tile, past closed doors with small nameplates affixed to them. From inside some of the rooms came unusual sounds. Unusual, at least, to me. Tinny hammering; ticking; a muffled mushy thudding that could have been heavy hail falling on a wet lawn; a series of sharp, rhythmic clicks almost like a dozen golf balls being hit in rapid succession, interrupted, then repeated over and over; and from one room a strange high bone-stretching sound, a tremulous humming, like a hundred-foot bow being drawn over a thousand-foot-long bass fiddle. That one was unpleasant, disturbing; it made my skin prickle and chill and I felt hairs on the back of my neck wiggle like splinters of ice or tiny half-frozen worms crawling out through my skin.

It says a great deal for Gunnar Lindstrom that though I first saw him while that nightmarish hum was still faint and cold in my ears, I liked the look of the man. Even then. And even though he was bending upon me a gaze of such probing intensity it could have bored holes in a Ping-Pong ball.

We had stopped before an open door about halfway down the long hallway. Inside, a short man with a large leonine head upon which a mass of pale brown hair streaked with gray was in great disarray, as though attempting to fly from his scalp in several different directions at once, stood staring at us from heavy-browed dark eyes. He stood behind a gray desk upon which were stacks of papers and several objects like parts of a three-dimensional jigsaw puzzle, arms folded over his chest, while fixing us—or, rather, me—with that pointed and penetrating gaze.

"Come in, Mr. Scott," he said.

The voice was soft, even gentle; but in it was something rather like a muted version of the bone-penetrating sound I could still faintly hear. The little man who'd accompanied me went silently back the way he'd come. I stepped inside.

"I am Gunnar Lindstrom," he continued. "You wished to discuss my stolen vehicle?"

"Yes. Among other things."

"Among other things? Are you a police officer?"

"No, I'm a private investigator."

"I see. All right. You may have three minutes of my time."

Lindstrom sat in a black-leather-padded swivel chair, and as I moved to another chair and sat in it, he reached for a small wood-and-curved-glass object atop his desk, and turned it over.

It looked like one of those little hourglasses with little bitty grains of white sand inside it. Sure, there were the little bitty grains starting to fall down to the bottom of the thing. I wondered what it really did.

"What's that?" I said.

"It is an egg timer. It requires precisely three minutes for the sand to be transferred by gravity flow from the upper chamber to the lower chamber."

49

"Precisely three minutes . . . ah. I get it."

"I would be astonished if you did not."

In a few more seconds it became clear that this guy wasn't going to be a lot of additional help. I stopped expecting any comments like "What is your problem?" or "How may I be of assistance to you, Mr. Scott?" or even "You now have only two minutes left."

"Well, sir," I said briskly, "you own a gray Lincoln Continental sedan. Last night I spoke to a man who was strolling a few feet from where it was parked on North Rossmore and asked him if he owned it. He denied that he did, but I have reason to believe he almost immediately drove off in your car. It is perhaps not significant, but of some interest to me, that about twelve or thirteen minutes after I braced this guy you phoned the police—at five-fifty-eight P.M.—and reported your car stolen. Do you know any of these men, Mr. Lindstrom?"

By then I had pulled from my coat pocket three mug shots and spread them on the desktop in front of him.

Before examining the photos, Lindstrom said, "I detect a certain emphasis upon the 'twelve or thirteen minutes' intervening between your—what was it, bracing?—yes, bracing this individual and my report to the police. Do you imply that there might be some connection between your bracing and my reporting?"

"I imply nothing at the moment. You may infer anything you wish."

"Hmm, you do not look like a strict logician," he mumbled softly. "Or even grammarian. Ah . . ." Lindstrom was glancing at the photos. "Yes, this gentleman is employed

50

here at Lindstrom Laboratories. I have on a few occasions seen him in the company of this gentleman. The other I do not know.''

He had indicated the mug shots of first, Elroy Werzen, and then Alvin Hauk. The man he professed not to know was the late Buddy Brett. I put the pictures back into my pocket and said, ''I don't mean to be picky, but those lobs are not gentlemen. You say Puffer Werzen works here?''

''Puffer?''

''Elroy—Puffer's his monicker, his hood name. Both of those creeps have lengthy arrest records, and Werzen's done time at San Quentin.''

''I am aware that Mr. Werzen is an ex-convict. I presume you agree it is better that ex-convicts be gainfully employed rather than continue to pursue the occupation that eventuated in their becoming ex-convicts.''

''It depends.''

''Upon what?''

''Lots of things, like do they maybe, after their hours of gainful employment and on weekends, go around hitting people upon their heads and borrowing all their money. But I hate to use my three minutes being so negative.''

''Ah.''

After a moment, Lindstrom eyed the hourglass—or, more accurately, threeminute glass—then turned it over on its side.

I considered that an encouraging thing for him to do, and said, ''From the little I know, not to mention the other-worldly sounds I've heard in this place, I would assume that many people with admirably convoluted brains work here

51

upon various complex items of machinery, invent great leaps forward, perform thunderingly abstruse operations—''

"You do not have to talk to me like a man with little bells attached to his epiglottis, Mr. Scott, simply because it is rumored that I am a genius.''

It sounded sarcastic, even nasty, but with the words Lindstrom smiled—his first unmistakably cheerful expression since we'd met—and it was such a bright, boyish, winning smile that twenty years fell from his face and his sharp features seemed almost to glow. There was also a definite twinkle in those dark eyes of his, I noted. Certainly, when accompanied by that smile, there was no sting in the words.

"O.K." I grinned back at him. "It's a habit of mine. I talk like a hood to hoods, and when yacking with doctors I sometimes sound like a vet myself. Well, I figure the people who work here, at least most of them, must have more than plenty of noodles, where as it's likely Puffer may not have enough for a thimbleful of weak soup. So—''

"Yes, I had anticipated your question. Mr. Werzen does think a slide rule has something to do with a close decision at home plate, but he is a man nonetheless of considerable physical strength, and also remarkable mechanical ability.''

"Uh-huh. So Puffer's employed to hold things up—strike that—lift and carry, fix nuts and bolts and such?''

"In an institution such as this there are many repairs necessary which do not require the talents of an engineer. Mr. Werzen is most efficient in repairing a wide variety of electrical instruments, constructing tables and platforms for which we would otherwise have to hire carpenters and several union vice-presidents, and fortunately, he approaches genius in his rapport with plumbing.''

"Fortunately?''

Lindstrom smiled again. "We have sixteen toilets here. Thanks to Mr. Werzen, never have less than fifteen of them been functioning perfectly at any one time. This is a prerequisite for optimum efficiency since, at Lindstrom Laboratories, it is not true that he also serves who only sits and waits. Mr. Werzen is virtually a Renaissance man of the toilet.''

"I would never have guessed it in a million years. I hope you got him cheap.''

"I'll admit, employing Mr. Werzen here in several minor capacities has saved us some money—which is a consideration not to be ignored. You see, Mr. Scott, Lindstrom Laboratories, unlike the many tax-exempt foundations in this country, is privately supported. It is a private enterprise, an institution designed to make money. The more we trim from overhead and operating expense, the greater the profit for our stockholders. All of Lindstrom Lab's employees are stockholders, by the way, which experience has shown to be most instrumental in stimulating employee loyalty and incentive.''

"Makes sense. Back to our Cellini of the can; you say you've seen him with Alvin Hauk?''

"Our what? With whom?''

"Puffer, the foe of constipation. With this guy." I showed him Hauk's mug shot again, and spelled his name.

Lindstrom nodded. "I did not know the man's identity. But, yes, I have seen that individual in Mr. Werzen's company on a few occasions.''

"Here at the lab?''

"Yes, on each occasion. Mr. Werzen does not drive, at least he does not drive his own automobile. Usually he comes to work with Mr. Collett, who is in charge of our bookkeeping department—our accountant—and leaves with him. On the few occasions I've mentioned, I happened to observe Mr. Werzen near, or entering, the vehicle driven by your Mr. Hauk."

"You remember what kind of car Hauk was driving?"

Lindstrom reached up and tugged on a hunk of hair, eyes half closed in concentration. Then he let go of the hair and it slowly fell down in front of his right ear as he said, "Yes, a Chrysler Cordoba, two-tone green sedan, this year's model."

"Would you mind describing Collett? I'm interested in any of Puffer's pals."

He gave me a brief but very clear description, which sounded like the fiftyish heavyset guy I'd seen with Puffer earlier, in front of the Weir Building. "It would be interesting," I said, "if Collett happens to drive a year-old Mercedes-Benz with a license plate ending in KDG."

"I believe he does, Mr. Scott. I have no idea what the license number is, but I'm quite sure his vehicle is a black Mercedes. A four-door sedan."

"What's his first name?"

"James. James M. Collett. Is it important?"

"Might be. O.K. if I use your phone? *Is* that a phone?"

It was. What I had thought might be a revolutionary breakthrough in communications attached to the thing was merely an oddly shaped metal doohickey resting against it, as I discovered when Lindstrom picked up the phone and placed it nearer to me, the object clanking against his desktop.

I dialed the LAPD and got Sergeant Gageron in Auto Theft again, mentioned the make I'd requested earlier and said the car might be registered to a James M. Collett, then waited slightly more than a minute for the check to be made. While waiting, I indicated the oddly curved and angled metal item on Lindstrom's desk, saying, "Interesting doohickey there. Something you're working on? Scientific breakthrough in—"

"It's a paperweight."

Then Gage was back on the line. Bull's-eye; registration was 033 KDG, and the Mercedes was Collett's. I listened to the additional info immediately available, Collett's description, address, and such. James M.—for Madison—Collett had no police record except for a couple of minor traffic violations. I thanked Gage, hung up, asked Lindstrom if he'd supply me with Collett's home address. He gave me the info; it was the same address Gage had given me.

I said, "I'm not sure what any of this means, Mr. Lindstrom, but at the Police Building this morning I learned that officers have been unable to locate Elroy Werzen or Al Hauk at their last known addresses, and that your employee, Mr. Werzen, has apparently been absent from his current place of residence for the past two or three days. Earlier, before I came here, I saw Collett, Werzen, Hauk, and another man chatting in front of the Weir Building, after which Werzen and Collett drove off in Collett's car. Hauk, you'll recall, is the guy who very likely was tooling your Lincoln around town last night. Mean anything to you?"

"No, it doesn't, Mr. Scott. Should it?"

"Beats me."

55

"Did . . ." He hesitated, then went on casually, "Did you say the Weir Building? That's on Wilshire, isn't it?"

I nodded. "You know somebody there?"

"No."

I waited, but he didn't add anything. "Collett and Werzen on vacation?" I asked him. "Taking some sick leave maybe?"

"Neither of them showed up for work today. Or yesterday, for that matter. I have no idea why."

"About the theft of your car last night. How did you discover it had been stolen?"

"I left here to go home for dinner, planning to return later. My car was not in its usual place in our parking lot. I made some inquiries among employees still in the building, but none of them knew what had happened to it, and I then phoned to report its disappearance. To be accurate, I did not then report my car as positively stolen, but merely as missing from its accustomed place."

"O.K. Just one more thing. I wonder if you know any of the other people who seem to be, or have been, involved with Werzen and Hauk."

"It doesn't seem likely, but . . . Perhaps."

"Can't hurt to try a few names on you then, can it? How about Virgil Kovick?"

Lindstrom pursed his lips and shook his head. He continued shaking his head slightly as I continued. "Charles Ellisohn? Aralia Fields? Norman Amber? Edward Brett—or Buddy Brett?"

Nothing much happened except that at the moment when I first said "Brett," he stopped shaking his head. At the same time, his brows moved closer together, a faint crease appearing at the bridge of his nose.

I stopped speaking, and without any further change of expression Lindstrom said, "No, none of those names mean anything to me, Mr. Scott."

But I'd have bet a sawbuck to a nickel that one of those names was familiar to him. At least one of them. Edward Brett, maybe; or the previous name, Norman Amber. Conceivably, but not likely, even a delayed reaction to Aralia's name. All I knew was that something had stuck Lindstrom.

"O.K.," I said. "I guess that's it, then. And thank you for your time and help."

"It's quite all right." He paused, pursed his lips once more. "But since I have answered several of your questions, Mr. Scott, perhaps you will now answer one of mine."

"Sure."

"*Why* are you interested in all these individuals you've mentioned?"

I thought a few seconds before answering him, but then said, "Reasonable enough," and gave him the top of what had recently occurred, commencing with the appearance of Aralia Fields at my door in the Spartan. Well before I finished, Lindstrom was gazing directly at me again, and once more with that same piercing intensity I'd noted when I first saw him.

As I stopped speaking he said, "Murder? Someone really intended to murder this girl?"

"Yeah, there seems little doubt about that. And not just someone, but the Buddy Brett I mentioned, who appears to have been pretty close to Al Hauk, among others, and in whose company your employee, Elroy Werzen, did time at San Quentin.''

"I am astonished," Lindstrom said, "truly astonished."

Maybe he was, I thought.

When I got up to leave, Lindstrom toyed with his interesting paperweight for a moment, then glanced up and said, "Mr. Scott, I—" He stopped, then continued. "I . . . have a few minutes more to spare. Would you like to look around a bit at some of the work we're doing here?"

I nodded. "Sure. I'd enjoy it." But I wondered what he'd really started to say.

We spent about fifteen minutes more together, and looked into half a dozen of the many rooms, including a couple of those I'd walked by earlier. I'd merely been making conversation when I told Lindstrom I would enjoy having a look around, but it turned out to be true. I possessed an almost total lack of understanding about what I was seeing, but it fascinated me anyway.

Our first stop was in a very large room at the end of the hallway where Lindstrom's office was located. The room was about a fourth the size of a football field, and, except for aisles down which the dozen or so men in view could walk, almost every square foot was occupied by machines or pieces of equipment, some of which were familiar and some of which were completely incomprehensible to me.

I recognized motors, generators, normal-looking television receivers, and what appeared to be a twenty-foot-high Tesla coil. Among the strange items was a shiny disc, its concave mirrored face displaying an empty space in its center; it looked almost exactly like those mirrors with little holes in them that doctors wear and peek through at you for mysterious reasons—except that this one was six feet in diameter. Another interesting something stood in the center of the big room, its base a six-foot transparent cube that appeared to be filled with a bluish fluid, and from which projected toward the ceiling a cluster of spiraling glass tubes ranging from half an inch to several inches in diameter. In each of those tubes something moved, slowly, like a viscous liquid, and in each of the tubes it was of a different color.

"That grabs me," I said to Lindstrom, indicating the colorful whatever-it-was. "What does it do?"

"We don't know yet," he said matter-of-factly. "We know what it's supposed to do—according to our computer model, at least—but it won't do it. So now we're attempting to find out why it won't, and then perhaps we can make it do what we think it should do. Or, again, it may tell us that its true function is something else entirely, or possibly nothing. Even then, we may not know for some time, if ever, what to do with what it does."

I squeezed my eyes shut and said, "Wonderful."

The last thing we looked at was in the room from which had come the oddly unpleasant humming or whining sound I'd earlier noted. I expected to see a two- or three-ton bullhorn, or something like that colorful apparatus in the center of the big room I'd first visited. But all the noise was produced through varying frequencies of electrical current fed into and inducing vibration in a pair of little buttonlike things six feet apart, sticking up from short metal or plastic tubes, atop a wooden table. One was the size of a boy's marble, the other no larger than a pea.

Lindstrom flipped a switch, played with a dial for a minute or so, talking animatedly about varying the rate of vibration to produce sounds below the level of human awareness, audible sounds, possibly even vibrations in the visible spectrum—or the production, not of sound, but of light. He mentioned Nikola Tesla, and some people I'd never heard of, then flipped the switch off. All the sound ceased, the sense of inner trembling or vibration inside me stopped.

That is, while it undoubtedly did stop, it seemed to have left behind it an echo, or almost-felt memory, of that weird and unfamiliar trembling or inner tumult. Or, as Lindstrom referred to it simply, vibration.

Whatever it might best have been named, it stayed with me as Lindstrom escorted me down the hallway to the heavy doors, which thudded shut behind me; with me even as I walked alone to my car; and it did not entirely fade away until I was miles from Lindstrom Laboratories, nearing the street where lived James M., for Madison, Collett.

The street, at least, on the outskirts of Hollywood where, I had been informed both by Lindstrom and the police, Collett lived. But because the alleged addresses of Hauk and Werzen had been conspicuously empty of Hauk and Werzen, I had not a whole lot of hope that I'd find Collett lolling about in his home.

The address was a sizable and rich-looking duplex with a driveway at both ends of the building, each leading to a covered carport. There was no sign of a black Mercedes with the 033 KDG plates.

Each half of the duplex bore a different street number, Collett's was the farther one from me. I pulled to the curb in front of it, cut the ignition. There was a drawing tightness at the base of my skull, and I wiggled my shoulders, shook my head a bit, before climbing out of the car. It was still bright daylight, only a little past four in the afternoon, and there was no apparent reason for me to be getting uptight; maybe it was a hangover from those distressing sounds I'd so recently listened to.

I stretched my shoulders again, then walked casually to Collett's front door and rang the bell. Nothing. I heard the buzzing inside, but there was no response. I poked the doorbell once more, waggled the doorknob. It turned; the door opened a crack.

I waited, telling myself that unless I thought about it for some time, I probably wouldn't be able to come up with a single good reason for inviting myself into another man's home, particularly a man presumably innocent of any wrongdoing.

I glanced around. The street was empty, nobody was in sight. And I was curious to know why Collett was so chummy with lads such as Werzen and Hauk. Besides, I asked myself, merely stepping past an unlocked door was hardly in the same category as kicking the thing down, was it? Of course it wasn't. And what harm could result if Collett—and therefore, Captain Phil Samson—never knew I'd dropped in?

Probably plenty, I told myself.

But I walked in anyway.

CHAPTER SIX

NSIDE, I closed the door behind me, stood silently in the living room, heels sinking into thick red carpet.

In the room were a low beige-gold divan, a large chair covered in the same nubby material as the divan, and a couple of straight-backed wooden chairs. A portable bookcase stood against one wall, and a bar on rubber wheels was in a corner. Plus the usual TV set, a low table, a couple of large ceramic ashtrays with a lot of dead cigarette butts in them.

I felt reasonably sure I was alone here, but I called, "Hello! Anybody home? Hello-hello." Nothing.

I walked over red carpet to a door on my left, opened it and peered into near darkness, the late afternoon sunlight outside blocked by heavy draperies. I flicked on a light, glanced around—bedroom, neat and clean, bed made, everything in place. It looked unused, unlived-in, almost sterile. I pushed the light switch down, stepped back, moved toward another door standing open a few feet away on my right.

Inside this room, too, was near darkness, a kind of thick grayness in which darker lumps were dimly visible, chairs or other furniture, presumably. I stepped into the grayness, brushing my right hand over the light switch as I entered the room.

The light flashed on, revealing a second bedroom—but this one unquestionably lived in. This one was about as far removed from neat and clean as a room could get without moss hanging from the ceiling.

As I took my first step through the open doorway, my eyes started to separate jumble into recognizable objects—king-size bed, unmade, tangle of sheet and blanket in a lump at the foot of the mattress, crumpled pillow; bedside table and lamp, newspaper on the table, lampshade awry; overstuffed chair, and another table next to it covered with a helter-skelter array of paperback books and magazines; bureau with clutter atop it, clutter reflected in the mirror, the mirror cracked, speckled with spots of white splatter, something moving swiftly at the mirror's edge.

Shock rammed up through my spine, from small of back to the still-tight knot at the base of my skull, a physical clench-ing that pulled my shoulders inward and squeezed my head down tighter against my neck. The movement was a man—not me, not my reflection—turning, swinging something dully glittering toward my head.

I'd taken only that first full step into the room, planted my foot, started swinging my other leg forward. When that reflection bounced from the mirror to my eyes, I wasn't solidly balanced, had no chance to spin or jump. I let the muscles of my leg go limp, or tried to, knee bending as my body started to drop.

Much of the tension in the long tendons of thigh and bunched muscle of calf went out of them, but not all; not enough. I felt myself falling slowly, and tried to push my head forward and to the left, thrusting against those involuntarily clenched and pulling neck muscles, and maybe all of that helped, a little; but not enough.

He got me.

He didn't get me with his best shot, but whatever the man was swinging in his hand banged and scraped against the right side of my head. If he'd hit me solidly the blow would have knocked me out for minutes or even hours and maybe for good, but even that partial blow, the glancing crunch against my skull, sent me the rest of the way down and into that lumpy grayness again.

For a second or two, perhaps longer, grayness swirled and billowed before my eyes and I felt myself hit floor that felt like mattress, knew I was turning, rolling. On my back, both elbows pushing against the carpet, I strained to see through the grayness and then, suddenly, the room was bright again and at the same moment—not until then—a shrieking pain like bruised fire exploded in one ear and half of my head.

But I saw the man clearly, knew him, recognized him.

Not Collett. Elroy. Puffer Werzen.

He was bent forward, the big bald head five or six feet away, above me. His right arm was stretched across his body, a heavy .45 automatic, its blunt butt projecting past his fingers, gripped in his fist. The force of his swing had pulled him halfway around but he'd kept his red face turned toward me, eyes fixed on me.

As I tried to roll farther left, get my elbow up off the carpet and my right arm free, I saw the widening of Puffer's eyes and the irregular line of his lower teeth as he stretched his mouth half open and let out a soft grunt, shifting his feet, getting both legs solidly beneath him again.

My left elbow dug harder into the carpet and I started to lift my right arm, heard the involuntary coughlike sound squeezed from my throat. The thick muscle between my right shoulder and the base of my neck felt mashed, torn, where the gun butt must have landed after ripping over my ear.

Puffer, in a slight crouch and with his weight balanced again, pulled back his arm, slapped his hands together. I saw him fumble with the gun, get the grip back into his right fist. In the same movement he jerked the pistol toward me and pulled—or, very likely, yanked—the trigger.

He did it all in too much of a hurry and the bullet whipped past my head as the gun's blast banged my eardrums almost as if the slug had hit them. If he'd taken a little more time, he could have emptied the automatic into me, but he didn't take the time. And, as he fired, my right hand slapped the .38 Special under my coat.

I'd raised up off the floor, legs still splayed out in front of me and my hand on the Colt's checked butt, but when that blast banged my ears I threw myself sideways, to my left and toward the floor, ripping the Colt out of its clamshell holster.

I don't know whether Puffer fired again before I did, or afterward. All I know for sure is that he fired twice more and the last slug smashed through his own foot, and when it was over, my revolver was empty and I was getting to my feet—as Puffer Werzen went down.

He went down slowly. Slowly, even with several—four, I found out later—.38 caliber pills in his stomach and chest.

That moment, for me, was just a kind of stiff blankness following and still part of hellish noise and me pulling the trigger until the hammer clicked on an empty cartridge. Clicked not just once, or even twice; more like four or five times.

It was his left foot he'd shot a hole in, and he went down on that side, the leg giving way just before he fell. He hit the floor with a pair of dull thumps, one right after the other, first his shoulder and then his head snapping over and hitting the carpet. There were two more very small sounds after that. He lifted his head an inch or so, silently straining, and it fell back against the carpet with a soft thud. Once more, up slightly, then down.

That's when he died, I guess.

At the end his fingers relaxed, but they were still curled around the automatic's grip. Puffer never did really let go of his gun—which was the reason I hadn't stopped firing until my Colt was empty. One of the reasons, anyhow.

I felt for the pulse in his throat, knowing there wouldn't be any. There wasn't. Then I sat down on the edge of the sloppy bed, breathing through my mouth, a thin trembling all through me, inside me—like the shivery feeling in my guts when I'd heard that goddamned humming or whining earlier today. I tried to swallow, but my throat and mouth were dry; my tongue felt as if it was sticking to my teeth.

Why the hell? I asked myself. Why had the sonofabitch

tried to kill me? He could have sapped me again, kicked me in the head—he could simply have held his heat on me and I wouldn't have given him an argument.

He'd known who I was, obviously. He'd known I wasn't a door-shaker or daytime thief or guy come to pick up the TV set. No, he'd known I was Shell Scott, and he had sure as hell been eager to kill Shell Scott.

Which awareness didn't make me feel wonderful all over. Any more than did the sight of Werzen's corpse, with four bullets from my Colt inside him. Nor, needless to say, awareness of the next little thing I had to do.

I lit a cigarette, had a couple of drags, watched smoke float in the air.

Then I sighed, found a phone in the front room, and dialed the LAPD.

When I hung up I smoked another cigarette, thinking, with some sourness, about Captain Phil Samson. At least I had been able to convey my report to a lieutenant of my close acquaintance in the Homicide Division, Bill Rawlins, rather than to the good captain himself as would have been my usual custom.

I snubbed out my cigarette, got up, prowled around a little. In the closet were one suit, a couple of sport jackets, two pairs of slacks, and some shirts. Not much clothing, but it all appeared to be Werzen's size. On the floor was a suitcase containing shorts and socks, a dirty T-shirt, and a nearly full box of .45 caliber cartridges.

I walked to the other bedroom I'd glanced into, checked it. Plenty of clothing in the closet, pants much bigger around the middle, half a dozen pairs of shoes. In a dresser drawer were letters addressed to ''James'' and ''J. M.'' Collett, plus a checkbook printed with Collett's name. On top of the dresser was a glossy slick-paper magazine, *Frolic,* with a very fetching unclad lady on the cover. She was facing the camera with one hand before her face, hiding her eyes but not anything else.

I picked up the magazine and it opened to one of the middle pages without any encouragement from me, the way magazines will when they've been folded back or left open, facedown, for some time. But once it was open, I kept it that way. Because there could not have been, in magazines anywhere, many pages more cleverly designed to catch and hang on to a red-blooded man's full and fascinated attention for some time.

The left-hand page was merely printed text, but on the right were displayed photos of three more lovelies, with a line or two of print beneath each of the three pictures. The half-page photo at the top was of a stupendously shapely gal clutching a shiny silver vase or cup, and below that were a pair of quarter-page pix, each of another young lady equally, which is to say totally, unclad.

Midway up the page were a few red marks—a word or two circled there, and some numbers written in the margin—but that merely tickled my eyes as they lingered on the astonishing bare curves of the luscious lass above them and then slid for a few moments over to the text on the left.

Even the text was of more than passing interest. At the top of that left-hand page was the heading, ''Winner in Miss Naked California Contest Chosen,'' and beneath that in smaller type, "Last of Fabulous Fifty Selected for Miss Naked USA Finals September 29."

News of the contest itself wasn't any surprise to me, but I hadn't realized the national wrap-up, or maybe more accurately un-wrap, was so close. This was Friday, September 21, so September 29 was only eight days away. I had known for several months not only that the national finals of this most beauteous of all beauty contests was in the works, but that its climax would be reached right here in California, only a few miles outside the L.A. city limits, at the Doubless Ranch owned by Doubless Productions, these being the less-than-marvelous names of, respectively, two hundred and forty acres on which still stood part of a movie set, and an independent movie production company—formed by two men each of whom had the initials "S.S."—which owned the acreage.

In fact, I had been looking forward to attending those festivities, and an even more imminent booze-and-barbecue bash, also sponsored by Doubless at the Doubless Ranch, if at all possible, because of my sincere interest in such cultural activities.

Culture, in this broad sense, had come a long way since the day when Mack Sennett's bathing beauties made three-fourths of a nation reel with righteous shock and the other fourth shamefully horny. Progress was somewhat inhibited from the first Miss America contests through the Miss Universe and Miss World extravaganzas, and the first "Miss Naked" contests of the late sixties and early seventies were therefore events cogently described, by some, as "a great leap forward."

True, it had taken fifty years to eliminate the zither playing and "Casey-at-the-Bat" recitations from "beauty" contests, but it had—as none who witnessed any of the results would deny—been worth the wait.

Those initial bare-pulchritude competitions could by no means have been described as national in scope, or even truly representative of the talent available in an entire county of the land, much less any one—and certainly not all—of the fifty states. Even so, those first almost casually planned and produced contests in which lovely young creatures posed and paraded publicly wearing nothing except, in more than a few instances, distinctly apprehensive expressions, were described by nine out of ten of those in attendance as lots of fun.

Baleful comments issuing from individuals in the ten-percent minority—ranging from doleful assertions that such flagrant exhibitionism couldn't last and the whole thing would peter out within a year, to dire predictions that even the losers were in danger of being carried off into the woods by monsters—all proved to be without any foundation in fact, or at least not much. This also proved, as it has been often and wisely said: There is nothing so powerful as an idea whose time has come.

The time for a real Miss Naked USA had unquestionably come. For, though to date there had been little coverage of the uncoverage by the news media, only a year earlier there had been real organization plus financial backing and know-how added to enthusiasm, and well-run competitions had been held in forty-two states, with the forty-two winners gathering for the runoff, or playoff, or showoff—it was called many things—in Miami, Florida.

This year, for the first time, the event could accurately be referred to as a truly *national* competition, with a winner from every one of the fifty states. At the finals there would be ceremonies, speeches, personal appearances by movie actors and producers, newspaper and wire-service reporters— but no television reporters, at least not with their cameras, not yet—and politicians. A fifty-piece all-girl orchestra would signal commencement of the event by playing "The Star-Spangled Banner," and its conclusion by "God Bless America" sung by the winner herself.

I was, actually, kind of excited about it all. Which was why I happened to know a little something about the contest. A little something. Not quite enough—as I was about to discover.

I merely glanced over the page of text—a *Frolic* staff writer's rhapsodizing about the "dawning of a new heyday" in America and promising that there would be in the next issue full-page pix of all fifty contestants plus a suitable-for-framing centerfold "of Miss Naked USA herself!"—then looked again at the naked lovely atop the right-hand page, who, I had by now deduced, was the very recent winner of the California contest.

Deservedly so, was my offhand opinion, as I again admired the full-color reproduction of those sweeping, thrusting, swooping, and sensational curves, and for the first time eyed the lady's face with some care.

The silver vase—actually, the wingéd cup awarded to the current Miss Naked California—that she held aslant in both hands concealed quite a lot of one breast, of which there was quite a lot to conceal, and part of her smiling face. Even so, it struck me that there was about that face—about the marvel-ous body, in fact—something . . .

I squinted, started shaking my head rapidly in little twitches.

My gaze fell to the word circled in red ink below the picture. One word, half of the name printed there. I shook my head some more, quite a lot more, opened my eyes wide, blinked.

"Aralia Fields," is what it said, and "Aralia" was the red-circled name.

I looked at that lovely, partly hidden face again, and said to myself:

"Aralia?"

CHAPTER SEVEN

I T was Aralia, all right. *My* Aralia.

The figures written at the margin of the page, in the same red ink used to circle the name, were 555-4489. It looked like a phone number; but because there wasn't a "55" prefix on any phones in the Spartan I knew it couldn't be Aralia's even though I didn't know what her number was.

But I did, for sure, want to call Aralia now.

So, carrying the copy of *Frolic,* I walked back into the living room, picked up the phone receiver, and started dialing Information—then stopped, looked at those figures again.

If that was a phone number, it was a reasonable assumption it had been written down by Werzen, or perhaps Collett, probably right here in this apartment. There would have been no need to make a note of the number if it was in the book, so it figured that Werzen or Collett had gotten the number from Information, or perhaps from a friend and jotted it down before making the call. A call very likely made—to continue

75

the reasonable assumptions—immediately after lamping the living-color display of Aralia's delectable charms, or her name.

I went ahead and dialed Information, got the number listed for Aralia Fields, gave her a call. A minute later, with the ringing phone still unanswered, I hung up, feeling only a slight sense of unease.

It took me several minutes more to run down the name of the man with the phone number 555-4489, which is what the figures turned out to be. It was listed, but not an L.A.-Hollywood number. The man's name was Vincent Ragan, of 1411 Hollyhock Lane. I'd never been on Hollyhock, but I knew where it was, a dozen miles north of Hollywood in largely undeveloped land that was mostly low hills and a lot of trees.

Because it was a toll call, I was able to determine that a call had been made to 555-4489, from the same phone I was using, on Wednesday night, September 19, at eleven P.M. And that was only two nights, less than forty-eight hours, ago.

I heard a car slowing for a stop at the curb, checked to make sure it was a police car, left the front door open. When the team of officers came inside I had just finished checking the L.A. phone directory for Ragan, Vincent. There was a listing, but only one. No home address in the book, or home phone. Just his business address. He was a patent attorney. His business address was on Wilshire Boulevard, a suite composed of rooms 38, 40, 42.

Yeah, on Wilshire Boulevard. In the Weir Building.

*   *   *

76

I knew both of the officers who'd arrived in the radio car, but the first man inside was Bill Rawlins.

Bill was a tall, slim, well-muscled guy a couple of years younger than my thirty, with wavy black hair, a dark handsome face and quick go-to-hell grin that had made a lot of ladies desire to go to hell with him. And very rarely, indeed almost never, had he denied any one of them fulfillment of her desire.

As Bill came inside he said, "Hi, Shell. You didn't make a mistake and just wound him, did you?"

"No such luck."

"You're sure it's Werzen?"

"Yeah. He's in there." I jerked a thumb at the open door.

Both officers went into the bedroom. I waited until Rawlins came out, alone, then took him over near the front door. "Look, pal," I said, "I know Sam's going to have a hemorrhage, but there was no way out of this one."

Rawlins rubbed his chin with a faint scraping sound. "He was still in his office when I left the squadroom. About to take off on his vacation, though."

I nodded.

"Wants everything cleaned up pretty well by midnight tonight—not planning to come in tomorrow. I managed to leave without conversing with the captain, but I'll have to fill him in about this when I get back. And, of course, so will *you,* you know."

"Yeah, I do know. And, ah, that's what I would like to . . . converse with you about, my friend. My dear old friend."

"Wait a shake, Shell. I don't like the way—"

"Bill, just listen for a minute, will you?"

77

I told him most of what had happened since my arrival here, and that I fully intended to visit the LAPD to dictate my statement, among other things, which other things included explaining all to the captain, and possibly throwing myself on his mercy, in case he had any. But, I added, I intended to do all that after some slight delay, if Bill could refrain a little longer from handcuffing me, because I had reason to believe I should make one quick trip first.

All Rawlins did during my spiel was shake his head and say, twice, "Can't do it." And when I'd finished he said, "Quick trip where?"

"See a guy out on Hollyhock Lane. Which is at least sixteen or seventeen miles from where we're at. If I have to go in the opposite direction first, clear the hell into downtown L.A.—"

"Why is it so important you see this guy?"

"Well, I'm not sure if it is. That's why I want to brace him, drop in without advance notice."

Rawlins glanced back toward the bedroom door, then said, "What's it got to do with this?"

"Man, that would take a little explaining."

"You could explain it downtown, old buddy."

"You're kidding. No, you aren't, are you?"

I told him the rest of what had occurred since my arrival at the duplex, plus much of what had happened before I decided to come here. Then I added, "Hell, I'm not going to leave the country. It's just, well, maybe an hour's delay. Naturally, I know you can't *tell* me to split, but if you'll just go to the can or something—"

"I dunno . . ." He paused. "This gal you mentioned—the

one lives in the Spartan—I was off last night. But I heard about her from some of the boys. Yeah, *did* I hear about her. It turns out she's really honest-to-God Miss *Naked* California?''

"That's right, you haven't met her—haven't even seen her, have you?" I paused. "Well, old friend, it just happens I have been carrying around a picture of my new friend, Aralia. And she is a dear, sweet girl, she really is.''

By then I had opened the copy of *Frolic*, which was still clutched in my hand—or, rather, held the magazine before Rawlins and let it slowly, as though by magic, open itself again—saying, "Bill, I want you to meet a dear, sweet girl, my pal, Aralia.''

"Oh, brother," he said, automatically flashing a go-to-hell grin at the picture. "I mean, sister. That's her, huh? That's really her?''

"See the name circled in red, Bill? Observe the name?''

"Yeah. You *do* know her?''

"Would I kid you?''

"Yeah. But, O.K., Shell old buddy, you'll introduce me to the lady, of course?''

"Are you out of your cotton . . . ah. Of course, Bill,'' I said sourly. "What are old buddies for?''

"You're a brick," he said. "Well, you wait right here, you understand? That's an official police order. I've got to go to the can.''

I almost missed Hollyhock Lane.

It was a narrow drive, black-topped with asphalt, perhaps wide enough for two cars to pass easily if they were both Volkswagens. It rose slightly away from me, a straight dark line going uphill for a hundred yards and then disappearing among closely planted orange trees. Another hundred yards or so farther on, the road passed out of the cultivated grove into land only slightly more open, with oaks, pepper trees, eucalyptus, and enough other trees and shrubs to qualify the area as Southern California jungle.

The trees cut off some of the sunlight, and there wasn't much of it left. The air was beginning to feel cooler, softer; it would be dark in another half hour or so.

I didn't expect to find much of a house out here in an area so sparsely populated, even though it was only a few miles from Hollywood. But I found a dandy. After passing two small places, much like mountain cabins, Hollyhock Lane curved left past a private drive rising to a beautiful ranch-style home at the top of a small hill. The house number was on a large metal mailbox at the beginning of the drive—the name "Ragan" was there, too, for that matter, in small cemented-on metal letters. This one wasn't a little cabin, but more like two hundred and fifty thousand bucks worth of stained wood and native stone. Whoever John Ragan was, he was doing pretty well.

I drove on up to an open area covered with pink gravel in front of the house, parked behind another car already there. It was a five- or six-year-old Chevrolet sedan, its once green paint job dulled by time and weather. The Chevy didn't look like a car the owner of this place would drive. I got out, carrying the copy of *Frolic* rolled up in my hand.

The sun hit only the top of the house, not the land or trees below. But there was plenty of light for me to see that Ragan—if he was the husky-looking man with his back to the front door—had company. A woman and a young long-haired individual were standing there talking to him. As I approached they both turned and walked toward me, obviously heading for the Chevy.

Before they reached me, the man called after them, "I'll phone you about it tonight, Mrs. Green."

"Mrs. Green" was middle-aged, maybe twenty or thirty pounds overweight, with a puffy face, wearing rimless glasses, shiny green dress, black shoes. The long-haired "individual" turned out to be male, a young guy in his middle twenties I guessed. Greasy-looking hair, pale eyes like pools of phlegm, heavy brows, thin nose, a small family of colorful pimples on his left cheek. He looked so unappetizing, I'd have given odds that only a starving cannibal would consider cooking him. As they passed, the woman gave me an artificial and joyless smile. The moldy-looking youth didn't glance my way, just trudged by.

After a few more steps I was standing on a pink-stained cement deck stretching across the front of the house, where the husky man had waited while I approached.

He was a nice-looking guy, around forty years old, wearing dark horn-rimmed glasses and a curious expression. He was five feet eight or nine inches tall, maybe a hundred and seventy pounds, with a lot of brown hair, obviously professionally styled—full over the ears and at the back of his head, long thick curly sideburns. He wore orange-and-white patterned slacks with an orange belt, crepe-soled white shoes, and a snugly fitting short-sleeved white T-shirt that revealed a muscular chest and flat stomach. He looked like a man who played a lot of tennis, or jogged every morning, or maybe worked out with weights.

"Hello," I said. "Are you Mr. Ragan?"

He nodded, one eyebrow raised above the curve of his horn-rims. "Yes, I am."

"My name's Shell Scott, Mr. Ragan. I'm a private detective."

"Detective?" The other brow rode up above his glasses. "You're here to see me?"

"That's right. Well, it's really about some people you know. At least, I think you know them."

He started to speak, then stuck out his hand, shook mine, and said, "Come in, please. We might as well be comfortable."

I followed him into a small hallway. Ragan walked to a door on our left, opened it, waved me through ahead of him into a living room, large and very attractive. It was bright, with a lot of reddish-yellow and burnt orange, a pair of white fluffy-looking hassocks, and an enormous white sectional divan.

"Sit down, Mr. Scott," he said pleasantly, indicating the divan. "Would you care for a drink?"

"Thanks, I wouldn't mind. Bourbon?"

"Sure. Soda?"

"Just water."

He walked toward the corner of the room. I didn't see anything that looked like a bar there. Ragan stopped before a barely visible foot-square screen in the wall, pushed a button next to it, and spoke into the screen. "Harwell, a bourbon and water for my guest, and my usual. Bring some of those little crab things, will you?"

And from the intercom's speaker, "Right away, sir."

Ragan came back to the divan, sat down, and said to me, smiling, "All right, who are these people you wanted to ask me about?"

He was so pleasant, and charming, I felt a little grieved at having to ask him about crooks and hoodlums. "Elroy Werzen, for one," I said.

He pushed his full lips forward slightly, and his neat brows lowered as he shook his head silently.

"James Collett?"

He continued to shake his head. "There must be some mistake, Mr. Scott. Am I supposed to know who these people are?"

"Well, I'm not sure, really. How about an Alvin Hauk?" He shook his head some more. "Edward Brett, called Buddy? Incidentally, the man Werzen I mentioned is also known as Puffer, and Hauk is called Al the Clam."

He scowled, beginning to look somewhat—quite a bit—less charming. "I really fail to understand why you're here, Mr. Scott. Who are these men?"

"Most of them are hoods, ex-cons. But—"

"Hoods? What the hell makes you think *I'd* know any ex-convicts?"

There was a little more starch in his voice this time, more muscle. But I couldn't blame the man for being somewhat bugged if he'd never heard of the characters I'd mentioned. "Just fishing," I said. "It's a large part of my job, and routine for me. I don't mean to offend you, Mr. Ragan—"

"Oh, it isn't that, but—well, I'm active in a number of civic and political organizations. If you have some reason to believe I might know these men, and presumably you must, I'd like to know what possible connection you feel there could be between such men and me.''

"Fair enough. It's all pretty thin, but for one thing, I saw Hauk, Werzen, and Collett outside the Weir Building earlier today. They were talking to a man who might have been you—I don't say it *was* you, Mr. Ragan. I'm not—"

"The Weir Building?" he interrupted, showing some interest. "I have a suite of offices there."

"I know."

He paused, head slightly lowered, staring at me. "What do you mean, this man might have been me? I assure you, it was not, Mr. Scott."

"I said 'might' because *I* wasn't sure. He was about your size and build, dark-haired, that's all."

"And these people were congregated somewhere around the building in which I have my offices." He smiled. "Thin . . . is hardly the word."

There was a nice sharp edge to his voice, and I had no doubt that Ragan could turn nasty enough to clabber milk if he put his mind to it.

I smiled, leaned an inch or two closer to him. "I'm not accusing you of anything, Mr. Ragan, so relax. If all I'm doing is wasting my time, and yours—"

Ragan glanced past me, saying, "Thank you, Harwell."

A short dark-skinned man wearing black trousers and a white shirt with long collars and French cuffs appeared, placed a tray on the table in front of the divan, smiled broadly at the far wall, and quietly left, still smiling.

Ragan handed me my drink in a squat gold-rimmed glass, and said more pleasantly, "Try some of these, Mr. Scott. I assure you, they're delicious.'' He pushed a small plate filled with crispy-looking oddities toward me.

I bit into one. It was one of the ''crab things'' Ragan had spoken of. ''Delicious,'' I said. It was.

''Crab Rangoon. Or Rangoon-Harwell. One of his specialties; he's a marvelous cook.''

''He sure is.''

''Was that all, Mr. Scott?''

I hadn't even chewed up the first crab Rangoon, or Rangoon-Harwell. ''Yeah,'' I said. ''I hate to eat and run, but . . . There is one more little item. Another name. Do you mind?''

''Why should I mind?''

''Beats me. Aralia Fields.''

''Who?''

I bit into another of the crab things, had a swallow of my drink. Ragan was shaking his head, the full lips pushed forward again. ''No . . . I—the name . . . I may have heard the name somewhere, but . . . No.''

''One of the guys I mentioned phoned you recently, from Hollywood, about her. I assume it was about her.''

He smiled. ''You assume a good deal, don't you, Mr. Scott?''

''Don't we all? You're certain you know none of the individuals I've mentioned, and that none of them phoned you about Aralia Fields—or anything else?''

He was still smiling. ''When should I have received this alleged call?''

''I was hoping you could tell me,'' I said.

''I'm sorry. I know you hate to eat and run, as you yourself phrased it—''

85

I'd been holding the rolled-up copy of *Frolic* in my left hand all this time. I tossed it over the couch toward him and said, "Page thirty-eight. She's at the top, name's circled in red. A phone number's written there, too, in red ink. Your phone number."

The smile faded slowly as the lips were pushed forward once more and the neat brows lowered. He looked at the nude shot of Aralia, cocked his head on one side. "That is my phone number. Of course, it wouldn't be difficult for almost anyone to find out what my number is—"

"It's not in the L.A. book."

He looked directly at me. "The number is unpublished, but listed. Which means anyone could get it from the operator."

"Let's assume that's what the fellow did."

His lips twitched, but then he gazed past my shoulder, cocked his head to one side again and said, "Ah, yes . . . of course." He paused, nodded. "Aralia. I thought that name was familiar." Ragan looked at the half-page photograph again. "So *this* is Aralia. I understand now."

"I wish I did."

"You shall, Mr. Scott. A few nights ago a friend of mine, another attorney, phoned me here. It was quite late. He was at the home of one of his clients. At least, he said he was with a client, and I assume he was at the individual's home. My friend had there seen a photograph of an extravagantly lovely young lady, as he described her—this must be what he saw—and asked if I might be able to arrange for him to meet her." He paused. "As I've mentioned, Mr. Scott, and as my friend is aware, I have a rather wide acquaintance here in

Southern California among, well, people who get things done, shall we say?"

"It's O.K. by me. Was it wide enough?"

"I beg your pardon?"

"Were you able to arrange the meeting?"

"Oh, no, I wasn't. I see what you mean; no, in this case my contacts were disappointingly narrow. I wasn't even able to learn where the lady lives. And, too, I was damnably busy, preparing an important brief that had to be filed with the court clerk by ten the next morning. So, after a perfunctory effort, I simply forgot about my friend's request, if you want the truth."

"That's what I want. Would you remember when this guy with the hots called?"

"With what?"

"When your attorney friend phoned to request your help in locating Miss Fields?"

"Oh . . . I'm sure, a few days ago. First of the week, I'd say. Monday, perhaps Tuesday."

I smiled. "Well, it would be the night before you had to file that important brief at ten the next morning, wouldn't it?"

I guess you could say he gave me a rather hard look then. "So it would," he said mildly. "You're very helpful, Mr. Scott. Yes, I filed the brief yesterday, Thursday morning. So I must have received the call Wednesday night."

"Maybe, like, around eleven P.M.?"

"It was before midnight."

"Right. Well, thanks, Mr. Ragan." I crunched the last of those puffy crab things between my teeth. They really were tasty little cookies. Then I got to my feet.

I held out my hand, and Ragan leaned forward and shook it. But after he dropped his arm, my hand was still stuck out there. He looked at it for a while.

"Something . . . ?"

"I'd like my magazine back."

"Oh, of course. Where . . ."

He felt around, found the magazine, which had somehow managed to get shoved down almost out of sight between a couple of the big cushions, next to his right leg.

"There you are, Mr. Scott," he said. "I certainly wouldn't want to deprive you of your reading matter."

I grinned. "Like you," I said quietly, "I only look at the pictures."

He flushed slightly and started to speak, but didn't.

I went on. "I guess we're safe in assuming the red-ink notations were made by the friend who phoned you. Right?"

"Why, I would assume . . . of course. Yes, of course."

"Would you mind giving me his name, Mr. Ragan?" I waited, added, "Which would wrap this little matter up, so we could file it all in the wastebasket."

He was silent so long, I thought he wasn't going to reply. But at length he said flatly, "Wallace Epplewhite. He's an important man, Scott. Married. With many powerful friends. I would strongly suggest that you refrain from—bugging Mr. Epplewhite."

"I try not to bug anybody, Mr. Ragan. But, sometimes, I fail. Thanks again."

We smiled at each other, much as two ladies in identical gowns at the annual ball might smile at each other across the crowded room. Which is to say, with no more warmth than a couple of one-watt light bulbs.

Then I walked out, into velvet dusk laced with the faint scent of distant fertilizer, and tooled my Cad back toward town.

Toward the "extravagantly lovely" Aralia, I hoped.

But also, unavoidably, toward the sometimes unlovely captain, Phil Samson.

CHAPTER EIGHT

I knew, and knew very well, that I should get down to the Police Building with reasonable, if not remarkable, speed.

But I intended to visit the Spartan first, at least briefly.

Both before and immediately after my visit with Vincent Ragan I had stopped at a phone booth to call Aralia again, and each time, which made it three times now, there had been only the phone ringing, and ringing, unanswered.

At the Spartan's desk I stopped and asked Jimmy, the night man, if he'd seen Miss Fields go out.

He smiled a dirty smile. "Not since I let her into your place, Shell. That was hours—"

"My place? She's in my apartment now?"

"Far as I know. She asked me to let her in. And like you once impressed on me with plenty of sincerity, any time a good-looking broad wants—"

"What's she doing up there, Jimmy?"

He gave me a dirty smile again.

He was young, diligent, ambitious. But his head was filled with fantasies. I told him what would happen to him if he didn't reform, then left him grimacing in mock horror and trotted up the stairs.

At 212 I banged on the door. Nothing for a while. Then I hammered some more and called, "For Pete's sake, let me in, will you? I live here."

That got results. Small shuffling or thumping sounds, somebody moving over the carpet, then click of lock and the door opened a crack. One eye, the clear hot blue of a small arc light, framed by a thick loop of strawberry-colored hair, eyed me.

Then the soft warm voice, "Oh, good! It's you!"

"Who else lives here? Besides *us*, I mean." I said it with a big smile.

"Come in, Shell, come in."

"Thanks."

I went inside, shut and locked the door, leered at Aralia, who was wearing a smooth white blouse held precariously together in front with four small pearly buttons, the blouse itself so thin it was pink where the points of those high heavy breasts thrust against the cloth, and a pair of brief white shorts that I guess are called hip-huggers, or should be, even if they are not.

"Shell, I hope you're not mad at me for asking Jimmy to let me wait here."

"Mad? I'm not even peevish—"

"The phone was ringing till it almost drove me out of my *mind*! Newspaper reporters, television men, all kinds of people, even that policeman."

I got a little twinge right there. But Aralia kept on going so fast, I wasn't able to clearly define its source, which was unfortunate.

"And I got a call from people financing a . . . contest—it's something I haven't told you about yet, Shell."

"I think—"

"But I will. Anyway, almost everybody knows everything there is to know about it, practically."

"What do you mean, practically?"

"And then I started getting, oh, a little scared, too. So I thought I'd feel better here in your apartment. I hope you don't mind."

By this time we were sitting on the chocolate-brown divan in my living room, she in the middle, me very close to the middle. "Mind?" I said, smiling. "Of course not. If I had a lick of sense I would have suggested it myself."

"You did suggest it. Last night." Her tender-looking lips were curving slightly in the soft start of a smile.

"Ah. Of course," I said. "I remember, I think. At any rate, I'm glad you're here, Aralia. For one thing, I have a few questions to ask you, and I've got only a minute—"

"I didn't get much sleep last night, anyway. Did you?"

"Once I fell asleep, I did. But getting there took most of the night—"

"I kept thinking about that naked man in my apartment. Is that what kept you awake, too, Shell?"

"Well, pretty close."

"Oh, I've just been babbling on, and I haven't even asked what you've been doing today."

She stopped, and smiled sweetly at me.

"Is that a question?" I asked her. "Well, I snooped around, shot a guy . . . Oh-oh, now I remember. I knew there was something I had to do. You really should wear serapes, or shawls, or an asbestos dickey."

"You shot someone? *Shot?*"

"Yeah. I'll fill you in later. Right now time is short, and shortening. Let me throw some quick questions at you, O.K.?"

She nodded, bright eyes interested, fixed on my face.

"A little earlier I was thinking back to our conversation here last night. I remembered you said your mother remarried a man named Fields. Charles Fields. Right?"

"Yes. Of course, Charlie ran off somewhere after a couple of years, so I never knew him. I don't even remember him."

"What I'm getting at, if your stepfather's name was Fields you weren't born with that name. So what was your real father's name?"

"Amber. Of course, he died before I was born, you know. And Ma wanted us all to have Charlie's name, so Petey and I just grew up with it. We didn't really have anything to say about it."

She was telling me something else, but I wasn't listening. I was staring past her shoulder, head bent to one side, thinking— much, I suppose, as Vincent Ragan had earlier gazed past me after I mentioned Aralia's name to him.

Amber . . . Norman Amber. He was one of the men who'd been serving a sentence in San Quentin Prison during the time Buddy Brett was an inmate there, had even shared the same cell with Brett for a while.

"Aralia," I said, "was your father's first name Norman?"

"Yes, but I never really knew him at all. . . ." Her bright

94

eyes widened and she held her lips in an "O" for a few seconds. "How did you know *that*?"

I almost blurted out that I'd seen some info about his prison record, but stopped. Because clearly Aralia believed—all her life *had* believed—that her father was dead. Which, for all I knew, maybe he was.

"I saw"—I began, then went on—"or read, heard, the name somewhere. I think. It's not important. How about your mother, does she still use the name Fields?"

"I suppose so, unless she married again after I left home. It was Laura Fields then, but I don't know if it still is. I told you, I haven't been back to Burbank since I went on my own."

"Uh-huh. Did she tell you much about your father? What he did, what kind of man he was?"

Aralia seemed surprised by the question, but after a moment answered, "Ma didn't say much about him, and never anything good when she did. Oh, she mentioned a few times that he was so smart—'smart-head' she called him, or 'old dumbsmart'—she didn't understand him half the time. He was some kind of engineer, and Ma said right after they were married he started puttering around and trying to invent things, instead of holding regular jobs—that was one of the things she couldn't stand, I guess." Aralia shrugged, apparently having exhausted her fund of knowledge about him.

"How did he die? He must have been a fairly young man, I'd imagine."

"I think he was like thirty, maybe not that old. One of his inventions—some 'dumbsmart thing' Ma called it—blew up, or electrocuted him, I'm not sure."

There were other questions I might have asked, but I let them ride and said, "Well, enough of this folderol, Aralia. Let's get down to the really important things—or, why are you sitting here with your clothes on?"

"What? Clothes on?"

"Exactly."

"Don't most people . . . oh. Do you think I should take my clothes off, Shell?"

"Exactly. Ah . . . What I mean, would a pilot try to fly without wings? Would a general make a speech without his medals? Why, then, would Miss Naked USA—or, at least, California—appear without her identifying . . . ah. Let me have another go at it."

I didn't get a chance. Aralia sprang to her feet, smiling joyously, and clapped her hands. "Oh, Shell, when you said '*Miss Naked USA*' it sounded so *wonderful*! I got a thrill all the way from my toes clear up to my nose."

"That's quite a ways," I said, as she wiggled her nose, and possibly even her toes, enticingly.

"You know then, don't you? I thought probably you must by now. I think I really *do* have a chance, Shell. To be Miss Naked USA, I mean. Maybe only a *little* chance, but I want it *so* much, and I have to think positively, don't I?"

"Can't hurt. Well, I was just sort of fooling around, working up to—"

"I never believed I'd win here in California, I really didn't think I had a chance. But when I *did* win, it gave me more—more—well, you know."

"Yeah. And you had quite a bunch to begin with."

"So I'm just *dying* for the finals to start, and that's only a

96

week from tomorrow! I'm going to walk out there, naked and proud, all charged up and sizzly with—with—"

"Yeah."

"—you know, thinking *positive*."

"Yeah . . . or, rather, no, Aralia."

"And day after tomorrow, this Sunday, I'll be the only woman guest at the Doubless barbecue! Isn't that something, Shell, the *only* woman invited to be there—with four hundred men?"

"*Wait* a minute."

I knew all about that barbecue. In fact, I was one of those four hundred invited guests Aralia had mentioned.

The two partners in the Doubless movie production company, who were also co-owners of the Doubless Ranch, were putting on the bash not only because they were both deeply involved in the Miss Naked USA contest, which they wished to promote, but in making horrible but profitable movies, which they wished to promote, and very likely were into other enterprises which they wished to promote, because if nothing else, they were high-powered promoters.

Because of string-pulling by another, much more successful and well-known movie producer—Harry Feldspen, president of Magna Studios and a long-time friend and sometime client of mine—I had received my engraved by-invitation-only card a couple of weeks ago. But I hadn't thought a great deal about it since then, and I had not been aware that Miss Naked California was scheduled to appear at the bash.

"Aralia," I said, "you're not going to the barbecue Sunday."

"But I *am*, Shell. Isn't it marvelous? It was suggested to

me the very day I won here in California, and I got a phone call just this afternoon—I mentioned it, about hearing from people financing a contest—to confirm it. So it's all arranged, and, really, it's an absolutely wonderful break for me—some of the important men who'll be judges for the *finals* are going to be at the Doubless ranch Sunday. And *my* being there—the only one of the fifty state winners even invited—won't hurt a bit!''

Aralia was still standing, and she threw her arms out rapturously, then wrapped them around her shoulders and hugged herself, giving the impression of a girl smiling all over. ''And you know what, Shell?'' she went on. ''Because of the title I won, you know, they told me to be sure and appear wearing the outfit I wore when I won it, isn't that cute?''

''Cute?''

She threw her arms wide again and cried, ''So this Sunday I'm going to walk out there, naked and proud, sizzly-positive—''

''No, you're not. Not *there*, you're not.''

''—and all. And then at the finals I'm going to give it everything I've *got,* and even if I come in *fiftieth* I'll know I put my best foot . . . What?''

''What what?''

''What do you mean, I'm not?''

''Well, dear, you sure used the right word earlier. Dying, I think it was. In fact, I know it was. You seem not sufficiently aware that there are two kinds of bad men. There are the bad men who want to do something bad to you; those are the good men. Then there are the bad men who want to kill you, and *those* are the guys you've got to stay away from. So you mustn't even think of parading around in the altogether—at least not publicly, ha-ha—this Sunday, or maybe even at the finals, Saturday, and perhaps not for several Saturdays and Sundays yet to come, so long as there's even a small chance you might thus get yourself permanently chilled, a thought too depressing even to contemplate. Now, about those nice bad men, like me—"

"But of *course* I'm going to compete in the finals. And appear at the Doubless barbecue, too!"

"No, no, you mustn't—"

"Don't tell *me* no, I mustn't. I am de-ter-mined! I *must*, and I *will*! I've made up my mind, and I just *know* everything will be all right. I can and I *will*—"

"What books have you been reading?"

"How did you know I read a book?"

"Easy. Look, I already shot one guy today, who couldn't, so far as I'm aware, have had any reason for instantly wanting to blast me except that I've been trying to find out why Buddy Brett came here—or was sent here—to knock you off. It happens that this thug I plugged was intimately associated with Brett. Also with the creep I braced downstairs on North Rossmore. And probably with others equally inimical to the longevity of people they become annoyed with."

"But nobody would try to do anything to me at the *finals*, or even at the barbecue Sunday. Not with all those people around . . . and all?"

At the end it was a question.

"Maybe. Maybe not," I said. "But you don't know. And

it would be a severe disappointment if you were wrong, wouldn't it?''

Aralia started protesting some more, but weakly, and I showed her the copy of *Frolic* magazine I'd picked up in Collett's apartment. She'd already seen it, and her own photo, of course, but when I explained the circumstances under which I'd found the magazine and asked her if she had any idea why one of the lobs I'd been checking on would have circled her name, she merely shook her head, looking puzzled.

Then she said, "What's that number? Is it a phone number?"

"Yeah. Belongs to an attorney." I looked from the magazine to her eyes, which were on mine, and said, "Name of Vincent Ragan, by the way. Ring any bells?"

She shook her head again. "I don't understand *any* of this."

"That's the key point, dear. Neither do I—yet. And until we know a lot more about what's going on, and there seems to be plenty, you'd better give up any idea of strolling hither and yon, incandescently nude and stupendously gorgeous, prior to the barbecue at the Doubless Ranch this Sunday."

"I suppose . . . Golly, that's almost like a poem."

"Huh? Barbecue at the Double—"

"The way you said that—about me, I mean. Stupendously nude and incandescently gorgeous . . ." She smiled blissfully.

"Actually, it was the other way around—skip it. Works both ways. But poetry? It didn't even rhyme, though they do say some of the *best* poetry—"

"Do you really think I'm gorgeous, Shell?"

"Well, hell, yes. Did I give you the impression I thought you were a scrawny old hag?"

"No. But you never said you thought I was pretty, either. Or anything. Oh, never mind."

She was silent for a few seconds, then took a deep breath and said softly, "What did you mean, Shell, when you said I mustn't parade around, like without anything on, 'at least not publicly ha-ha.' "

"You've got a good ear. That's exactly what I said. Well, it was a little joke thing, sort of. Fun thing. Implying that nobody would shoot you or wreak terrible havoc upon you if you thus paraded privately. See? For example, if you practiced your, ah, parading here—in my handy apartment, that is, where we're at—well, you can bet your boots *I* wouldn't—"

"Do you want me to?" She was smiling sweetly. "You know when I entered my first Miss Naked—way back last January—I was really nervous, embarrassed. But I got over that right away, almost. And then I started to enjoy it. I mean, I really did *enjoy* it."

"That's nice."

"I guess I just like being naked, if you want the truth. And walking around, and feeling all those eyes in that big audience on me. It's exciting, it's *fun*!" She took another deep—even deeper—breath. "What do you think of that, Shell?"

"I think it might be almost as much fun here, even without the big audience."

She moved her tongue around inside one cheek, lids slightly lowered over the long-lashed blue eyes. "It might . . ." she said. Then, smiling, she added, ". . . even be more."

Her left hand moved to the top of that thin white blouse, and with a little *flick* of her fingers the first pearly button was undone. Her hand moved down, *flick,* and the second little button was out of its little hole. That was two of them undone. I was getting, you might say, a bit undone myself; there were only four of those little pearly buttons. Then, *flick-flick*.

"Boy, isn't that something," I said.

"Are you just going to sit there, staring at my buttons?" Aralia asked me gently.

"I didn't know that's what I was doing."

"I'm not going to have to do this all by myself, am I?"

"How could you?"

"I mean, shouldn't *you* be taking some things off, Shell?"

"Good thinking. Yeah. Sure, I'll start with my gun, how about that? Then my holster. Then—"

"Oh! Your gun!"

"Huh?" I had it in my hand already, but I wasn't doing anything with it. "Just putting it on the table, dear," I said. "I wasn't going to plug you with the thing."

"It's just that seeing it reminded me of something."

"Of what?"

"I'm not sure I should mention it."

"Go ahead. It'll bug me now if you don't."

"Well, guns, and holsters, they made me think of the police, and I suddenly remembered that policeman calling here so many times. I meant to tell you about it when you came back, but I forgot."

"Policeman? Calling here?"

Aralia had pulled the blouse apart with both hands, was sliding it back over her smooth shoulders, and down. As she arched her back those magnificent bare breasts seemed to swell, to grow, to thrust themselves buoyantly forward as if they possessed a vibrant and vigorous life of their own, which I wasn't entirely certain they did not.

"Yes, after Jimmy let me inside, the phone rang and rang. I didn't want to answer it at first, here in your apartment, but it rang so *many* times I finally couldn't stand it. The policeman—he said he was a captain, I think—"

She stopped, and looked closely at me. "Did you say something?"

"No."

"I thought you made a crazy noise."

"I did."

"Are you in pain?"

"Yes."

"Can I help?"

"Not this pain, you can't. Go on. Tell me everything."

"Well, this captain, I don't know who he was—"

"That's all right. I know who he was. Did he sound like the Wolf Man?"

"No, silly . . . Except—it's funny you should say that."

"No, it isn't."

"When I first answered the phone, and said hello and all, at first there wasn't anything except, oh, like heavy breathing at the other end, and a kind of funny chomping or chewing sound like . . ."

"Like the Wolf Man? Chewing on a cigar, maybe? Or a human thigh bone? Well, I've got to go. It's sad, God knows, but I've really got to—"

"Then when he found out who I was, and that you weren't here, he said when the scourge of evildoers came back to bed—I don't know why he said that—"

"It's O.K. Don't worry about it."

"—to tell him to get in touch with the man. Without fail, he said. He didn't even say a name, in touch with who."

"It's O.K. I know who. You'd better put your blouse back on."

"He really did say 'scourge of evildoers.' I'm still not sure what he was talking about. What's a scourge?"

"That's me."

"But of evildoers, he said."

"That's me, too. Don't take your shorts off, dear. Just be a waste. Oh-h, what a waste. I don't think you really heard me before, but . . ." I sighed, stood up. "I have to go."

"Go?"

"You got it."

"Like that?"

"I'll wait a minute or two. But it is now clear to me that my good friend, Captain Samson, has not yet departed from the Police Building. And that he will not under any conceivable circumstances depart before I present myself there, and afford him the opportunity to . . . ah, reason with me."

"What about?"

"You will recall my telling you of this Homicide captain who feels my investigative procedures leave a little something to be desired?"

"He's the one who's mad at you for kicking the wrong door down and then—"

"Yes. We need not go over it all again. Well, I deduce that he has by now learned that this afternoon I lay in wait and assassinated a Good Humor man. Consequently, he will wish to hear my side of the story before he boils me in cooking fat—"

"Shell, don't talk like that! It's *negative*."

"Who said anything different? Dammit, I told you not to take your pants off. What *for*? I've got to *go*. Would I kid you at a time like this? Aralia, Aralia, will you *please* . . ."

She stood up, facing me, gently rubbing her fanny, and smiling an inscrutable smile.

"Why are you doing this to me?" I asked.

"*I* believe," she said, "in finishing what I start."

It was tough, believe me, to leave Aralia there in my apartment, gently caressing her own bare derriere and smiling, saying things like, "So, go," and "Who's stopping you?" and "Maybe you'd like to borrow my book."

But I knew that if I did not soon, very soon, placate Captain Samson in at least a small degree, there was every likelihood that I would not again see Aralia, or anyone else, for a large number of days. And nights. It was, I think, the thought of all those nights that gave me strength to leave.

I did try to make Aralia understand that I was, so to speak, taking the long view, as does the boy who saves his pennies till he has a whole dollar, or the man who—like the good captain himself—forsakes his annual two-week vacation for three years in a row so he can eventually take one two-week vacation all at once.

Of the boy, Aralia said sweetly, "But what if he loses the whole dollar all at once, Shell?" And about the man no comment was necessary, since I'd blown that one myself.

At least, she had not stalked out and down the hall to her

own apartment, partly, I suppose, because she really did feel ill at ease there now, and partly because I vowed that if I lived—I kind of exaggerated the terrible dangers—I would return with champagne, and little edible goodies, and a big surprise.

I think she listened to my argument. I couldn't be certain, since during it she strolled about the living room, humming—I couldn't place the melody, but I was pretty sure the lyric began, "*There* she is . . ."—and when I went out the door she wasn't even facing me, but was bending over to place a stack of records on the stereo's spindle.

It wasn't easy, leaving her like that.

In fact, as I walked out the Spartan's front entrance and down the steps into the balmy night, I saw vividly before me, not shadowy North Rossmore and my Cadillac parked across the street, but a good part of what had won for Aralia the title "Miss Naked California."

So that's what I walked happily toward and, simultaneously, sadly from. With a small smile on my lips and a small bittersweet sound in my ears. That sound, in its odd way, though not really unpleasant of itself, seemed—like Gunnar Lindstrom's vibrations of earlier in the day—to possess faint or possibly even unheard unpleasantnesses within it, an almost menacing tickle at the ear.

It wasn't my imagination. The sound was really there, not merely a product of the abstracted mind. There and getting louder. Something on my right. Close now.

I was in the street, maybe ten feet from my Cad. I pulled my head around, squinted up Rossmore. Nothing much, after all. Just a car approaching. Not speeding, not racing at me, just perking along at about twenty miles an hour.

With its lights off.

I didn't even think about what I was doing. When my right foot hit the asphalt I took one fast step and jumped straight ahead at my Cad, slammed against its side, started dropping to the street.

I never did see the gun. If I'd moved half a second later I never would have seen it. It wasn't a handgun or even a rifle. That booming blast was from the muzzle of a heavy-gauge shotgun.

Fat chunks of shot ripped the air inches behind my back. As I fell to the street clawing for the .38 under my coat, the car, a dark sedan, was only feet away. I could see the blur of a man at the near window, another blur like part of him that moved and gleamed, swinging back and down toward me.

I landed on the asphalt with a solid jar, gun in my hand but face down with my right arm beneath me. I rolled, fast, but I didn't even try to aim the Colt and fire, just kept rolling, over all the way and face down once more, then scratching and grabbing and kicking to get farther under the Cad.

The sonofabitch fired again before I'd made it all the way under, but he missed, shot high. He'd expected to get me with that first booming blast—understandably. You don't have to aim at the bull's-eye when you're spraying more than a dozen lethal slugs at once. That second, and last, shot was high but not by much.

I heard the ugly ripping sound of metal pellets crashing through the Cad's door above me, imagined I felt the car rock, scratched some more, and squirmed over next to the

107

curb. The engine of the other car was suddenly louder, whining as the driver hit the gas, picked up speed.

I couldn't get out from under the Cad's right side with the curb filling much of the space there, so I shoved myself forward, got my right arm thrust out in front of me, .38 firm in my fist. I could see only part of that dark sedan, only its spinning tires and glitter of back bumper. Another six inches forward and I could see most of the car's rear end—in line with my gun.

I squeezed off two shots as twin red taillights flared bright red, winked dim and bright again. I pressed my body flatter against the asphalt, pulled my other arm up, and got my left hand beneath my right, steadying the gun. Squeal of sliding rubber came back to me, punctuated by three more sharp cracks from my Colt as I squeezed the trigger, pulling the revolver's short barrel right, trying to keep it aimed at the turning car.

Then the sedan was gone.

Twice more I heard that screech of rubber skidding on asphalt, each time fainter, more distant. After that, just the normal soft hum of traffic on Beverly Boulevard, sounds of the city. And, after a minute or so, some kind of nightbird singing.

Yeah, a minute or so.

I just lay there for a while, the side of my face resting against the street. I could feel muscles in my right forearm quivering, as if an electric current were running through them. Then that stopped, the tightness between my shoulder blades eased a little, my pulse slowed down reasonably close to normal.

I sucked air into my throat, filled my lungs, oily dirt-and-tar smell of the street sticking in my nostrils. Then I inched sideways, out from under the Cad again. Taking my time. It seemed, then, as if I had all the time in the world, that there was no reason for hurry, that there could never be a reason for hurry.

I heard nearby windows sliding up—or maybe down, now that the excitement appeared to be over—and a voice calling something, another more distant voice answering, and the sound of running feet. Soft, not the slap of leather, like someone running barefoot.

That's what it was.

She came tearing down the Spartan's steps and over the walk and into the street, then slowed, stopped a couple of yards away as I straightened up and stuck the Colt back into its holster.

"Shell?" Her voice wavered. "Are you all right?"

"Yeah. So get back in the Spartan, will you? I've got enough to worry about."

"God, I thought—I thought you were dead."

I'd noticed she was not in the same condition as when I'd left the apartment, but only now did I recognize her outfit as an old trench coat of mine.

Aralia looked past me, at the black holes in the sky-blue paint job of my Cadillac, then she stepped closer, lifted one hand, and let it fall against my chest.

"I thought . . . I thought you were dead," she said. "I thought you were dead."

"Will you quit saying that?"

"What happened?"

109

"What the hell do you think happened? Two, three, I don't know, bastards tried to saw me in half with a shotgun. You crazy broad, what the hell are you doing out here on—ah, I'm sorry." I stopped. "I'm sorry, Aralia. I'm not mad at you. Mad, yes, but not at you."

"I know." Her voice was soft. "I understand."

Maybe she did.

She went on. "Mad. And still scared, a little."

"Me? Scared? *Me?* Yeah, you better believe it. Well, I have to run, downtown to see . . . Oh, boy." I shook my head, forcing my thoughts into another channel. Looking at Aralia, I said, "I'm pleased that you got dressed instead of running out here naked as a jaybird. Surprised, but pleased. You just keep on taking old Shell's advice. Aren't you glad I told you to put on your pants, and things? Why, you might—"

"But I didn't," she said.

"Didn't what?"

She made no verbal comment, just tugged at the belt and then pulled the trench coat open wide, held it open for a few seconds.

"Will you put that *away*?" I barked. "I mean, goddammit, are you *trying* to get me murdered? It was that gorgeous goddamned ass of yours that almost got me killed *this* time. It was hanging in the air out there"—I pointed—"and I just ambled along, asking for it. That was bad enough, but now . . . Well . . . give me another peek. Who wants to live forever?"

She looked at me soberly for a few seconds, then smiled.

"Flirt," she said.

We grinned sappily at each other, and after a while she

said, "you're so poetic, Shell," and I said, "Yeah, ain't I? Me and Iron-Guts Goober—I'm on to you now," and she said, "Not yet, you ain't," and I opened the Cad's door—with some difficulty, since it was slightly sprung—saying, "You get your sweet, uh, tootsies up to the apartment, O.K.?"

She nodded. "Tootsies to apartment. Message understood."

"*My* apartment, that is."

"Of course."

I climbed in, got behind the wheel, slammed the door. "In case you're asleep if—when—I get back," I said, "why don't I wake you up?"

She smiled again. "Why don't you?"

"Why don't you?" Sam said.

No matter how hard he tried, Captain Phil Samson would never get out of those words what Aralia put into them.

Needless to say, he was not trying to.

CHAPTER NINE

I'D made it to the Police Building in downtown L.A. in not more than fifteen minutes after leaving Aralia.

I had taken the elevator to the third floor, walked down the hall to 314, strolled through the Homicide squadroom into Sam's office, grabbed my wooden chair, and straddled it, saying, "Hi there, Sam. Working late again, I see. Got lots of things to tell you, Sam. You wouldn't believe . . . Cat got your tongue, Sam?"

Me saying, "Job must be getting to you, huh? I do dislike adding to your woes, Captain, but . . ."

Me saying, finally, "Maybe it would get a rise out of you if I cut my throat and dripped black blood all over your desk."

That's when he said, "Why don't you?"

That is not all the captain said.

Three nonstop minutes later the flow of extraordinary monologue slowed. Then stopped, temporarily, with Sam's comment, "What have you got to say for yourself? Don't answer that."

I answered it anyway.

I covered the episode in Collett's apartment and the shotgun shooting on Rossmore, even mentioned my visit with Vincent Ragan and explained the logic of Aralia Fields's presence in my apartment. Through it all I stressed the point that because of a perverse streak in my nature, it went against the grain for me to cooperate with numerous assassins attempting to massacre me, which was why I had not done so.

Then there was quiet for about half a minute.

I lit a cigarette. Samson dropped a mangled and soggy-ended black cigar into his wastebasket, dug a fresh one from a drawer and clamped it between his teeth.

Finally, he looked at me, shifting the cigar from one side of his wide mouth to the other. And I really looked at him, too, during those moments, noticed the comparative pallor of his usually pink face, puffiness beneath the sharp brown eyes, deeper than usual lines around his mouth. There was even a rarely seen stubble of beard on his cheeks and chin, faint, but noticeable.

He took the cigar from his mouth and said—quietly, even wearily, "Well, Shell, we've chased our tails around before. Plenty of times. But this time it's different."

He examined his cigar as if considering lighting it, something he seldom did. When lit, they exuded an overwhelming odor, like burning manure from constipated giraffes, and I don't believe he enjoyed the scent himself. Sometimes he lit one as a weapon, and puffed on it, knowing this would put me to flight, get me out of his office. But I was pretty sure he didn't want me out, not yet.

"Within the hour," he said, "I have been privileged to appear in the chief's office. From hints dropped here and there, I apprehend that the captain of Central Homicide, our mutual friend, may just possibly have overlooked certain felonious actions of one local private investigator—"

"One local private—?"

"—often in the past. Too often. Actions which, had they been committed by anyone else would, and should, properly have stirred said captain to decisive action."

"I get it."

"Not yet, you don't."

"Then quit stringing it out and lay it on me."

"O.K. When I was in the chief's office, we hadn't yet heard about the shooting on Rossmore—"

"Sam, I didn't exactly plan on that myself—"

He didn't say anything. He just paused briefly, hit me with eyes like brown ball bearings, and went on. "But even before then I'd made up my mind. You can have it one of two ways. You can turn over to me your gun, and your license—I'll accept your pocket card, and your word that you'll cease representing yourself as a licensed investigator until I hand the card back to you—or—"

"Godalmighty, Sam, why don't you just put me—"

"—I'll lock you up myself."

"—in a . . . cell?"

"Where else?"

"You've got to be kidding."

"I'm not."

115

"That's not—not reasonable."

"Who said anything about reasonable?"

"Look, without my gun I'm a dead duck, how can I defend myself from—"

"You can't. So maybe you'll quit asking to get killed. Maybe it'll get you out of circulation, instead of the circulation out of you."

"Look, my license can't be officially jerked without action by the director of the Bureau—"

"I didn't say officially. I do mean effectively."

"—and you can't just grab my gun. It's not . . . legal."

"I can't?"

Yeah, he could.

I realized, too—even though I was more than a bit hot— that Sam wouldn't be leaning on me like this unless he had heavy reasons. It was also probable that without plenty of behind-the-scenes arguing by Samson, I wouldn't have even the limited choices he was offering me.

I said, "Give me those two ways to go again."

He did. Slowly, with an edge in his voice. But I listened carefully and did not hear him say I couldn't roam unarmed around the city if I cared thus to expose myself, or ask a question here or there, or conduct myself as might any curious private citizen lollygagging about.

So when he finished I mumbled, "Yeah, great. Just great. I might continue to do a little, uh, research—"

"Don't press your luck, Shell. I might add to what I've already said, that if you do hand over your gun, with it goes your guarantee that you won't replace it with another one. If you so much as point a loaded gun at an escaping felon, that's *it*."

It would be wise, I decided, not to give him a chance to get more specific, or lay any additional particulars of my probation on me. Particulars I would then be morally bound to observe. So I sighed, stood up, snapped my .38 from its clamshell holster, looked at it, and placed the gun before Samson on the desk.

While I pulled from its plastic window in my wallet the pocket card issued to me by the Bureau of Private Investigators and Adjusters, Sam broke open the Colt, ejected the shells.

When I handed him the card he looked at me, holding five spent shell cases in the palm of his hand, one unfired hollow-point Super Vel between thumb and forefinger.

"What happened?" he asked innocently.

"I got a cramp in my trigger finger. And right now I've got a severe cramp in my—"

"I would remind you, my boy, if you get into any difficulties during the next couple of weeks, old dad won't be around to make everything nice."

I took a last look at my gun, turned, walked to the door.

Then I went back to Sam's office, opened the top drawer, took out one of his black cigars, bit off the end, spit it into the wastebasket, lit the thing, blew foul smoke at him, pretended delicately to throw up, and handed him the cigar.

"Have a fun vacation," I said, and left.

Just walking from the Police Building to my car was a queer experience. Queer, because of the empty holster at my

117

left armpit. I felt undressed, vulnerable, not complete. So I drove quite speedily toward home. Not straight home, however.

Before leaving the Police Building I'd spent some time doing a couple bits of the research I'd told Sam I might do. Specifically, I had done a little checking on "One-Shot," and put together all the info I could get from the LAPD on Norman Amber.

Nobody I talked to had any information that One-Shot was in the L.A. area, but men in the Intelligence Division knew who he, almost surely, was. The only man in their files with that monicker was, as my informant had told me, from New Jersey. His real name was Melvin Voister, and he'd been a criminal specialist—his specialty, shooting people—for the almost incredible period of three decades, interrupted only by one five-year jolt at an eastern prison.

He was now fifty-nine years old, ancient for a man in his occupation, and apparently still not only in business but in demand among those willing and able to pay for his services. An expert marksman with everything from .22 target pistols on up, Voister almost invariably used a high-powered scope-equipped hunting rifle for his jobs, preferring to be as far as possible from the victim, thus facilitating his getaway from the murder scene. The hoodlum nickname, One-Shot, was a natural for the man, since according to the "raw" I.D. files Voister never, or almost never, required more than that first shot to dispose of his human target, after which he split for Jersey. And was generally there, with a carefully prepared alibi complete with shifty-eyed witnesses, before anybody, at least any official body, knew he'd left town.

Consequently, among the boys on the turf, One-Shot Voister

was something of a living legend, and in the hoods' back rooms and bars there were innumerable stories told about him, most of them obviously ninety-nine percent exaggeration. Still, what boozy Bernie Hooten had told me now carried more weight, and had to be considered a bargain at the price of three shots of Early Times.

As for Amber, there were gaps I hoped soon to fill—hopefully from Amber himself, since I now knew he lived at 4811 Wisteria Lane, which was where I was planning to stop on my way home—but the picture wasn't quite so fuzzy as before.

Norman Amber was now fifty-four years old. He'd been born in San Francisco, graduated with honors from Stanford University, with a B.S. in electrical engineering, and after that spent four years at the prestigious California Institute of Technology, where he earned his Ph.D. in physics, ending his formal education at the age of twenty-five. Police records didn't show what subjects he'd studied or degrees he'd earned, but listed him as a "physicist, and engineer; inventor." Nor did those records indicate what kind of patents he owned, only that he did hold a couple of dozen patents in his name.

There hadn't been anything available—not tonight, anyway—about Amber's former wife or wives, or children; just three rather cold words, "Divorced, no dependents." What lay behind those words could be discovered easily enough tomorrow, and perhaps even tonight from Amber himself.

I did know, finally, what the crime was for which he'd done just over a year in San Quentin. At the time of his arrest nearly three years ago, Amber had been employed by Horizons, Inc., a company engaged in the development and manufacture of solid-state components and circuitry, elements for closed-circuit television systems, photographic equipment, and a dozen varieties of lasers, among other things. It wasn't clear just what Amber's function there had been, but he'd been accused of appropriating for his personal use—stealing—half a dozen small, but complex and staggeringly expensive, items of equipment belonging to Horizons, Inc. They'd been found in his home, in one of two rooms filled with much other paraphernalia Amber used for his personal investigations and experiments.

Accused, arrested, booked, jugged, tried, and convicted—though his formal plea was not guilty and he was quoted in a newspaper clip I'd read in his package as declaring, moments after being sentenced to San Quentin, that he was ". . . the victim not only of a gross miscarriage of justice but of a deliberate frameup. The innocent man knows of but cannot always prove his innocence. I will. In time, I will."

It had a sort of stentorian blast to it, even in newspaper print; but I'd read or heard the same thing a hundred times before. Essentially the same thing, anyway. Usually simpler and shorter, like, "I was framed," or, "Charlie, I wasn't even there, how could I of done it?"

I found the house in the 4800 block on Wisteria Lane, one of only two in the block—not many people lived out here on Wisteria—and there was little traffic, little noise. The house was dark. I rang, hammered for a while on the door. No response. I did not remove the door from its hinges, or try to pry open a window. Instead, I went back to the Cad and headed for home again.

*   *   *

I didn't try to be quiet letting myself into the apartment, and made no attempt to tiptoe into the bedroom. But Aralia did not rise up with a glad cry to greet me.

The small shaded light I sometimes turn on in the bedroom, not for reading, was filling the room with a very soft lovely glow. Aralia lay on her back in my bed, eyes closed, sheet pulled halfway up—or down—her body.

"Yoo-hoo," I half whispered. "Which, translated, means Guess who's back?"

Nothing. No glad cry. Not even "Yoo-hoo yourself."

At least, she wasn't dead. She was breathing. Above the crumpled edge of the sheet, gentle movement of her rib cage was evidence of the rise and fall of her breath, on which rise and fall rose and fell those bare and super-beauteous bazooms. She wasn't dead by a long shot. She was merely asleep.

I didn't awaken her. Not immediately. But soon I commenced to slither between the sheets, on the opposite side of the bed from Aralia, moving very gingerly. Which, of course, is the moment when she chose to open, or just happened to open, one eye.

"What in God's name is *that*?" she said in a muffled voice. Or maybe it was something else she said. It was pretty muffled. But both of Aralia's eyes were now open.

"What?" I said.

"Shell? Is that you?"

"Of course it's me. Who else do you think would be in this dumb position? Were you expecting someone else?"

"Shell, you weren't going to sneak into bed, all naked like that, without even waking me up *first*, were you?"

"Well . . ."

121

"*Were* you?"

"Well—look—it's . . . see, I thought it would be fun to—you looked so lovely and, ah, alone . . . lying there alone. Like—ah!—like Sleeping Beauty. That's it. You remember her, don't you?"

"Sleeping Beauty. I'm—did you just make this up?"

"How can you say that? It just swept over me, *there* she is, Sleeping Beauty, waiting for her prince to come."

"Don't let that mistake I made about your being poetic go to your . . . wherever it's gone to."

"O.K., so *I* made a mistake. You can be snoring Dracula if you want—"

"You're my prince, right?"

"Well, not if it turns you off. Of course, I guess you haven't been turned—"

"Shell, you can get into bed. It bothers me, the way you are. It's yours, you know—"

"It is? I was hoping—"

"*It's your bed.* Listen carefully. I am Sleeping Beauty. All right? And you are Prince Charm—you're the prince."

"Whatever you say."

"I've been sleeping for a thousand years. Well, you're here, finally. Awaken me, Prince."

I could understand her reaction better now; it really sounded horrible when someone else was saying it. However, I got more comfortable, and leaned forward to give Aralia—who at last was smiling, I noted, not a whole lot but quite sweetly—a kiss that would wake her up even if she'd been snoozing for two thousand years.

I don't know why it happened right then, but suddenly I

remembered that when I had left Aralia earlier I promised her I would return "with champagne, and little edible goodies, and a big surprise." And I hadn't kept my promise.

"This may not be the time to mention it," I said. "But I forgot the champagne and little goodies."

She seemed not to have heard me. But I guess she forgave me anyhow.

Because later, really asleep, she seemed still to be smiling.

CHAPTER TEN

Aralia was out of bed, and making small noises in the kitchenette, when I woke up. At least, somebody was making little clink-and-clatter noises in there.

I stretched, rubbed my eyes, stuck my tongue out, almost forgot to pull it back in again. After a while I scratched the hair on my chest, scratched the short hairs on my head. I was sitting on the edge of the bed, not scratching anything, not doing much of anything, when Aralia walked in.

"What happened to the man who was in here last night?" she asked me.

"In where?"

"Here in Sleeping Beauty's room."

"Don't ask dumb questions. I've had it with those dumb fairy tales. But to answer your dumb question, he always leaves before I wake up. He knows I'd kill him—"

"Want some breakfast?"

"No."

"No?"

"Is it a complicated answer?"

"But I just fixed breakfast for you, Shell. It's all ready."

"Huh."

"Goodness, you really are a bear in the morning, aren't you?"

"Yeah. And I'll bet you've been cooking porridge. Who's been sleeping in *my* bed? That was another dumb bunch—"

"I scrambled some eggs, with mushrooms and herbs and things I found."

Aralia walked into the room toward me. I noted she was wearing one of my old white shirts with the sleeves rolled up. The front of it wasn't buttoned. She was very casual about buttons. It looked like she was wearing a big scarf.

She sat on the bed next to me. "You ought to eat some eggs."

"You're out of your mind."

"But you have to keep your strength up, don't you?"

"That has never been a problem. But I suppose you're right. I just never thought of it that way."

I rubbed my eyes, stuck my tongue out.

"Do you have to do that?" she asked me.

"Yeah. It's how I wake up."

"Well, you ought to be wide awake by now. So, upsy-daisy. You really should have a little something, Shell."

"Upsy-daisy, huh? Cutesy-pootsy." I looked at her, beginning to see, dimly.

She smiled.

"Well," I said, "maybe a little . . ."

* * *

In the Cad, rolling along on Wilshire, I felt splendid. Simply splendid. This despite the fact that my breakfast entree had been two bites of a scrambled egg that tasted as if it had just hatched in the refrigerator. That was all right; I almost never have more than two bites of an egg. But I had also consumed toast, milk, and lots of coffee, and felt ready for whatever the day ahead might throw at me. At least, that's what I thought then, in my innocence.

Earlier, at the LAPD, I'd learned that efforts to locate Al Hauk or James Collett, in whose duplex apartment I'd shot Werzen, had proved unavailing; they'd just dropped out of sight. The police were not yet officially interested in talking to Norman Amber, or even to One-Shot Voister.

As for me, by noon—after spending most of the morning digging up all the additional info I could about Norman Amber—I had driven to his home again, and once more found nobody there. But by then the picture that had started taking form last night was, though still far from complete, a good deal clearer.

Perhaps most important, there was no longer any doubt that the Norman Amber who'd done time at San Quentin and had since been living in the house on Wisteria, was Aralia Fields's natural, legal, and now-ex-convict father—the same Norman Amber who, according to Aralia, had died before she was born. Which, when I got around to telling her about it, would undeniably be a more than mildly perplexing circumstance for her to consider. Assuming, of course, that Aralia had not been fibbing to me somewhere along the way, which was an assumption I had no reason to make, and therefore didn't.

127

Official state records showed that Norman Leonard Amber and Laura Aralia Blengrud had been legally married a little over twenty-eight years ago in Pasadena, California, when he was twenty-six years old and Laura was twenty-four. They'd been divorced in the same city three years later, one year after the birth of a son, Peter, and three months before the arrival of their daughter, Aralia Ann.

Divorce had been granted to the plaintiff, Mrs. Amber, on the grounds of mental cruelty, which in those days covered everything from boredom to wife-beating. Through the promise of fifty bucks to a long-time contact in Sacramento, and a little luck, I learned that the real reason Laura split from Norman was that she discovered him in flagrante delicto; which is Latin for she caught him banging the nineteen-year-old baby-sitter; which does not mean that Norman had been hitting the girl on the head with a board.

Even more interesting, less than a year after the marriage was dissolved Norman Amber applied for and was later granted the first of his many patents. That first invention was essentially the combining of a redesigned sixteen-millimeter movie camera with a compact, built-in, battery-operated gyroscope of Amber's design, so that when taking pictures with the camera hand-held it would be nearly as steady as though mounted on a tripod. Apparently, it worked, since Amber had been awarded patent protection, but the idea seemed never to have caught on or made any money.

Even though my scientific education ended approximately with my learning where the washer went on the faucet, one impression did emerge during the time, including a half hour on the phone to Washington, D.C., that I spent checking on

Amber. It was that—in contrast to what I knew of Gunnar Lindstrom, who was apparently a genius in half a dozen very different, even basically unrelated, fields of science and technology—nearly all of Amber's work was directed toward improvements and entirely new concepts in the area of "images."

That is, nineteen of the twenty-four Amber patents had at least some bearing on the production or reproduction of images or pictures—snapshots, home movies, the cameras and films used by professional moving-picture makers, as well as television cameras and receivers and tubes and tapes.

His most recent inventions, including the only one on which he'd been granted a patent since his release from prison, were not only more complex and thus less comprehensible to me, but apparently indicative of the direction he'd taken during and since his five years with Horizons, Inc.

Those were years when the growth of cable television, TV cassettes and discs, and the use of "laser-printed" holograms for everything from information storage and retrieval to production of the first crude but astonishingly real three-dimensional movies began their still-continuing explosion. I had myself seen one of the first—I believe *the* first—three-dimensional moving pictures produced by the embryo holographic technique. I'd seen it because I have long enjoyed raising, feeding, ogling, and even breeding tropical fishes, and the film was of fish swimming in an aquarium.

The "picture" was projected not onto a silvered screen but simply into a couple of cubic feet of air, and it was in three dimensions. It was perhaps not as vividly alive as the two aquariums in my living room at the Spartan, though from a

129

few feet away the shape, color, and rippling movement of those exotic little aquarium fishes had certainly appeared solid and real to me.

But the one unforgettable impression that had stayed with me ever since was that the aquarium remained solid and rectangular, in perspective, filled with swimming fishes, even when I walked around it—examined it from both sides, from the rear, from the front again.

I watched a small *Corydoras paleatus,* or catfish, wiggling over sand at the aquarium's bottom on the side next to me, moving from my right to left; then I walked around behind the tank and observed that same catfish continuing to wiggle over sand, from my left to my right, at the aquarium's bottom on the side opposite me.

I looked for some time at that aquarium, and the fishes, and especially the scavenging *Corydoras paleatus,* blinking quite a bit more than merely a little, because there was nothing there. Nothing at all. At least, not anything tangible or alive; just color and movement and light that sure as hell looked solid and wet and wiggly and real.

It was therefore with some interest that I learned Norman Amber, during his years with Horizons, Inc., had been in charge of Research and Development, or R & D, on several secret projects in the "image" field, concerned with the storage and reproduction of both still and moving images or pictures, this time through employment of lasers, holographic techniques, computers, and I don't know what all. Since the projects were secret, I wasn't able to find out a great deal about them.

I did know that the patent so recently granted Amber on

his latest invention was for some new kind of camera-and-projector combination that was supposed to produce a greatly improved three-dimensional picture, but just how it might accomplish this I didn't know, and probably didn't need to know.

But I did have several reasons for wanting to know more about Amber himself, and especially for wanting to find and talk to the man. So by one P.M. I was pulling into a parking slot in front of the Weir Building.

According to the board in the building's lobby, Vincent Ragan, patent attorney, occupied offices 38, 40, and 42. I took an elevator to the third floor, walked to the door numbered "38," and opened it.

A bright-looking, middle-aged secretary stopped typing when I stepped inside. She seemed surprised when, after giving Ragan my name over the intercom and saying I had no appointment, he said to send me right in.

Ragan was seated at a small desk made of highly polished grainy blond wood, but he stood up and extended his hand as I entered his office, gazing steadily at me from behind the dark horn-rims.

I shook his hand and said, "Thanks for seeing me, Mr. Ragan."

"It's all right. Just got back from lunch, and I've a minute or two." He smiled slightly. "Not much more, though."

"Shouldn't take more. Wanted to check one thing I left out last night. Didn't know enough to mention last night, I mean."

"What's that?"

"I wanted to know what you could tell me about Norman Amber."

"Norman?"

I pricked up my ears. One does not respond to a question about a total stranger by repeating his first name.

The word, that first name, came out easily and naturally, but then the question—or, more likely, Ragan's automatic reaction to it—stuck him for some reason. It wasn't obvious, just a twitch of his neat eyebrows, quick compression of his full lips.

Then he rubbed a finger beneath his nose, as if a stray hair had tickled him, saying, "Can't tell you much, Mr. Scott. I hardly know the man." He paused. "Which makes it surprising that you'd come here to ask me about him."

"Just fishing for bits and pieces, Mr. Ragan." I lit a cigarette, took a drag. "I've learned he's an inventor, has had several patents granted over a period of about twenty-five years. Since he's a local man, I wondered if you'd handled any of those patent applications for him."

Ragan shook his head. "No. I don't really know much about Norman's—Mr. Amber's—work, but I met him at a couple of conventions, the last one here in Los Angeles. He's a charming man, quite brilliant. A little odd, of course."

"Why of course?"

Ragan smiled. "I shouldn't have put it that way. But he *is* odd, eccentric. I've noted that a good percentage of my own clients depart quite widely from the norm. Nothing wrong with that; if they didn't, they probably wouldn't be researchers, inventors. The tried-and-true may be comfortable, but it isn't new, it isn't—invention."

"Can't argue with that," I said. "Do you mean Amber is a bit balmy?"

He laughed. "Not at all. It's just that he's . . . difficult at a personal level, in conversation, that sort of thing. Extremely opinionated, intolerant of other viewpoints. Brusque, very sure of himself, almost messianic, and he has some very queer ideas. Of course, I'd be the last to denigrate that element of his nature—he's patented some of those very queer ideas."

"Do you know where I could find him?"

Ragan shook his head.

"I've been out to his home," I said, "but nobody's there. You don't have any idea how I might track him down?"

"No, I don't even know where he lives. As I mentioned, we met at a couple gatherings of researchers, engineers, inventors, patent lawyers—addresses by politicians promising to expand capital-gains treatment of royalties in return for votes, company presidents looking for new-product ideas, that sort of thing. The most recent convention was in March of this year, and that's the last time I saw Norman Amber." He paused. "I rather regret that, actually. He's irritating, decidedly unpleasant at times, but damned stimulating. I wish he *was* my client. I like him."

"What do you do for your clients? I mean, what's the function of any patent attorney?"

"That's simple enough to explain, a bit more complex in actual practice. But let's say you've invented or improved some new and useful thing—process, machine, manufacture or composition of matter—or think you have. Most would-be inventors have merely come up independently with an idea already discovered by at least a dozen or a hundred other people. From your explanation of the invention, the technical information, I prepare the required patent application in formally correct form, including the written specifications, drawings, and claims at the end of the patent application.''

I interrupted. "Sounds like you almost have to be an inventor yourself. Or at least some kind of scientist.''

"Well, no, but . . . it helps.'' After a moment he continued. "You can expect a year or so to elapse before the first examination, or initial decision on the merits of your invention, which usually results in rejection of the application. Three months are allowed for preparation of a response—called an amendment—and if there is *not* a second rejection, you will get your Notice of Allowance, which makes everybody happy.''

"That's the patent?''

"Not of itself, but it does mean you've won, you will be granted protection. I see that the issue fee is paid, and then the Patent Office sends the quite impressive Letters Patent, and you are from that moment forward an honest-to-God inventor. I make sure your legal rights are protected and that you understand all of those rights, and defend against possible suits for infringement. In time, with luck, you may safely attempt to sell, assign, or manufacture your disposable ashtray liner or magnetically cushioned pogo stick.''

"Wonderful. I just happen to have a brand new idea, for a car clock that ticks. What's new about it is, it keeps ticking.''

"I'll handle that one for nothing, Mr. Scott. Speaking of clocks.'' He glanced at his watch.

"Right. Just one last quick question. I tried to phone Wallace Epplewhite, but I'm informed he's out of town."

Ragan's eyes narrowed behind his horn-rimmed glasses, and I could see movement of muscles in his forearm as he drummed fingers briefly on the desktop. "You mean you went ahead and phoned Wallace after I advised you not to bug him?"

"Oh, come on, Mr. Ragan. All kinds of people give me all kinds of advice. Would you know where I might get in touch with Mr. Epplewhite?"

"No, Mr. Scott, I would not."

I stood up. "Thanks for your time, Mr. Ragan."

He nodded, opened a desk drawer, and placed a stack of papers before him. I went back the way I'd come in, pausing briefly to thank the efficient-looking lady who'd announced me to Ragan. I got the impression that not many people thanked her for much around here.

The L.A. phone book listed a Fields, Laura on Glenrosa Street in Burbank. I didn't phone, just drove out the Freeway to the Burbank turnoff, rolled along to Glenrosa.

I'd been checking house numbers, and knew the address I wanted would be somewhere in the middle of the next block, across the street on my left, about where a car was parked at the curb. Its hood was raised and a long-haired guy was standing there with his back to me, bent forward and apparently fiddling with the engine.

There was something about the look of him—and the car, a sedan. Chevrolet, far from new, a muddy green. And then I noticed the woman with her head stuck out past the front door. As I rolled slowly by—without stopping, not yet, not until I'd sorted out the impressions beginning to jangle in my head—I saw her mouth moving.

The Cad's window was down on my side, and I heard her yell, very clearly, "Told you to get your ass *in* here, Peter. Hurry *up!*"

That's who it was, the somewhat weather-beaten overweight lady, and the lank-haired youth who need have no fear of cannibals.

CHAPTER ELEVEN

THAT'S who it was, all right. The marvelous pair I had observed leaving Vincent Ragan's house less than twenty-four hours ago.

I rolled to the next intersection, my thoughts jumping in several directions at once. By the time I drove around the block I had decided to head back toward Hollywood. I still wanted the chat with Mrs. Fields and her magnetic Peter that I'd come here for, and I still intended to have it—but not until I had a better idea of what the hell was going on.

The sound of typing stopped when I came through the door.

The middle-aged, bright-looking secretary looked up, smiled slightly, and said, "It's—Mr. Scott, isn't it?"

"Yeah," I said, but without pausing. I tromped across the room toward the adjacent office, adding, "You need not announce me—"

"Mr. Ragan isn't in his office, Mr. Scott. If it is he whom you wish to see."

I paused with my hand on the doorknob. "Oh? Where did he go?"

She didn't know. Ragan had left about five minutes after my earlier visit, without saying where he was going. She didn't know if he had made, or received, any phone calls before leaving. Several names I mentioned, including Norman Amber and Laura Fields, were unfamiliar to her. Nothing but blanks until, instead of names, I gave her a couple of descriptions—that of Mrs. Green and her unappetizing boy.

They had both been here in Mr. Ragan's office, she was quite sure, on Friday of the previous week. For about an hour. She checked Ragan's desk calendar, on which he usually listed special appointments. No names there, just the notation "LF & P" on the page for Friday, September 14, eight days ago, and the time, 2:00 P.M.

But that was quite enough for me.

The plainclothes car pulled in behind the spot where I was parked at the curb on Wisteria Lane.

I waited next to my Cad as Bill Rawlins got out, walked up to me.

"Thanks for coming, Bill," I said.

"Don't thank me yet. You left a lot out on the phone, pal. Fill me in."

"I didn't leave much out. I told you, this is the third time I've been here, third time no response. I've checked; the guy should have been seen in a couple of places, at least once or twice, and he hasn't. Ordinarily, I might sort of sneak in myself and mope around a little, only . . ."

"Only maybe you're getting smart. With a little help from the captain."

"Help, he says. Did Sam tell you—"

Rawlins lifted the left side of my coat, looked at the spot where my holster and Colt ordinarily were.

"Yeah, he told you," I said.

"I wouldn't have believed it." Bill shook his head. "No wonder you called a cop." He glanced at the house. "Who did you say lives here?"

"Norman Amber."

He looked toward the house, then at me, scowling. "You want me to go in there—uninvited, without a warrant—and do your moping around for you, right?"

"That's right."

"I must be out of my skull. If the guy's snoozing in there, or say his aunt's cooking in the kitchen, what the hell kind of excuse—"

"Sam get away on his vacation?" I interrupted.

"Yes, he did. Shell, don't pretend I haven't known you a long time and thus might fail to notice your crude attempts to change the subject or remind me that the captain is on his merry way. His way may be merry, but that ominous presence still broods over the Police Building, nay, over the entire city—"

"Good God, Bill, you're starting to talk the way Sam does when he's sick. Ah, look, you're here. You're either going to go in or stay out. And would it make sense not to go in there when you're already out here? Of course not. So—"

"Not so fast." He shrugged. "All right. You get around

in back, hammer on the door, yell, or make noises. I'll investigate the disturbance. Don't overdo it.''

Half a minute later I'd walked over a rock path in a dichondra lawn to the back door and was banging away on it and yelling a bit, but not excessively. Then I waited.

Not very long, no more than two or three minutes. The back door opened and Rawlins said to me, "O.K., come on in.''

"He's there?''

"Yeah. He's dead, all right.''

The rest of it used up an hour—getting the detectives, lab men, and deputy coroner out to the address, Rawlins's report at the scene and mine—but checking the place ourselves took only the first five minutes.

Amber lived in a normal house, bedroom and kitchen and bath and such, except for two large rooms filled with a lot of equipment. Some of it was recognizable, things like meters and motors, test equipment, switches and rheostats, coils of wire, several different kinds of small metal bars. But some of it was like nothing I'd ever laid eyes on before.

There were also two boxes about the size of packing crates, or large trunks, each with several dials and lenses on its face, an "on-off" switch, and a black-painted lever in a slot at one side of the box. We could only guess at what might be inside the things, but with all the gadgets on their outsides there had to be a lot that couldn't be seen until the boxes were opened. And they'd be opened; one of them would, anyhow.

Because Norman Amber's body was crumpled on the floor

near, almost touching, the base of one of those boxes. He'd been dead, Rawlins and I guessed, at least a couple of days. The Coroner's Office would be able to give us a more accurate estimate of the time, but rigor mortis, the weird stiffening of the corpse's muscles, had slowly formed and slowly melted away, so he probably hadn't died within the last twenty-four hours.

There was a clearly visible mark across the palm of his right hand; possibly there were others on his body, beneath the trousers and shirt and stained rubber apron, but that would be checked later, too.

A couple of feet above his head, the black-painted lever was midway down its slot, projecting out parallel to the floor—rather than up at the top of the box and angled toward the ceiling as was the other one of the pair. Too, the lever's paint wasn't shiny black, wasn't smooth; it was bubbly; it looked burned. As did Amber's right palm.

Rawlins and I were standing a yard or so from the body when he said, "We'd better keep the hell away from that whatever-it-is with the dials and stuff. Looks like he pulled that lever and got electrocuted."

"It stinks." Rawlins glanced at me as I went on. "This guy wasn't a kid playing with pretty sparks; he knew what he was doing."

"Things go wrong, Shell. Accidents happen, even to the pros."

"I just don't buy it."

"The experts can tell us, maybe. I'll call in."

While Rawlins phoned downtown I squatted on my haunches near the body, looked at the dead man's face.

141

You can't tell from the face of a corpse what the man really looked like. You can match it with a photograph—like a mug shot and a newspaper picture I'd seen of Norman Amber—eyes, nose, lips, hairline, but you miss whatever it is that rests in the movement, animation, lift of brow or smile or sneer, the living part of the man. The puppet was here on the floor, but the guy with the strings was gone. Still, while I knew Amber had been some kind of high-powered brain, he'd also been a damned good-looking man. I could tell that much from what was left of him. Strength in that face, in the jaw, shape of mouth, even without any power behind the mask. Fairly tall, six feet or over, lean but not skinny. In addition to the outstanding think-pot, he'd been a better-than-fair physical specimen, too. He had undoubtedly been looked at with admiring eyes by more tomatoes than a few.

And—now—so what?

I straightened up, looked around some more, waiting for Rawlins. In shelves along one wall, a lot of books; piles of magazines, technical and scientific journals, papers and reports. Also at least two dozen cameras, movie and still, among them a couple of contraptions that might have been either cameras or parts for a three-dimensional jigsaw puzzle.

Rawlins came back in. "On the way." He saw me looking at the shelves and asked, "Anything new in here?"

"Nothing important," I said.

The last thing, just before I left, was watching the remains of Norman Amber being rolled along on the collapsible four-wheeled stretcher to the waiting coroner's wagon. From there he went to the morgue, Rawlins headed for the Police Building, and I went to Burbank again.

Up Glenrosa, to the Fields' address, and to the door. The green Chevy wasn't in front of the house, and nobody answered my ring or knock. Ten minutes of checking with the neighbors and I knew both Mrs. Fields and Peter had left some time ago. Exactly how much time ago I was unable to find out for sure; but it couldn't have been very long after I'd driven by earlier today. Half an hour, say, or even less.

A couple of the neighbors told me the same story: When the pair of them left together, Mrs. Fields had been carrying two suitcases, which she put into the backseat of the Chevrolet before getting behind the wheel and driving off. That's all they'd taken with them, a pair of suitcases, but it was enough to tell me I needn't anticipate their speedy return.

It also told me at least one other thing: dynamic Peter hadn't been carrying any suitcases.

The big heavy door slowly swung open.

"Hi," I said. It was the same evil-looking guy who'd let me in the first time I visited Lindstrom Laboratories.

"Oh, it's you."

"Yes, it is. I'd like to see Mr. Lindstrom again, if I may."

"Come in, Mr. Scott." He pulled the door wider, stepped back.

I blinked. "Just like that? It's easier the second time, huh?"

"Mr. Lindstrom informed me that you were to be allowed admittance right away if you returned."

That was a little odd, I thought. "Right away? Anytime at all?"

"He didn't specify any conditions. But only, of course, to

see him. Not to enter any of the other areas, unless in his company.''

''That's fine with me.''

The massive door swung slowly closed behind us, as though sealing us in forever. He preceded me down the long dimly-lighted hallway. It was quiet, and I was happy to note that, in contrast to my previous visit, those disturbing sounds almost like silent pressure on the eardrums, or the brain, were not in evidence this time.

I commented on that to my guide and he explained: Because it was Saturday afternoon, only he and Lindstrom and a couple of other men were still at the laboratories. That was fine with me, too, since I was not overly fond of walking past heavy doors into windowless places without my familiar gun in its shoulder clip.

We turned left at the intersecting corridor, and my guide said over his shoulder, ''I'll let Mr. Lindstrom know you're here,'' and speeded his pace, moving on ahead of me. I saw him open a door, lean in and speak, then step back, leaving the door open. He smiled absently as he went by me, moving silently over the smooth dull-gray flooring.

I paused in the open doorway. Gunnar Lindstrom, as before, was behind the cluttered dark-gray desk, seated this time, drilling me with that piercing gaze of his.

But he said pleasantly, ''Come in, come in, Mr. Scott,'' and as I entered he smiled. It was merely a small smile, a polite facial gesture, but it brightened his sharp features, made him look rather like an aging boy.

He indicated a chair before his desk. I sat down, saying, ''Thanks for letting me in again, Mr. Lindstrom. Especially so speedily.''

"I left instructions that you were to be admitted without delay if you wished to see me again."

"Would you mind telling me why?"

He answered easily, "On your first visit, you informed me of certain circumstances and events that"—he paused briefly, then continued—"were of interest to me. That I was not previously aware of. That clarified in some degree questions to which I had not—and still have not—found satisfactory answers. I believe I assisted you also, to a degree, in your own search for answers. Therefore, it seemed not unlikely that, even between two individuals of such disparate backgrounds and professions, there might result a further quid pro quo, shall we say, should you have reason to return."

"Would you mind telling me what it was I told you that you found so interesting?" No response. "Specifically?" I added.

He didn't say anything, just sat there like a stone, drilling me with those almost-glowing eyes. This went on for a while.

I remembered that during my first visit, after our introductory comments—when Lindstrom had started his little sand machine going, it was—there had been what might be described as a stupendous lull in the conversation. Unrelieved by even a hint of any comment or aid from Lindstrom.

"I suppose you know you make me uneasy doing that," I said jocularly.

"Well," I went on fairly soon, "I can tell you that much has been happening, Mr. Lindstrom. Some of which, I've got a hunch, will provide you with at least small tremors of excitement.

"Yes," I continued, "small tremors. For example, yesterday I asked you about Elroy Werzen, whose hood monicker was Puffer. I say was, because within an hour after I left here I shot and killed him."

"Yes, I know."

"How did you find out he was dead? Or that *I* plugged him?"

I waited.

It was pretty clear now. When Lindstrom didn't want to answer a question, or felt no overwhelming urge to speak, there was just a—lull.

"O.K.," I said. "Just sit there and keep your ears open. I'm sure you recall everything I mentioned yesterday. Add that when I saw Puffer and Collett and Al Hauk at the Weir Building, they were with a fourth man I didn't get a look at. But in the Weir Building—along with numerous other individuals, of course—there is a Vincent Ragan, patent attorney, who for an as yet unexplained reason apparently does not wish me to know he is, in some way, involved with Mrs. Laura Fields and her decaying darling-boy, Peter. The same Mrs. Fields who—lo and behold—is the mother of Aralia Fields. Said Aralia being the lady Buddy Brett—remember him?—failed to live quite long enough to murder, in the Spartan Apartment Hotel. Outside which hotel was parked, last night and at that lethal moment, your Lincoln Continental. Near which allegedly heisted heap strolled Al Hauk, bosom pal to a couple, or maybe several, of your employees, as already demonstrated. Now, it is a circumstance of surpassing interest, at least to me, that the aforementioned Laura Fields turns out to be none other than the one-time wife of very recently deceased Norman Amber, also mentioned in passing here yesterday. And the late Norman Amber, whose profession should prove of interest even to you—"

"*What?* Wife of—late? Deceased—dead? Norman *Amber*? What are you saying?"

It was so sudden, I almost went over backward in my chair.

During my spiel Lindstrom had appeared quite unmoved, as though he'd turned off an invisible hearing aid and was merely watching, with reluctant interest, my lips wiggle. With—until the explosion—only one small exception.

That was when I mentioned "Vincent Ragan, patent attorney." It wasn't anything dramatic, just a fractional lift and compression of the brows, perhaps a slight increase in the amperage of his steady gaze, and his lips parted slightly, though quickly. Not much from which to draw any exciting conclusions.

I recalled that during my recital of names here yesterday Lindstrom had reacted minutely to one of them, either Norman Amber or Buddy Brett I'd thought then. It did not now seem likely it had been Buddy Brett.

During my last comments Lindstrom had suddenly sat bolt upright in his chair, then leaned forward, mouth opening. He was still like that, big leonine head with its used-mop tangle of gray-streaked brown hair thrust toward me, body pressed against the edge of his desk.

"What did you mean by that?" he continued. "Deceased? But he isn't dead."

"He is dead," I said.

"Norman? Norman Amber?"

"That's right."

"Perhaps you're mistaken. How long—"

"I don't know for sure how long he's been dead. Not more than a few days, though—his body was discovered only a couple of hours ago, by a police officer and me. By now it's at the L.A. County Morgue."

"You're sure it was Norman?"

"Yes. That was checked out before the dead-wagon took him away."

He winced when I said dead-wagon.

Then he ran a hand through his bushy hair, which judging by its appearance was how he combed it regularly every week, and slowly turned his swivel chair around until he was facing in the opposite direction.

I presumed he was staring at the wall, but that was a guess. All I could see was the black-leather padding of the chair's back. Half a minute went by. I assumed Lindstrom was making some kind of mental adjustment to what was obviously surprising, perhaps shocking, news. Again, it was a guess. Maybe he was hiding. It was possible. There are people who close their eyes and think nobody can see them.

After another half-minute I began to wonder if there was a hole I didn't know about in the floor over there, and he'd disappeared into it the instant he got out of my sight. Then the chair swiveled around. I was actually relieved to see Lindstrom still in it.

Even before he'd turned the full 180 degrees he began speaking: "I am not sure of the man's name you mentioned, the patent attorney. Vincent . . . ?"

"Ragan."

"In the Weir Building?"

"Yes."

"He was there in the company of the three other men you mentioned, two of them my employees?"

"I'm not sure of that. I strongly suspect it. The three of them were there with a fourth man. I don't know who that fourth man was."

"Ragan," he said softly, not to me. "Hmm. Well." Then to me again, "You were one of the men who found Norman's—Mr. Amber's—body?"

"Yes."

"Where was this?"

"At his home. Out on Wisteria Lane."

"Had he been . . ."

Lindstrom was stuck again.

He fell silent, eyes dropping from mine. After about thirty seconds he picked up the small sand-filled glass, his egg timer, turned it over, and placed it on the desktop. He still didn't say anything, just watched the tiny grains of white sand silently falling.

Half of them trickled through into the bell-shaped bottom of the glass, then Lindstrom looked up at me. He blinked his eyes, as if bringing them back into focus, and finished what he'd started to say perhaps two minutes before. He didn't even repeat the first part of the question, just went on from where he'd left off, completing the question.

". . . murdered?"

"What?" Two minutes is a long time for me.

"Had he been murdered?"

"Why do you ask that? Do you think someone had reason—"

149

The brows pulled down and inward slightly. "Mr. Scott, dammit, will you answer my question?"

Then his body seemed to relax, his face smoothed, he smiled gently, and his expression grew much warmer. "I'm sorry. I have concluded that you may be of great help to me. So I have already decided to tell you everything you want to know. More, since it is almost a certainty that I have answers for which you could not possibly be prepared with questions, I intend to ask myself those questions, for your edification, and answer them. Believe me, it will be quicker that way."

"I think I believe you."

"Excellent."

"Especially if I don't know the questions."

"Tell me, then. Was Norman murdered?"

"I'm not sure. We found his body on the floor next to some kind of equipment that was wired in to a transformer, connected in turn to a two-twenty-volt power source. The piece of equipment wasn't grounded—had been, but the ground connection had come loose one of the lab men told me—and it looked as if something had shorted out and electrocuted him. That'll be checked by the experts. But, for reasons of my own, I think he may have been murdered."

"Oh, yes," Lindstrom said.

"Would you mind expanding on that a little? Does it mean you're agreeing with me, or—"

"Agreeing, yes. Definitely. I assumed, as soon as your words convinced me that Norman truly was dead, he had been murdered. It was something I had difficulty allowing myself to believe." He ran a hand through his tangled hair again, his expression grave. "But I have refrained from

150

looking directly at many obvious truths for a long time now. You will better understand this, and much more besides, when I have related to you certain incidents.''

"I hope you're going to include your reasons for thinking Amber was murdered. And why. Do you know, or think you know, who killed him?''

"To the last part of your question, no. Not specifically. Why he was killed? Yes, I'm sure I know the reason for that. But all in good time, Mr. Scott. I must have certain assurances from you.''

He stood up, moved out from behind his desk. Then, with his hands clasped behind his back, Lindstrom walked slowly to the far wall, back again, kept pacing while he spoke.

"Since your visit here yesterday, Mr. Scott, I have made certain inquiries about you. Further, I have observed you closely. I believe there is in you an almost disturbing force, perhaps not sufficiently disciplined but capable, given minimal direction, of thrashing through to the solution of a problem, a dilemma, that has long faced me.''

"Thrashing through, eh?''

He went right on, turning to pace toward the wall. "And I expect if you give me your promise to act, or refrain from acting, in a specified manner, you will honor that promise. I believe there is in you a kind of raw, ebullient integrity—''

"Couldn't you try a little harder to win me over?''

He stopped pacing, returned to his swivel chair, and sat down. "I am usually more decisive, Mr. Scott. But I have been avoiding this moment for nearly five years, and it is difficult to suddenly overcome that conditioning.''

He was silent for a few seconds, then looked at me and

151

said briskly, "I have certain information—I cannot call it evidence—of monstrous and unique fraud and deception, the ingenious theft of hundreds of thousands of dollars, soon inevitably hundreds of *millions*—completely unsuspected by anyone other than the conspirators themselves until now. Worse, the corruption of truth, the bastardization of genius. And the murder of at least one man, perhaps others."

He paused, and I said, "That's quite a mouthful. If you can back it up."

"I can. And I am willing to tell you everything I know and suspect about this conspiracy, this monstrosity, but solely for *your* information, as a possible guide to your actions. You must give me your word that you will not reveal to anyone else—without my express permission—what I am prepared to tell you, or even reveal that I have told you anything. You must not in any way involve me personally. You may *act* on the information if you wish—I, of course, hope this is what you will do—and I am certain from comments you have made, Mr. Scott, that what I tell you will explain many things you desire to understand, answer many of your questions which, without what I can tell you, might forever remain unanswered."

"Forever's quite a while—and that's another mouthful. How can I promise not to spill any of this info when I don't know what it is?"

"You must answer that question yourself, Mr. Scott. You should also know that if it becomes necessary, I will not hesitate to deny I have told you anything whatever. I will not corroborate a single thing you might say. I will not repeat to the police or anyone else what I am prepared to tell you— when and if you agree to my conditions."

"Well, I don't know. . . ."

"I will not tell you unless you give me your word. But I hope you . . . agree. I would . . . like to tell you, tell someone."

There was a strange note in his voice when he said that. His expression didn't change, not a bit. But there was something in his tone, an almost tortured twisting of his words, that would normally accompany an expression of pain.

So it seemed. Maybe I was imagining things again. However, he did have me interested. I wanted to hear his tale. I thought about it.

Then I said, "Do you mind if I smoke?"

"Not at all. May I assume this means you intend to stay awhile longer, and listen to what I shall tell you?"

"That's right."

"You fully understand my conditions."

"Fully."

"And you agree? I have your word you will not violate those conditions?"

"You've got it. You're really putting me in a bind, you know. Especially on top of Captain Samson's bloody—skip it." I sighed. "You've got my word, Mr. Lindstrom."

"Fine. Fine." He folded his hands before him on the desktop, gazed at me with those penetrating eyes. "We begin."

CHAPTER TWELVE

"LINDSTROM Laboratories was incorporated in the State of California nineteen years ago," Gunnar Lindstrom said. "In the beginning it consisted of only myself and four assistants, but it grew and prospered over the years, became quite well known, at least in the scientific community."

He paused. "But that's all a matter of record. As is the fact that we work on many things, some developed internally, some from 'outside' inventors who bring their ideas, both patented and unpatented, here for help in development and possible commercial placement—exploitation, sale of rights to appropriate manufacturers, that sort of thing. This function of ours is not unique by any means, but we've been very successful. Are you familiar with the tax laws as they apply to inventors, Mr. Scott?"

I shook my head.

"The essential comment I would make is that an inventor's patent income is, in most cases, treated not as ordinary income but as a long-term capital gain. Are you acquainted with the considerable benefit that would thus accrue to the owner of a valuable patent?''

"That I can understand. Instead of seeing as much as fifty percent of his net income gobbled up by the IRS, he'd pay a capital-gains tax of at most twenty percent and keep the rest of his money. Right?''

"Essentially so. Only forty percent of his capital gain would be added to other income and taxed at up to fifty percent maximum rate, while sixty percent of that capital gain would be entirely tax exempt. You can understand, then, that in the case of a commercially successful product or process worth many hundreds of thousands, or even millions, of dollars, the capital-gains treatment could mean thousands or millions saved—not dissolved by taxation—for the patent owner or owners.''

"I sure can. Dissolved is a good description. It melts away and is never seen again—''

"I suppose it should have been obvious that such a situation would inevitably appeal to the criminal mind. The possibility of great and essentially 'legitimate' profits, subject even legally to minimal taxation, would surely impress an imaginative criminal with its inherent potential for huge and continuing gain. Gain that might be assured through his natural methods of corruption, manipulation, intimidation—that is, by the employment of extra-legal techniques with which the criminal is already of necessity familiar. Including force, extortion, even murder, to ensure the criminal's participation in this financial bonanza. Perhaps it should have been obvious, but it simply never occurred to me.''

156

"Or to me, either, Mr. Lindstrom. I don't quite understand how some bright hood would make it work, but his reason for trying to make it work is clear enough."

"I should say that it never occurred to me until it happened to me. About five years ago I was approached by two individuals who invited me to participate with them, and associates of theirs whom I would not meet—to my great financial benefit they assured me—in illegal and immoral activities such as I have just suggested are possible. I refused, of course. At first. However, I am able to assure you that these suggested activities *are* possible, Mr. Scott, and immensely profitable, since I have been involved in just such a corrupt scheme for nearly five years. I have been a key member, we might say, of a very successful criminal conspiracy."

He fell silent briefly, but I didn't interrupt.

"With hindsight, I can see that from their point of view I must have appeared an almost ideal choice," he went on. "Certainly it soon became clear they had decided upon me, and were determined that they should have me. My scientific credentials were impeccable, my integrity unquestioned, and I possessed an outstanding record of continuing research and invention, having had, at that time, more than seventy patents granted to me. Moreover, I was president of an already established and successful corporation, Lindstrom Laboratories. It became clear that my fellow conspirators intended to present me with plans for, and even working models of, new and potentially profitable inventions, products, processes—some already with patent protection, which would be assigned to Lindstrom Laboratories, and some for which I would make patent application in my name."

157

He hesitated, frowning, then went on slowly. "Quite simply, it was expected that I would apply for patents on work
done by others, by scientists or inventors I might never have
heard of . . . and allege that the work for which I asked
patent protection was my *own,* the product of my *own* thought
and researches."

"Did these characters give you any idea how they expected to come up with those goodies—patents or models,
whatever they had in mind?"

"No. I was assured that all of this would be taken care of
by others—that word, *others,* was often used, but never from
then until now have I been told *who* those others might be. I
was not to be involved in that area of the conspiracy. My
function was what I have already indicated, plus the exercise
of any talents and abilities I possess to improve, if possible,
upon the ideas presented to me, make working models if such
were called for, proceed, in other words, as if the idea or
concept were truly my own. And to arrange for *legal* protection of the ideas. Isn't that ironic?"

He pulled his hands apart and squeezed them into fists a
few times, as if he might have been clasping his fingers
painfully tight during the last minute or two. But the expression on his face didn't change as he went on. "I must say,
without modesty, that they chose well. I have been very
successful in doing what they asked of me."

"I get the impression you must have refused to go along
with these guys in the beginning. But that you did go along."

"In the end, yes. Their appeal to the human emotion most
familiar to them, greed, having failed, they endeavored to

appeal to another basic emotion, fear. Fear of pain, of death. I was beaten. Crudely but thoroughly beaten.''

He shook his head, a puzzled expression on his face. ''I am still unable to comprehend such men. Well, I was hospitalized for several days. I was warned not to protest to the authorities or the same thing, or worse, would happen to my son. I am a widower, Mr. Scott. Except for my work, my son is the only thing I love, all I have. In the hospital I could not be with him—he remained at my home, in the care of a friend. When I returned from the hospital, this friend had been called from the house—a telephone call, a ruse—and my son was gone.''

''There's something in the local police records about that,'' I said. ''Didn't you report him kidnaped, then later claim he'd just stayed away overnight?''

He nodded. ''I felt he had been kidnaped, and I reported it. I was . . . terrified, not thinking clearly. And it was not until later in the evening that I was visited by the same two men who had originally approached me.''

''Maybe you ought to tell me who these guys are, Mr. Lindstrom. I assume—by now—you know their names.''

''Oh, yes,'' he said. ''Though at that time I did not. You are acquainted with both. It was Mr. Hauk and Mr. Werzen.''

''Al the Clam and Puffer. Well, I don't feel as bad about plugging Puffer now. Not that I was all broken up to begin with.''

''I confess I was not dismayed by news of his death myself, Mr. Scott. To conclude this, they told me they held my son. If I did not cooperate with them, he would be further injured, and if necessary he would be killed.''

Something in his last sentence bothered me. At first I didn't know what it was, but then I tagged it and said, "Further injured? Had they already roughed the boy up?"

"My son was at the time twelve years old. Approximately eight years earlier his left hand was injured in an accident, and the little finger of that hand failed to respond fully to treatment. It remained crooked, with a prominent bony mass at the second knuckle. When Mr. Hauk and Mr. Werzen visited me that night, they gave me my son's finger."

Lindstrom stopped speaking. When he went on, it was without further comment concerning his reaction, his logical conclusions, his capitulation. He merely said quietly, "We live among savages, Mr. Scott. I suppose you know that better than I. I am aware of this now, but I was not then."

After a while he added, "I suppose, too, having informed me of much that they planned to do, they considered it essential that I join them in their criminal activity, become a co-conspirator with them and thus doubly silenced. Perhaps you better understand the restrictions, the conditions, I placed upon you earlier."

"Yeah, I do. And I imagine there's a reason or two you haven't gotten around to yet."

"Yes. I might mention that during these past five years I have applied for a total of twenty-one patents, of which seventeen have been granted or the patent is pending and will probably be allowed. Of the seventeen, eleven represent the result of my own labors."

"Does that mean your crooked associates brought only six ideas to you?" He nodded, and I said, "That doesn't seem like much in five years."

160

"It is not quantity, but quality, that is important. To them, at least. And by quality I mean the likelihood of commercial development, with consequent financial gain. Of those seventeen ideas worthy of patent protection, five will probably prove to be extremely profitable—two of them, in fact, already are. And only one of those five was originated by me. The other four were brought to me by my associates. You would probably not appreciate the function or potential of most of them, so I will mention only one, Mr. Scott."

"You'd better keep it simple."

"I intend to. This one is a storage battery. Not merely an improvement over batteries now in use, but based upon an entirely different principle. The basic unit is a small cell I might describe as a sandwich of several metals plus a printed circuit, a rather complex marvel of solid-state microengineering about the size of a mustard seed."

He smiled at that for some reason, and went on. "I'll not burden you with figures, but merely say it is more compact, more powerful, more efficient than any other storage battery available today. Very adaptable for use in automobiles, for example—or in flashlights, tools, kitchen appliances, and battery-operated equipment—so you can make almost any estimate you desire of its profit potential."

"This is one of the things the hoods brought you, and you've since gotten a patent on it?"

"Yes. I had some difficulty in gaining the approval of the patent examiners. It was necessary that I make two trips to Washington, D.C., taking with me a working model of the device—originally supplied me, you understand, by my partners in criminal invention—and demonstrate that it *did*

161

work, after inventing a fairly reasonable explanation of *why* it worked. It is a good, logical explanation, in accordance with known physical laws. But I am certain it is not the true explanation—the thing may operate in accordance with physical law *not* yet known. However, my theory satisfied the patent examiners, which was my purpose.''

"You say the designs and a model of this battery were brought to you by Hauk and Werzen? Those two specifically?''

''Yes, they are the only two individuals I have ever dealt with. I have much evidence that several others are involved, but I've not discovered their identities. As I indicated earlier, Mr. Scott, I have not tried very hard to learn more. Until now.''

He mussed his hair absently with first one hand, then the other. It looked neater when he got through mussing it. ''I preferred to know as little as possible,'' he went on. ''But it was glaringly apparent that neither Mr. Hauk nor Mr. Werzen was intellectually capable of devising a scheme of such inherent complexity, or of beginning to understand the nature of those things they brought to me for my attention.''

"What I'm getting at, if they turned over this battery to you, do you have any idea who really put it together, invented it, and therefore knows why it works?''

He sighed. ''That would naturally be one of the things a man in my position would most desire *not* to know, wouldn't it, Mr. Scott? However, again, certain conclusions force themselves upon us. Because I was always interested in and familiar with his work, and because the battery was brought to me three years ago, I am quite sure it is one of the inventions of Petrocini.''

"I missed something. What does three years ago have to do—"

"Petrocini was killed in an automobile accident three years ago. About a week before the designs and model were delivered to me."

I grunted. "That could lead to some pretty ominous conclusions about the five other—"

"Perhaps," he interrupted. "However, there may be a certain warped integrity among hoodlums, some of them—I have allowed myself to hope so. Because I was assured in each case, *except* that of the battery, that all rights to the invention had been legally secured, paid for, with cash and . . . I believe Mr. Werzen's exact phrase in all instances was 'some udder inducements.' I recall wondering where he picked up the word *inducements*."

"I wonder more what those inducements were. Like maybe operating on a guy's kneecaps with a hammer? Or threatening to carve . . ." I let that one ride, thinking of young Lindstrom's little finger again.

"At any rate, Mr. Scott, my suspicions about what may have happened to Petrocini—suspicions long and deliberately suppressed but nonetheless often agonizing to me—are now reinforced by what you have today told me about Norman Amber."

Lindstrom shifted in his swivel chair, sighed heavily. "You see, Mr. Scott, I have had in my possession for three days now half a dozen of Norman Amber's brilliantly executed inventions—I mean, the actual working models, prototypes, in various stages of development, either apparently finished, the work concluded, or else capable of completion with

163

minimal further effort.'' He sighed again. ''Also several pages of description, design, mathematical formulae. Plus a dozen notebooks, obviously gleanings from Norman's mind over a period of at least twenty years. Notebooks, which it is obvious to me even after only cursory examination, contain thoughts, ideas, concepts of astonishing brilliance and value.''

''Three days? That would be since—Wednesday?''

''Yes. Shortly before noon, Wednesday last.''

''So we can assume he was dead Wednesday morning.''

''That is what I assume. And since he *is* dead, I am morally certain he was murdered by my co-conspirators, and therefore in a very real sense by . . . myself as well.''

''Mr. Lindstrom, you may have gone along with some hard-case hoods, perhaps more than you should have, but that doesn't make you a murderer. I wouldn't reach that far for—''

''I would.'' He snapped the words out, then went into one of those still, quietly staring sessions of his—brief this time, only a few seconds—after which he straightened up, spoke in a brighter tone. ''Yes, I would, I'm afraid, Mr. Scott. Or—is it Shell?''

''That's right.''

''You may as well call me Gunnar, Shell. For *we* are now co-conspirators, are we not?''

''Uh . . .''

''In one sense, at least. Perhaps more than one. Together we conspire to confound and make impotent the professional thieves and hoodlums. More, you have most solemnly agreed not to repeat without my permission what I have told—and will tell—you, not to involve or incriminate me. Thus you conspire with me to conceal my participation in monstrous—"

"Hold it. Please. I wish you could meet Phil Samson. Together, you and the captain could get me at least twenty years—"

"I do not wish to meet any captains. Not just yet. But back to the matter of Norman Amber. And his death. If it can be shown that he was murdered with deliberation and forethought, a crime of epic dimension has been committed. I shall not, I am certain, be able to convince you of the enormity of that crime."

"Well, it's pretty bad, sure. Murder is almost always an enormity of one kind or another, Gunnar—"

"You do not even begin to understand. Perhaps only another scientist—more specifically, another professional scientific investigator and inventor, such as myself—can fully understand what the death of Norman Amber means. You had never heard of him, had you?"

"First time was . . . day before yesterday? Yeah. It seems longer."

"Even so, your own life has been affected in at least a dozen areas, though perhaps only in small ways, because Norman Amber lived as long as he did. Your television set, stereophonic-sound components, moving pictures you have seen in theaters, films and cameras you may have used—all of these and *much* besides are more efficient, more valuable, because of contributions made by Norman Amber. And his most recent contribution—which I think of as the Amber Effect—is the greatest of *all* his inventions."

"The Amber Effect? What's that? One of the gizmos the boys brought to you Wednesday?"

"Gizmos. Ha! Yes, one of those. But I will explain this to you in a moment. What I am trying to say to you now, Shell, is that Norman is . . ."

Lindstrom winced slightly, as he had when I'd mentioned the "dead-wagon," then continued. "Norman was not necessarily the most brilliant man I have met in my lifetime, but he was unquestionably the most brilliant inventor I have ever known, a man not only of magnificent intellect, brilliant unorthodoxy, admirable courage, but of magical faith."

"Magical?"

"He was a scientist with a mystic's faith, then. Consider, he was almost unique among scientists in that he did not deny the possible existence of a law—rule, principle, natural habit—simply because he was himself unaware of its existence, for he knew that *his* denial for the law's possibility would inevitably make it *for him* nonexistent, incapable of existence. Are you beginning to comprehend now?"

Lindstrom examined my expression with apparent concern. "How can I make this simple enough so you may grasp my meaning?"

"Maybe there isn't any way."

"Don't say that! Let me approach this from a different quarter. In science there are many questions which are never asked because they are obviously unanswerable. Therefore, nonmystical scientists do not ask them. Norman, however, often asked these questions to which there are not and cannot be any sensible answers."

"Hold it—"

"And sometimes, answered them. Do you understand?"

"No."

"I feared as much. I will try one more time. The virtue of Norman Amber was his realization that a thing is impossible because we believe it to be impossible. So long as this remains our belief, the thing is indeed impossible. Even if our belief changes, the thing may remain impossible. But it is *only* through this reversal of belief that the impossible thing *may* become possible. And perhaps, in a larger sense, that is the real Amber Effect."

"Suits me," I said.

An expression best characterized as "bleak" overcame his features. He frowned, concentrating, then his face smoothed and he brightened considerably.

"I have it. I need not further attempt to explain anything to you. Instead of trying to tell you, I will *show* you."

"That might help. I guess. Show me what?"

"The Amber Effect."

"Swell," I said. "So what is it?"

Slowly Gunnar Lindstrom smiled. Slowly but widely, joyously—perhaps fiendishly. He just kept on smiling, almost athletically; and, even then, I had a hunch I would remember that smile for a long time.

"This Amber Effect," I said soothingly. "What the hell is it?"

Still smiling, he replied, "You will see. . . ."

CHAPTER THIRTEEN

GUNNAR left me alone in his office for fifteen or twenty minutes, mysteriously avoiding any comment about where he was going or what he intended doing when he got to wherever it was.

At least, it struck me as pretty mysterious, particularly when he came back in through the door "washing" his hands, rubbing them together and smirking.

"If you're trying to act like a mad scientist, Gunnar," I said, "that's an extremely convincing performance."

"Come," he said. "Come along."

"Where? And, listen, if you say 'you'll see' once more—"

"To the central laboratory. We were there yesterday, Shell."

I stood up.

He was already going out the door, gazing—and very peculiarly did this strike me—at a large round watch in his hand.

"The big room? With all the junk in it?"

"Yes, the large central room. We have some new—junk in it." Smile, smile, smile. Maybe he really had gone a bit off the deep end, right here before my eyes.

He was moving along the corridor at a brisk pace. I caught up with him as he glanced again at the watch. It was a stopwatch, I noted. Tick-tick-tick, long needlelike hand sweeping past the seconds.

"When does the bomb go off?" I asked him, only half serious.

"I realize I have placed severe restrictions upon you, Shell," he said, apropos of absolutely nothing germane to what was now happening, it seemed to me. "And I realize this places you in a difficult position. However, I have endeavored to make you understand why this is necessary, at least until there is immense improvement in my situation. I hope—in fact, I expect—that you will be the agency to bring about that immense improvement."

We reached the intersecting corridor, turned right, simply scooting along. The double doors of the central lab were ahead of us, about fifty feet away. "I believe you possess a certain blundering determination, a kind of savage intensity of purpose, that might—"

"Will you quit it? If you're going to start that blundering-thundering stuff again—"

"—solve for me this horrible problem that I have long felt was well-nigh insoluble. I have hope—*hope!*—at last. I simply never assumed my succor might come from an individual so obviously enslaved by animal appetites, a man of such fearsome mien and lumpy muscularity."

"Gunnar—"

"Who else, however, who else but such a one could extricate me from the predicament in which I find myself, a predicament fashioned by criminals and hoodlums? Yes, I have hope—and, Shell, if you *do* succeed in delivering me from this predicament, I intend to pay you one hundred thousand dollars."

"You've got a big mouth, you know. Maybe your brains are full of, ah, uh, brains. . . . I don't think I heard that last bit."

"It is not 'tainted' money, Shell. I was a millionaire before being joined by my criminal associates, and the money I have earned since then from others' work is, essentially, held in trust. I believe the laborer is worth his hire, and—"

"What the hell are you doing?"

He had stopped in the corridor, a few yards from the entrance to the lab, and was placing his stopwatch on the floor, near one wall.

He straightened up—not replying—and walked to the double doors, placed one hand on a knob. I followed him there, gnashing my teeth slightly, and he said, smiling, needless to say, "Will you retrieve my watch, and bring it into the laboratory, Shell?"

"You just *put* the dumb thing there. Have you really gone off the deep—"

"Perhaps I am testing you, Shell, testing your reflexes—"

"Wouldn't it be easier to pound my knee with a little rubber banger?"

"—or, more importantly, your conduct under peculiar stress, under conditions totally foreign to anything in your previous experience. After all, a hundred thousand dollars is—"

"A hundred thousand dollars, yeah."

"The watch, please?"

"Sure. I'll go get it for a thousand bucks."

But I stomped back up the hallway.

By the time I picked up the stopwatch and turned, Gunnar had opened the doors, stepped past them, and closed them behind him. Probably locked me out, I thought. And plans to accuse me of stealing his watch. It surprised me a little when the door opened easily.

I stepped into the big room, recognizing several items of equipment I'd seen yesterday, including the spiraling pattern of big glass tubes filled with pretty colors. But I didn't see Lindstrom anywhere. Didn't see anybody.

I took three or four steps into the room, glancing around, and heard Gunnar calling from my left, "Over here, Shell."

There he was, about ten feet away, stepping toward me. And smiling, smiling. "I'd like for you to pretend we have just met, Shell," he said. "Never mind why, just yet. Please do as I say, all right?" He continued to walk toward me, raising his right arm, hand extended.

His voice sounded a bit odd, perhaps because of the acoustics in the high-ceilinged room. Or maybe it was just illusion, the effect a ventriloquist gets with his dummy. I didn't like that thought, when it was increasingly apparent that Lindstrom was pulling some kind of strings here, and maybe my leg.

But, what the hell, I thought. What can I lose? Which, when you think about it, was not a wholly rational attitude.

I stepped toward him, sticking my right arm out, and feeling a *little* bit silly. The stopwatch, I noticed, was still in my right hand, so I transferred it to my left and said, "Well,

172

I got your dumb watch. Didn't explode, as I expected it to. So you owe me a G.'' I put on a false smile, and said with totally unconvincing exuberance, "Well, how do you do, Mr. Lindstrom? I've heard a lot about—''

And right then I almost had a heart attack.

I mean it. My ticker is probably strong enough and healthy enough to pump ten invalids out of hospital beds, but for an eternity—a two- or three-second eternity—I thought it might not only stop, but split.

Because as Gunnar and I met, I slowed, then came to a stop and grabbed his hand and nothing was there—nothing was there—and he kept walking slowly, smiling, walking straight at me *and on through me.*

And then I was falling.

Nothing pushed me or pulled me, there was no blast of air or pulse of light or shock of electricity—plenty of *shock,* though. It was much like stumbling in the dark on the last step at the bottom of the stairs when you were sure there was one step more; or, more accurately, like reaching with your foot for the top step that *isn't* there.

I was reaching for his hand, and my hand went right through it, and then I saw with perfect clarity his solid and substantial body moving closer to me, and while my hand clutched and squeezed tight in an involuntary convulsion of muscles, I was automatically trying to draw away, avoid the gentle but unanticipated collision, and as he walked through me—the stupid goddamned Cheshire cat smile six inches from my face—I was twisting, off balance, and falling.

And, I'll admit it, gripped with a cold quick kind of terror. Real terror, not for long, for a shrieking second or maybe

173

only half that, but *real* while it lasted, and *terror* while it lasted. It was the terror of sudden disorientation, of the false become real, of the fearful unknown that kids imagine under tight-clutched covers in the dark, a flickering jagged glimpse of that tiny part of death people wonder about when depressed, or bone-weary and worn, or mad.

But then I hit the concrete floor and got a little mad myself, a different kind of "mad." My left knee cracked against the concrete and the impact sent a stab of pain up my thigh, and then my elbow was pushing against the cement and I had myself sort of half balanced—or half-assed balanced, because I was still wobbling and my butt was thrust up into the air contributing to what had to be a supremely ridiculous posture, and I shoved with my left arm and elbow, starting to roll over, and at the same moment I did not fail to yell, "You sonofabitch!"

Then my butt hit the cement, I got my feet under me, and bounced up. "I don't know how the hell you did that," I roared, "but it's ten to one I'm going to knock your block—" I paused, right arm raised, fist clenched. "Even money? No . . ."

I wasn't the least bit panicky now—that uncharacteristic trifle of petrified gooeyness *couldn't* have lasted more than half a second anyhow, maybe only a quarter—but I was sure as hell confused.

Gunnar—or he—it—whatever the dumb thing was that had just plowed through me real as the Rock of Gibraltar but silent and soft as a sigh—still walked ahead, receding from me, the helter-skelter mass of gray-streaked brown hair mov-

174

ing slightly in . . . it had to be . . . in the thin movement of air against it.

I squatted, turned all the way around quickly, flicking my eyes at and behind equipment, up, down. Nothing. I slapped my hand across my chest to grab my Colt Special, grabbed air, scratched my armpit instead, straightened up.

Gunnar—it—walked on to the wall. And disappeared.

I said aloud, "You're all under arrest. Now hear this: This place is surrounded. By a lot of other places. Everything you may say will be taken down and used against you. If I can find you." And other nonsense.

During which chatter I looked around, found a wavy but straight-enough rod of steel with a sharp point at one end; also another unidentifiable hunk of metal shaped approximately like a ten-pound sap and capable of being similarly employed.

Thus armed to the thumbs with a weapon in each hand I turned around, to see Gunnar Lindstrom stepping from behind a wooden platform, or large box, appearing distressed.

At least he—or that which several of my senses told me I was observing—was not smiling.

He said, "I must apologize, I do apologize, Shell."

"You stay the hell away from me," I yelled. Then, "Stamp your foot," I said.

"What?"

I didn't say anything.

Then he nodded slightly, stamped his foot on the cement—it made a nice smack—and clapped his hands a few times.

"Splendid," he said. "In fact, *all* of your reactions have been excellent, even those not closely reasoned—"

175

"That's quite a bunch—"

"—and it was clever to make me stamp my corporeal foot, so you would know I am real."

"I don't care if you pull off your sergeant leg, I'm still not sure. So I believe I shall run this wiggly steel rod through you. If there is copious bleeding, I will have a clue—"

"Shell, I *am* sorry, I *have* apologized." He was giving me a very dubious look. "My error arose from the fact that I had not before this moment observed anyone *else's* reaction to what I must admit is a . . . profoundly moving experience."

"It sure moved me. Well . . ." I dropped my wiggly bar and overweight sap. Walked close to Gunnar. Lifted a hand. Poked him with it in the gut.

"Oopf," he said.

"Sorry," I said, poking him again.

"Oopf."

"That's reassuring, Gunnar," I told him. "It's really you, huh? How the hell did you do that? *What* did you do?"

"You have just witnessed," he said, "or experienced, one small demonstration, one *tiny* demonstration, of the Amber Effect."

Fifteen minutes later we were still in the big central room.

Gunnar had run his "film"—for that, in the final analysis, was all he'd really done before—twice more, and each time I was nearly as impressed and flabbergasted by the effect as when it had literally bowled me over.

"Well," I said to him, "I told you about those aquarium fishes, but this is a stupendously long way from a solid-looking *Corydoras paleatus*."

176

"What is a *solidellking Corydoras paleatus*?"

"Some scientist you are. It's a catfish. That's the Latin, of course," I added a bit smugly.

"Ah, you are familiar with Latin?"

"*Sí*. At least, I speak a little of it. *Cómo está?* Gunnar, I have now seen that mind-blowing demonstration three times, and have twice watched you perform the hey-presto, but I still haven't the foggiest idea what happened."

He smiled. "Look at me closely, Shell. What you see is not really *me* in the strictest sense—"

"Let's not get off into Magicland again—"

"Wait, please. When we become visually aware of any material object, it is because light is being reflected from the object, bouncing from millions, billions of areas, points, let us say, and then entering the pupils—lenses—of our two eyes. A myriad of varied vibrations of light impinge upon the eyes, that light energy is transformed into chemical-electrical impulses which travel along nerve pathways to a pair of visual cortex centers in the back of the brain, and it is the effect of that vibration upon those brain cells that results in the binocular three-dimensional picture, or the condition we call 'seeing.' "

"But there wasn't anything *there*—"

"Ah, but there was, Shell. Not anything solid, tangible, no. But do not confuse the sense of touch with the sense of sight—the identical myriad of varied vibrations of light I just spoke of *were* there. More accurately, an exact reproduction of them. I hope this much, at least, is clear."

"Yeah . . . If you can make light waves, or whatever they are, shoot out of a spot in the air the same way they bounce

177

off a guy, I guess you'd think you were seeing the guy. Even with no guy there.''

"You have it. Of course, you don't *think* you see, you *do* see. But, all right, that's enough. Except—do you recall what I said to you yesterday when you were producing sounds from those small Nikola buttons?''

"Yeah. Vibration, vibration—''

"Everything *is* vibration.''

"I'd just as soon not believe that, even if it's true.'' I was thinking of Aralia when I said it. And, in an odd way, I kept thinking about her for a while as Gunnar continued speaking.

"Very simply, then, one virtue of the Amber Effect is that it allows the *exact* three-dimensional reproduction of those patterns and intensities of light vibrations I just spoke of. All that is required is possession and use of the equipment of Norman Amber's design—and you have now seen what I refer to, for convenience, as the camera, film, and projector.''

I had closely examined the three items Gunnar spoke of, but none of it resembled any photographic equipment I'd ever seen before. The "film,'' for example, looked like a solid block of semi-transparent plastic about three inches on a side, with faintly visible curving lines and blobs and squiggles in it.

The camera, or at least the main part of the items that combined to capture the image of whatever was being filmed, at least approximated the appearance of a large television camera. But the "projector'' looked more like a Buck Rogers ray gun with a couple of doodads and one dingus attached to it.

Looking at the thing, I said to Gunnar, "This is part of the stuff Hauk and Werzen brought to you Wednesday, huh? I suppose that projector there is the only one in existence?''

''Oh, no, there are a half-dozen more, all slightly different in design, but all based on the identical principles and essentially the same. This particular model is the one Norman demonstrated for the patent examiners in Washington. However, except for the projector units in this room, there are no others in existence, since only Norman Amber was working on this particular approach to the production of three-dimensional images.''

He paused, then went on. ''At least, so far as I am aware. No matter how much creative scientists and inventors may wish it were otherwise, I am inclined to think that each great advance creates itself, so to speak, or at least awaits its own time. Certainly production of three-dimensional images of such remarkable fidelity as these had to await invention of the laser, the hologram, microcircuits, perfection of the transistor and modern computer, and a great many other marvels of modern technology. This three-dimensional aquarium which so impressed you, and its little catfish, when did you see it?''

''Quite a while back. Sixty-nine, I think.''

He nodded. ''Yes, lasered light reflected from mirrors for the production of holograms was used in the sixties for making three-dimensional still photos. Also the first simple three-D moving pictures which did not have to be projected onto a screen, such as your aquarium, were produced before the sixties ended. Even quite recently, although techniques had improved immensely, the image—a man's figure, for example—was not *free*. That is, movement of the astonishingly realistic image was restricted, limited to a few cubic yards of space, in much the same fashion that Hollywood's previous two-dimensional images were limited to the few square yards of a movie screen. Among other things, what Norman Amber has done is *free* the three-dimensional image so that it can be projected in any direction to a considerable distance.''

"Any direction, too, huh? I'm glad you didn't think of having that—that you I shook hands with walk up in the air at a forty-five-degree angle.''

He smiled. ''My purpose was merely to impress you with the value of what I call the Amber Effect.''

"You succeeded.''

"To be accurate, I should explain that though this free image I speak of can be made to appear—be projected—at almost any desired distance from the viewer, the image does not necessarily remain constant in its dimensions. It may, or it may not, depending upon how the operator programs the unit's computer. For a theater audience, the image would actually be made to grow smaller in order to give the *illusion* of an individual's movement to a distant point.''

"Sure, same deal as with a flat screen,'' I said.

"Exactly. And, in Norman's patented designs and diagrams, and of course these working models, all is compressed, miniaturized, built in, so that it will be a simple matter to mass-produce portable units the average man might purchase and use, merely by pointing, pushing switches, following simple instructions to produce his *own* perfect three-dimensional movies should he so wish. Just as he now produces his own two-dimensional photographs and films. But that is only the beginning. I expect, within a few years, the many possible commercial applications will produce a yearly dollar volume of a billion or so.''

Quite a number of questions were crowding my mind, but some of them got crowded out by the last thing he'd said, or what I thought he'd said.

"Did you say something about volume of a million? You mean bucks? Dollars?''

"Yes, dollars, commercial gross. But not a million, a billion. Per year.''

I opened my mouth, closed it again.

Lindstrom said, ''You have perhaps not visualized many of the other obvious commercial applications. Such as a wall in a home, with beautiful paintings hanging upon it—*exact* reproductions of Raphaels or DaVincis if desired—and niches for priceless vases, figurines, jewelry . . . but there is no wall; it is a projection, a picture. Or it could be, not a wall, but a sunlit patio, a forest pool, a stream and splashing waterfall, the only limits are the limitations of our own imaginations.''

"Yeah . . . You could put some fancy chairs in the corner, just so you didn't sit in any of them. Only cost you a nickel. Right?''

"Right.''

"Or a piano . . . Why, hell, even a few guests—*people*.''

"Of course.''

"*Real* people, if you didn't try to carry on a conversation, or make them go *oopf*.'' I found the idea increasingly stimulating. "I'm beginning to see what you mean, Gunnar, about all the possibilities in this thing.''

"Not quite all, I think,'' he said.

181

"¡Maybe not. But—well, so *glad* you could come to my *pah*ty, dearie, over there in the corner is the famous movie star Tootsie Tickle. And I'm simply thrilled to goosebumps to introduce *the President of the United . . .*"

I stopped. "You know, Gunnar, this could get a little scary."

"And we have barely begun, have we not?"

"Yeah, I guess so. Barely, you said. Barely . . ."

"Something?"

"You better believe it." I thought about it a little more. "Gunnar," I said, "you actually made that brief but astonishingly real and lifelike film of yourself during the time I was alone in your office?"

"Yes, of course. Making the film required only the half minute or so of actual action. I assume you realize there is no processing necessary, that is to say, no form of film development, since the holographic impression in the cube is made instantaneously. This should not surprise anyone familiar with television's instant replay. I spent most of my time positioning the laser and cube, which were already connected to the unit's power source—what we refer to as the projector— to ensure that my image appeared where it would be most effectively presented to you. And in estimating the minutes that would elapse before you entered the laboratory, so I could time our arrival here moments before appearance of my image."

"Hence, your stopwatch."

"Yes."

"And sending me to pick up the watch, so you could sneak in here, and sneakily hide."

"Yes. This is all extremely elementary."

"*Now* it is. But how elementary would a moon shot have been to the Wright brothers? You have to think of me, for a while yet, as one of the brothers, not an astronaut."

"I believe I can do that."

"But I did think of a couple . . . Yeah, barely. That was it. Bare—"

"Of course. I should have perceived the reason for your preoccupation before now. Indeed, instantly."

"Oh?"

"Pornography. Perfectly lifelike, and life-size, three-dimensional flesh-and-blood—so long as you merely watch them—individuals furiously coupling, and perhaps even tripling or quadrupling, before your interested gaze. Not on a flat screen in two dimensions, but big as life and quite as real, in living, loving color—right there squirming in your living room, even bedroom, kitchen—"

"Well, I wouldn't go quite—"

"That is what you were wondering, is it not? The new realism and thus improvement of vicarious titillation that will be afforded by the inevitable emergence of such 3-D pornographic films?"

"Well, that did sort of brush my—yes."

"Unquestionably, the market for pornographic films, large even now, will become huge in a very short time. As I said, even a minimum of thought provides many, many additional insights into areas of vast potential."

I was getting several insights. Among them, the desirability of my asking a couple of questions of the lovely Aralia, and sensible detective-type questions they were—but the si-

183

multaneous thought of 3-D movies and Miss Naked California was almost too much all at once.

So I pushed that out of my mind, mentally groping for something else that moments ago had been in it.

"Gunnar, I've got to take off. I'd like to hear more about all this, but later. You did say something, though. . . . Yeah, a comment about Amber's patented designs? You've mentioned the several ideas and gizmos of his that were turned over to you Wednesday. Are they patented?"

"Everything I have alluded to under the embracing term the Amber Effect is. Norman applied for patent protection nearly a year and a half ago, his application was allowed, the Letters Patent was issued this past July in Norman Amber's name. But none of the other processes or inventions I mentioned have patent protection, with one small exception."

"What's the exception?"

"A strange new film emulsion, containing a surprising amount of the element mercury—of little importance just now, really. I could instruct you more fully, but it is quite technical. . . ."

"So forget it. I have to get going, Gunnar, but I'll keep you informed."

"Please do. I did wish to discuss further my intention to reward you, if all goes as well as I hope, with a payment in the amount of one hundred thousand—"

"It's a little soon to talk about that much money, Gunnar. Besides, even if we made a deal, my usual fee is a hundred bucks a day and expenses."

"This, however, is an unusual situation. With enormous amounts of money involved. More important to me, there is my now-resurgent hope that I may yet reclaim my life, be able to call it my *own* once more.''

"I'll work on it." I grinned at him. "Maybe we'll work on it together."

Then I waved a finger at Gunnar, and took off.

To see Miss Naked California.

CHAPTER FOURTEEN

WHEN I let myself into my apartment, Aralia was sitting on the chocolate-brown divan, legs tucked underneath her, reading a book and taking a bite out of an apple.

She was wearing a bright print dress, and apparently not much else. A pair of low-heeled shoes rested on the carpet near where she was curled up on the divan.

As I entered we exchanged exuberant hellos, and what have you been doings, and then she said, "You told me not to go out, so I've eaten almost everything in the refrigerator. This is the last apple."

"That's something I wanted to talk to you about, Aralia," I said, joining her on the divan.

"The last apple?" She smiled in a way I had come to know. "Like Adam and Eve's?"

"That was the *first* apple. And it had a big worm in it. But, no. I meant your not going out. Have you—I hope—changed your mind about attending that gathering of dirty old men tomorrow at the Doubless Ranch?"

"No. And I won't, Shell. I told you, it's just too important to me."

"I was afraid of—"

"But forget that for now, Shell."

She went on for a while about Adam and Eve and apples, asking me if I wanted a bite, things like that, but without much success in distracting me from my purpose, which was to talk about her planned appearance at the ranch tomorrow.

Finally, she eyed me with some dubiousness and said, "You . . . aren't the same, Shell. You were more—more *fun* last night. And even this morning."

"I was, huh? Well, dear, fun's fun, but there is a time for everything, right? And time's a-wasting."

"It sure is."

"I mean, if you're really set on going to that barbecue, I have some proposals and suggestions to present to you, and some of these will require your strict attention, not to mention considerable rearrangement in your thinking."

"You're all business, aren't you?"

"Sometimes—during business hours. But wait till I tell you what happened today. First, you don't want to get shot tomorrow, do you? And killed? No more fun, or anything, just killed? Dead, dead—"

"You're really not a ball in the afternoon, are you?"

"—dead . . . Will you stop quibbling? I'm trying to keep you from getting killed."

"I know. Dead, dead, dead."

"Now you've got it. So will you listen?"

"I might as well."

"Good. Now, pay attention, dear. First, your father is dead."

"So what else is new?"

"I didn't mean to hit you with it all of a sudden like . . . Yeah. Aralia, there is a great deal you do not know. But you are soon going to know it all, even if I have to sock you. So will you *listen*?"

She listened. With a few interruptions at the beginning of my spiel, but none at all after that. Nearly five minutes later I leaned back, saying, "Well, what do you think?"

And, this time, it took Aralia a while to reply. She asked a couple of questions about her father, was silent for almost a minute, then said, "It's as if we're talking about someone else. I don't—feel any different."

After another brief silence she went on. "Shell, do you really think somebody might try to kill me tomorrow? *Really* shoot me maybe? Right out there with all those people around?"

"I'm honestly not sure, Aralia. It depends on a lot of things. But there's a damned good chance, particularly if I make it easy for them."

"That's nice. It's nice to know you care—"

"You haven't been listening with all your might, have you? Besides, I did leave a little out. So listen some more."

Two minutes later she shook her head silently, then said, "Well, golly. I don't know. It sounds *crazy*. But . . . you promise, if nothing happens—if you're wrong, I mean—I can really do my thing? I can wait there on that movie set they used for their last picture until it's time for me, and then walk right *out* there—"

"Yeah."

"—and then mingle and all afterward? With the people, the *producers* and everything?"

189

"Right."

"You promise?"

"I promise. Look, I've told you I know the president of Magna Studios. Harry and I don't usually, or even often, see eye to eye, but he's a good friend of mine. So, dear, you go along with all this and I'll introduce you to Harry Feldspen."

"Personally?"

"You bet. Personally. Which, I have just realized, is about the only way I could do it."

She liked that. Judging by her smiles, and happy wiggles, she liked it a whole lot. But she was still dubious. Aralia simply could not bring herself to believe that anybody would actually try to kill her, murder her, in the presence of so many people, a number of them men well known throughout California and even the nation.

I couldn't fault Aralia for that. I had large doubts about it myself. Even if every single link in my chain of reasoning was a perfectly logical link—which was not a sure thing to begin with—she might not be in the slightest danger. But I thought I knew the hoodlum mentality better than she did, and I therefore knew there was at least a chance, if she appeared in public tomorrow without taking any precautions at all, it could be her last public appearance anywhere. No matter how small that chance, I figured, why risk it—when there was a way to avoid that risk, or at least avoid most of it?

Finally—I'm not quite sure what process of reasoning led me to it, but logic is not always the victor—I asked, "Incidentally, dear, who was runner-up in the Miss Naked California contest?"

"Felice Dumonnet. That's what she *calls* herself. I think she got her name off a bottle of wine."

Her tone was the clue I needed.

"I know she's not in *your* class, Aralia—who is?" This rewarded me with a smile. "But she must be a real doll, anyway," I went on. "Even second in a statewide contest is nothing to be sneezed—"

"I'd swear she's had silicone injections in *four* places. And *picky*? After I won, she had the nerve to say—not to me, you can bet, but to the other girls—that I must have—"

"Wouldn't it be something if you got killed, Aralia? You know, dead-dead-dead. And Felice whoever went on to the Miss Naked USA finals in your place? I suppose, if the state winner cannot, or does not choose to, compete, the runner-up—"

"I'll do it."

Strange are the workings of the female mind. It was undoubtedly true that I knew much more about the hoodlum mentality than did Aralia, but I do not even kid myself that I understand women, or what really goes on among the delicate neurons and synapses when a doll thinks.

But sometimes I get lucky.

"You will?" I said, as though overwhelmed.

"Of course, Shell. It makes a lot of sense to me, now you've explained it all."

Gunnar opened the heavy doors of Lindstrom Laboratories himself this time, and led us—Aralia and me—along the silent corridors. We left Aralia in his office, then he and I continued on to the big central room.

191

"I arranged everything immediately after you called, Shell," he said as we entered the large high-ceilinged room again.

"Fine. I guess. I suppose it's natural I'd be a little nervous. But . . . fine. I guess."

We had walked into a cleared area approximately fifteen yards square bordered at one end by a large white screen. Opposite the screen and thirty feet or so from it was the 3-D camera Gunnar had used earlier in the day to make the film of himself, calling, "Over here, Shell," then stepping toward me and extending his hand, and the rest of it.

A few feet to the camera's left, on a small wooden table, rested the "projector." This consisted primarily—not counting the framework holding the components together in their proper relationship, and electrical cord leading to the power source—of the ray-gun contraption, or laser, this mounted atop a sealed black box and aimed at the innocent-looking cube of what appeared to be semi-transparent plastic. Gunnar had told me the black box was a microminiaturized and extraordinarily efficient computer that controlled "plane scanning, and in-depth movement at right angles to the plane" of the laser beam, which had not exactly contented me at the time. But, at the time, it had not seemed necessary that I become a private-eye Einstein.

Earlier this afternoon, too, of course, Gunnar had—after literally "bowling me over" with his projected three-dimensional image the first time—twice more demonstrated the simple operation while I watched. And it was simple; once the "projector" was set up and correctly aligned, there was nothing to be done except to turn the thing on. Which was merely the flipping of a toggle switch, like turning on a light or starting anything else.

So now he repeated the process once more, causing that same familiar but still astonishing image of himself to appear instantly and miraculously from nothing and then as instantly disappear, and then had me play with the apparatus for a few minutes.

After which I said to him, "Well, so far it's easy enough. You just set it up, then I push that little switch there. But I have this . . . uneasy feeling. In case something should go wrong—not that anything *will*—maybe I should have a better idea of how and why this thing works."

"I agree. In its essence, the process is quite simple, Shell. Once you understand the basic principles, and their specific applications in this case."

"Quite simple. Once you understand it. So is Chinese. So teach me Chinese in ten minutes."

"It is not necessary that you have a degree in electrical engineering in order to turn the lights on. You have seen the demonstration; you know it works. I cannot make a physicist of you in ten minutes, but you are a detective, so I shall at least provide you with some clues."

Gunnar then launched into a brisk but, to me, dizzyingly technical—and clueless—explanation replete with comments about solid-state circuitry and molecular switches and feedback-from-computer-thus-controlling-laser-beam-scanning-of-pre-selected-holograms, all of which almost surely would have been of exceeding interest to at least a dozen people in the world, but was pure Chinese to me.

So I interrupted him by saying, "Gunnar, think of it this

193

way. Pretend I have just graduated from kindergarten, and you're the first-grade teacher. Like, twenty years from now, when everybody knows about this sort of thing, instead of now when practically nobody knows anything about it except you and me. I mean, except you. O.K.?''

He started to speak, nodded instead.

I pointed to the small three-inches-to-a-side cube, saying, ''I know what you said about that thing. But something's awry here. I don't see how you could get a bunch of snapshots in there. Even *one* snap, much less a moving picture. In three dimensions, yet. No, the damn thing just doesn't seem possible—''

''Don't say that!''

''I forgot. Obviously, you can get everything from all the Laurel and Hardy comedies to a dozen late-late shows in there, with room left over for commercials.''

''You do exaggerate. But not very much.''

''Not very *much*—''

''Look at this, Shell.''

He fumbled in his coat pocket and pulled out what looked like a little cube of glass. I couldn't figure out what it might be.

''Look at this little cube of glass,'' he said. ''Its top face is one inch by one inch, and thus has one square inch of surface. How many parallel lines would you say could be drawn, inscribed, on that surface?''

''Oh . . . a hundred?''

''More.''

''A thousand?''

''Thirty thousand.''

194

"O.K. Thirty thousand."

"Actually, more. However, assume we have inscribed that number of lines from left to right. Now, we inscribe an *equal* number of lines at right angles to the first ones. Wherever those lines intersect, we have a *point*, is it not so? Thus, on this one square inch of glass, on this single face of our little cube, we have how many individual and separate *points*? Thirty thousand times thirty thousand, or . . ." Gunnar rubbed a hand in random movements over his hair, accidentally bringing it into a semblance of order. "Or nine hundred million points," he continued, before I could answer.

"Right."

"Are you familiar with modern mathematics?"

"Not really."

"You aren't?"

"Not really."

"Well . . . I ask you to visualize a computer that operates only with the figures 'one' and 'zero'—or with only two integers, as plus and minus, or positive and negative. As either a positively charged *point* or a negatively charged *point*. All right?"

"So far."

"Some computers do operate with such positive and negative points, which are called *bits*. Now, each of our nine hundred million points here"—he held the small cube of glass before me—"may be charged, or magnetized, either positively or negatively, thus providing us merely in this one square inch of surface with nine hundred million *bits*. We will say ten bits are required to form an average letter, and

195

one hundred bits for a word. From this point on, I will simplify for you.''

"Good."

"To our computer we join a laser, which projects an extremely narrow or threadlike beam of light extending to, but only to, the precise distance or depth we desire. The minute tip of this laser beam we will consider a—a stylus. Think of it as similar to the tip of a phonograph needle that rests upon the groove of an LP record for the audible reproduction of music, voices, words, except that this stylus is a moving point of light, and instead of resting in a microgroove it touches, moves over—scans—those *bits* we have discussed. All right?''

"Sure."

"We have determined that our computer can 'recognize' and reproduce a word when its laser-stylus scans approximately one hundred bits. Assume the average book consists of seventy-five thousand words, equivalent to seven million, five hundred thousand bits. We have available nine hundred million bits. Simple mental division reveals that we can record—*on this one square inch of surface*—one hundred and thirty-three point three books! Is it not marvelous?''

"Sure is. You figured it out in your head, huh?''

Gunnar was getting all excited. He fumbled in his pocket again and pulled out a felt pen. With the pen he marked a few faint intersecting lines rapidly on one face of the cube, then handed it to me, saying, "There. This is a one-inch *cube.* Each of its faces, therefore, presents one square inch of surface. We will imagine that those ink marks I've made represent our thirty thousand parallel lines with thirty thousand more drawn at right angles to them. Now, turn the cube a quarter way around . . . that's it . . . so the inscribed face of the cube is to your left. Look at the side of the cube now facing you and mentally inscribe thirty thousand more lines from top to bottom, and consider each of those divisions as a—a *slice,* shall we say? A slice of the cube's material. Do you understand?''

''Yeah. Pretty thin slices, though.''

''You do understand. Fine. Yes, thin, but much thicker than a molecule, or many molecules.''

''I'll take your word for it.''

''Now, then, visualize that first square inch we spoke of—the plane surface of the cube, to your left—as the first slice. And, looking from left to right, visualize the second thin division as the second slice, and so on. How many *slices* have we now in this entire cubic inch of material?''

''Well, we drew thirty thousand lines, so—thirty thousand slices. Or thirty thousand and *one*? Yeah—''

''Call it thirty thousand. Each of which we may consider as identical with the first slice, the original plane surface. Each of which thus also provides us with an additional nine hundred million positively or negatively charged points, or bits. Now, how many books—we could, of course, translate this into storage of art, music, newspapers for transmission to homes over telephone lines, stock market quotations, many things, but for clarity we will consider only additional books— can be stored in this single cube?''

''A lot.''

''Um, yes. Obviously, one hundred and thirty-three point three times thirty thousand, or . . . ?''

"A lot."

"Approximately four million books. Or the entire contents of forty libraries each containing one hundred thousand books."

I was nodding my head, and Gunnar observed me nodding it, then he said, "I thought this was quite exciting."

"It is. I'm all agog."

"But—do you *truly* comprehend what I have been telling you, Shell?"

"Yeah, I think I do. Really, Gunnar. It's just . . ." I looked at that little cube in my fingers trying to believe there were forty big libraries in the thing. "It's just . . . wow!"

"You do understand!" he cried, sounding pleased. "Yes, wow! That sums it up nicely."

I tipped the cube over a bit. "Seems like it ought to be heavier," I said. Then I smiled at him. "Even if they're paperback books. Or lending libraries? Just a joke. No harm in—"

"What I have so simply described has been possible for some time, Shell. We are already capable of much more. Future possibilities are endless."

I was still looking at the cube. It fascinated me now a lot more than it had when it was empty.

"Man," I said, "if you lost this thing, you'd really lose something, wouldn't you? Or, say the nurses' auxiliary lady came around and asked, 'Have you got any old used books to donate?' and you tell her, 'Yeah, lady, I've got four million or so around here somewhere. Let me look in my other pants—' "

"At any rate," he interrupted, with a trace of asperity, if I had not lost all powers of observation, "perhaps you can now accept the possibility that it is possible for this one small cube to contain more than . . . what was it? A bunch of snapshots?''

"Yeah, I can. And do. I think. Yeah, I do.''

"And you understand that the image, or sound, of each word may be produced by scanning those preselected positive or negative bits with the infinitely tiny tip of a precisely controlled laser beam?''

"Yeah. Sure.''

"Excellent. Then we may proceed from words to pictures. For production of the three-dimensional image of our present interest, we no longer scan those individual bits, since we are dealing with a much more complex problem, but the *principle* is essentially the same, and you should therefore now be able to perceive from your understanding of the one how we arrive at the other, is it not so?''

"You bet.'' I smiled at him.

"For production of the three-D image, our laser scans not bits but a large number of individual holograms. Assume that the face of the cube you hold—the first of those thirty thousand slices we have discussed—bears upon its plane surface not nine hundred million magnetically charged points but a mere thousand or so tiny holographic impressions, each representing one fragment of the complicated movement of a three-dimensional body.''

"Only a thousand or so, huh?''

"Somewhat more. But, remember, there are thirty thousand slices, each of which may be inscribed, or impressed, with additional holograms representing additional fragments of the continuing movement.''

199

"O.K."

"And do not forget that the laser beam that scans these separate holograms can be extended or retracted so that its tip may probe surface, middle, any slice of the onion, so to speak. It can scan the outermost skin, or the second layer, or the cube's precise middle, or slice number twenty-one thousand and eighty-two."

I nodded, still smiling.

"And you realize, of course, we have been discussing the capacity of a one-inch cube, whereas the cube actually employed with our projector is a three-inch cube, as you have seen. Thus the capacity is somewhat greater, is it not so?"

"Sure is. Hadn't thought of that, but you'd have nine times as much stuff, wouldn't you? Or—three times three is nine, and there's another . . . *Twenty-seven* times as much, right?"

"Wonderful. Three times three times three is . . . Wonderful. You are right again. Indeed, Shell," he continued enthusiastically, "once the projector's computer has been programmed correctly by the operator—a job requiring the services of an expert, I'll admit—the rest is automatic."

"That's good enough for me, Gunnar. And you're an expert, aren't you?"

He shrugged. "As expert as anyone else alive," he said, "now that Norman Amber is dead."

"O.K., then. I know enough." I smiled some more at him. "You just set it up, then I push that little switch there."

He gave me an odd, sort of semi-bleak look, then ruffled his hair. "Does the young lady understand what is expected of her, Shell?"

"Well enough. Why, she knows nearly as much about this operation as I do. I'll go—"

"She is a remarkably attractive child," he said.

"You ain't seen nothin' yet," I said. "And, Gunnar, I have a hunch you will not, from this moment forward, ever again consider the word 'child' as properly descriptive of Aralia."

"Indeed?" he said, raising both eyebrows—not for the last time, as it turned out.

"Indeed," I said. "I'll go get her."

By ten-thirty that night Aralia and I were sitting once more on my divan, both of us just about talked out.

We had discussed not only her most recent experience at Lindstrom Laboratories, but everything that had happened since we'd met. And, as well, what might happen tomorrow, particularly in view of what we'd just listened to on the ten o'clock news.

Even before driving with Aralia to the lab, I had phoned a television newscaster of my acquaintance who was widely seen and listened to on a local channel. He felt that he "owed" me one, and agreed to introduce into both his six P.M. and ten P.M. "local action" segment of the news a fifteen-second mention of Aralia Fields, recent winner of the Miss Naked California title—transformed to "Miss Nudie" on TV—along with the intelligence that Miss Fields would be making a personal appearance before a private group of interested individuals at two P.M. tomorrow, Sunday, at the Doubless Ranch.

I turned off the TV set, went back and sat next to Aralia

201

again. "That should do it," I said. "If there's anything to get done."

"That's what you meant earlier, isn't it, Shell?" Aralia's voice was softer than fuzz on a baby chick's tummy. "About making it easy for them?"

"Sure. I'm starting to think I was being supercautious even to imagine somebody might try to plug you. Probably nothing to worry about, but just in case anyone really *does* want to try, it's better if we choose the time and place—and target, which means we have to let them know where to find you, right?"

"Absolutely. And I thought you were being—well, *mean*."

"Mean? Me? Why, Aralia, I don't have a mean bone in my whole body."

"That's not true," she said, "thank God. Why don't we go to bed, Shell?"

"Yeah. Why don't we? After all, we've got a big night— big *day* ahead of us. Tomorrow. Don't we?"

"Yes, we do." She leaned closer, lids starting to droop over those big blue eyes, long lashes quivering slightly. "We sure *do*," she whispered. "And don't forget, you promised."

"Promised?" I moved toward her, beginning to smile.

"To introduce me to Harry Feldspen," she said.

CHAPTER FIFTEEN

THE Doubless Ranch, two hundred and forty acres of hilly brush-covered land partly shaded by clumps of oak and eucalyptus trees a few miles from Los Angeles, was not only a land investment of Doubless Productions, Inc., but had also been used as a location for the two—so far—movies put together by the independent producing company. Put together in at least haphazard and possibly entirely accidental fashion, according to some unkind critics.

But whether critics were kind, unkind, or pathologically sadistic mattered not to the two geniuses who controlled Doubless, so long as those critical carpings and mewlings failed to significantly affect their pictures' B.O., which is also and coincidentally an abbreviation for "box office." The alleged negative cost and actual gross were the factors of real interest and importance to Sammy Shapiro and Schwerin Schicklmeister, the genius pair, who, it perhaps need not be stressed unduly, were often at odds.

They were, however, a successful team so far. Their latest release, *Rich Butterfly,* had according to their own reports cost only "seven hundred thou and some change" to make, and had grossed eight million five in the U.S. alone. It was expected to equal that gross from foreign releases, "except maybe in Japan," said Sammy.

A few minutes after nine A.M. that Sunday morning, with black coffee still sluggishly infiltrating my bloodstream, I stood alone on the once green but now beginning-to-shrivel lawn on which Mitsui Hochikuchi had danced wearing only huge gossamer wings, in the scene which ended with her using a pair of giant sharpened chopsticks to commit hara-kiri, or maybe it was chop suey; anyway, it killed her and she fell into the shallow pool—only a couple of yards from my feet—there to be devoured by the giant goldfish. Which were actually fat carp, painted yellow. Or, rather, yellowish. Those carp, or carps, were typical of the budget problems plaguing Sammy and Schwerin during the shooting of *Butterfly.* When they finally found a paint that would stick to wet fish, they had to capture the scene in one quick take, getting Mitsui's pathetic sueycide in the can only half a minute before all the carp died.

It was with some misgivings, therefore, that I gazed about me at what remained of the *Butterfly* set—including pool, lawn, small garden, teahouse, painted wall—acutely aware that this was where Aralia was scheduled to make her brief center-of-all-eyes appearance at two o'clock this afternoon.

Everything was done, in place, ready to go. At least, everything I could think of was.

But that, I realized, did not necessarily include everything.

I sat down on the lawn, yanked out a blade of grass, and bit it. Considered my misgivings. Attempted to reason them away. Last night I had been enveloped by a kind of dizzy euphoria in which all things seemed possible; more, seemed probable. Where had the euphoria gone?

Last night, I had been here for the first time, equipped with steel tape measure, pencil and pad, and high enthusiasm. Leaving Aralia back at the lab with Lindstrom—who by then, with full understanding at last of what I had in mind, was making final preparations for what I shall always think of fondly as Aralia's initial 3-D film test—I had examined the location, gotten the "feel" of the place, carefully checked several objects and distances with my tape, and completed a rough but precisely measured sketch of the limited area in which Aralia would later appear "in person."

Appear for not more than one minute. Possibly less.

The making of that sixty-second "film" took nearly an hour, and a singularly interesting hour it was, though nearly all of it was occupied by making measurements, chalking marks on the floor, having Aralia move from mark to mark, pause, speak, until she could do the scene easily, and without obvious downward glances to find the chalk lines, or unnatural pauses in either movement or speech.

It was, however, the last ten minutes, which included the final "take" preceded by what might be euphemistically described as Aralia's dress rehearsal, that not only totally absorbed my attention but also gave rise in Gunnar Lindstrom to behavior I had not previously noted in Gunnar Lindstrom.

I plucked another blade of grass, merely nibbled on this one, checked my watch—9:10 A.M.—glanced around.

I was sitting where Aralia would later stand—or within a yard or two of where she had *better* stand—near the edge of the shallow pool into which Mitsui had toppled, fluttering her gossamer wings. A microphone would be placed here to carry Miss Naked California's brief remarks to the small crowd that would be assembled—wisely, I thought, at the *opposite* side of the pool, or in a space extending from approximately five to fifty feet beyond its far edge.

Four hundred guests, all male, had been invited to attend the ceremonies; and only one, a chap who would be having a gallbladder operation at the time, had declined. A small crowd, yes; but the adjective is relative. The number was minute for attendance at a pro football game in the L.A. Coliseum, but huge for an orgy; and it was because of the latter consideration that all the men would be required to sit, in wooden chairs later to be assembled there, with the pool between them and Aralia.

I tried to ignore my misgivings. Concentrated on the good side of things. First, the film itself was splendid, truly a work of genius, magic—and art. Second, the location here satisfied me in virtually all particulars. I had been mentally quibbling, thinking there wasn't a chance in ten, maybe even a hundred, that an attempt on Aralia's life would be made here, before four hundred witnesses, when her death would thus so obviously be deliberate murder. But, so what?

Even if there was only one chance in a thousand, that justified all the trouble we'd gone to, and more. And if there was an attempt, it would have to come from one of only two places, both straight ahead—or due north—of where Aralia would be standing later today. I got to my feet, looked across the pool to where the guests would be seated. That would be one of the spots, the gathering of four hundred men.

Then I looked past that area and up, to the hillside beyond, rising at a steep angle of about thirty degrees. Plenty of oak, pepper, eucalyptus trees, along with wiry-looking shrubs and some other small bare-branched trees. Especially was there cover, plenty of it, near the crest of the hill about two hundred yards from where I stood. Not too distant; not for a fair marksman with a high-powered scope-equipped rifle.

I'd already been up there, prowled, covered the entire area. Prowled, yawning prodigiously in the early morning sunlight, true; but I'd checked it with care. So I knew that only fifty yards on past the hill's crest was a one-lane asphalt-covered road. Nothing else, that was all.

Behind me, as well as on both my left and right, the painted cardboard "Great Wall of Japan"—*Butterfly* hadn't exactly turned out to be the year's most historically accurate documentary film—rose thirty feet into the air. Only from the north, on that hill, might anyone not invited perch or hide and be able to see anything down here, or take aim, or simply practice a little titillating voyeurism.

The small plywood "teahouse" where Mitsui had waited in vain for her oriental lover, Honi Sakitumi, was about ten yards away on my right. Actually, since I had measured the distance from its open doorway to this spot, I knew the doorway was precisely twenty-eight feet four inches from my right foot. Which rested on a nail I'd forced into the grass, to mark the spot where a microphone would later stand.

From that teahouse, Aralia would walk. In that teahouse was everything necessary to create the Amber Effect. The laser-and-cube projector, microminiaturized computer, cord already plugged into power source—all was ready. Even including the separate audio components spliced into the PA system and ready to go.

Once the "projector" was switched on, audio and video—or perhaps more accurately audio and holeo, since the image projection hadn't been given a name yet—would be automatically synchronized. The sound might fall a bit oddly on the ear, as had Gunnar's voice on my ears when I'd been viewing his projection for the first time, but very likely that would not give rise to comment. Particularly when those listening were simultaneously eyeballing the totally bare, and undeniably exceedingly gorgeous Miss Naked California.

I looked at my watch again. It was 9:12 A.M. There was no point in delaying the acid test any longer, so I shrugged, turned, and walked to the little teahouse, gave everything inside a last check.

Then at exactly 9:14 A.M. I performed the scientific maneuver for which I had been educated by Gunnar Lindstrom: I pushed "that little switch there," and simultaneously started his—now my—stopwatch.

Nothing happened. But nothing was supposed to happen. Not just yet. Timing was crucial to the success of this operation, and I refused to think about what *could* happen if the timing was a minute or more off. Or even off a few seconds.

I walked around to the far side of the pool, sat again on the grass. Lit a cigarette. Checked my watch. Waited.

When we'd made the film, Gunnar, knowing I would have a few things to do today immediately after switching the unit on, suggested that he provide a few minutes of blankness, of "nothing," before Aralia's appearance—much as you can splice a few feet of blank film on at the beginning of a reel so that, before the show starts, you'll have time to get back to your chair, or couch, or do whatever it is you have in mind.

What I had in mind was leaving Aralia—the real Aralia—in the teahouse, giving the microphone's position a last quick check, and getting—hopefully unobserved—to the top of that hill where grew the many trees. One or two minutes wouldn't be quite long enough for all that; but the more time that elapsed between my pushing the switch and "Aralia's" appearance and immediate exit from the teahouse, the more time there would be during which some little thing could go largely wrong.

I told Gunnar to give me a three-minute blank. That was cutting it close, but it would be barely enough—if I was not delayed.

9:16. Plus a few ticks. In less than a minute Aralia would—should—step smiling through the teahouse door.

Just as, last night, before the large white screen in the big room at Lindstrom Laboratories, she had stepped forward smiling, glancing to her right while walking briskly ahead at a ninety-degree angle from the suitably distant camera, then turned sharply, paused, hand on flaring hip and brilliant smile on beautiful face, nothing else on anyplace. Like that, five seconds. Then fluid movement again, straight toward the camera—toward the not-yet-there microphone, the future audience—four steps, four memorable mind-burning eye-branding seconds, firm stride of flashing thigh and calf, rippling shudder of big warm white breasts.

It had been, even for me, a sight worth seeing. And for the producer-director-cameraman, Gunnar Lindstrom?

Well, I guess it is simply not entirely true that forewarned is forearmed. Gunnar knew what was going to be done, had to be done. He knew Aralia would take her clothes off and walk to her chalk marks, turn, smile, wave, make her little speech. Moreover, it was revealed to me that he had seen before not merely one or two nude ladies but so many bare broads of such varying virtue that I concluded even "pure" science might be slightly soiled without becoming totally ruined. Also, Gunnar was at least partially preoccupied with directing and filming-holographing the action.

All that hadn't seemed to make much difference.

After Aralia finished the "dress rehearsal" prior to actual recording of the action, she clapped her hands and asked sweetly, "Did I do it all right?"

She was asking Gunnar, naturally, since he was the expert who had to approve the scene. He was at that moment perhaps forty feet away from her, and I watched him walk thirty-eight feet forward with his jaw hanging down like the posterior flap on a pair of old BVDs.

Slowly his mouth closed, jaw gradually lifting toward his upper chops as might the scoop on a child's steam shovel, and when he finally got it all together there, he apparently did not have it together anyplace else, since he said nothing at all for some time. At length he moved his lips oddly, like a man preparing to spit out a chew of tobacco, and eventually I heard: "What was it you asked me?"

"Did I do it all right?"

"I believe so. I'm not sure. Yes. Of course, you did. But you'll—we'll—have to do it over."

"Oh, I'm sorry, Mr. Lind—"

"It's not your fault. Not exactly."

"Well, I don't mind doing it again. I *like* doing it."

Down went the scoop again. Up. "Who"—to me this time—"did you say this young lady was, is, Shell? Miss what?"

I said, "Well, Gunnar, among other things, she's our official Miss Naked California. Might even be Miss Naked USA before long."

Gunnar, just before returning to his camera for another run-through, seemed to peek covertly at Aralia for the last time, or at least the last time up close. His head was still turned a bit toward me, and he sort of glanced slantily leftward and downward, eyes pausing upon Aralia's abundant breasts, moving down, down and up, pausing once more at her breasts.

"You, Miss Fields," he murmured, "could tell me you were Miss Naked Milky Way and I would believe it."

Then, back to the camera, and lights, roll 'em, speed, quiet!, action, cut, print it. Well, not much like that; not at all like that; but after one more rehearsal the sixty-second classic was filmed, completed, and in the cube, so to speak.

9:17 A.M. Exactly one-hundred and eighty ticks of my stopwatch.

I glanced toward the teahouse door.

And there she was. . . .

CHAPTER SIXTEEN

1:50 P.M.

Even here inside the teahouse I could see that Aralia's face was flushed from excitement, skin pink and healthily glowing, blue eyes so bright they were like small cool suns.

Maybe part of it was the undoubtedly stimulating effect upon her ears of the boisterously bubbling sound of four hundred masculine voices, a noise like a gang of restless bull apes getting playfully tickled in sensitive areas.

The whole gang was here; most had been here for an hour or more. I'd looked them over before escorting Aralia into the teahouse, and had taken a peek from time to time since then. At first they'd all mingled, most with drinks in hand—a good deal of booze was being consumed—but the last time I'd checked, all but a handful of those interested citizens over there on the far side of the pool were seated in their wooden chairs, waiting for the MC—Sammy Shapiro—to come back.

Several announcements and a couple of brief talks had

been made, and all the guests knew the next event was the
pièce de résistance, which is French for Miss Naked California.

Miss Naked California was at the moment wearing a pair
of white jersey shorts tailored so smoothly she appeared
merely to have sat down briefly in cream from healthy cows,
and a sleeveless white jersey blouse so snug on her skin that
it had pores in it.

"Is it time yet?" she asked me breathlessly. "Is it time
yet?"

"Seven minutes. For me, that is. Ten minutes before you
make your entrance. I don't mean *you,* but the film we
made."

"I know. *Me.* Not even *I* can tell the difference."

"Yeah. And, baby, don't get all wacked up and go leaping
out there smiling and blowing kisses while *it's* out there.
They'd be hauling guys off in padded ambulances by the
dozen. Some never to be heard from again."

"I won't, Shell. I know what to do—you've told me
enough times. I just stay here while my picture's out there. . . .
Doesn't that sound funny?"

"Funny. Yeah, funny. Somehow I don't feel very—"

"Then when *it* comes back I just wait. Until *you* get
back."

"Yeah. Now, if it happens that I *don't* return speedily, if
ever, and you hear sirens . . ."

I was doing it again.

It was true that I had curiously ambivalent feelings about
this operation. I had become almost convinced that nothing
wildly exciting or dangerous was likely to occur, that nobody
was going to get killed. But at the same time I could not

escape the nagging little suspicion that *if* anybody got killed, I'd be the one; and very likely my painful murder would occur while I was poking my head about up there among the pepper and eucalyptus trees. Obviously, only one of those assumptions could be true, and the other therefore had to be false, which wasn't great comfort to me, since I didn't know which was which.

Besides, for quite some time I'd had the perturbing feeling that I'd forgotten something. Maybe an item of no real importance, merely enough to give rise to these little whisperings from my subconscious, but possibly something essential, vital, catastrophic—

"They sound horny, don't they?"

"Aralia." I looked at her, while the gurgling half-hooting half-howling cacophony of muscular voices clawed at my eardrums. "I'm beginning to think if a guy got his nuts caught in a swing when he wasn't even swinging you'd think his howl was a proposition—"

"Shell, don't say nuts. That's crude."

"O.K., balls. What difference—"

"Anyway, you're a man. So it wouldn't sound sexy to you."

"Praise the Lord. Incidentally, while we're on this subject, if I am delayed in returning to our enchanted little teahouse, I would suggest you let as much time as possible elapse between your—that is, your other—*nude* appearance before this festive throng and your *real* appearance fully dressed . . . if that's a fair description . . . following the stimulating, um, exhibition."

"You already told me that, Shell, but I still don't really

215

understand why. I know they're supposed to think I'm in here putting my clothes back on afterward, but what's wrong with my pretending to get dressed fast in a half minute or so and then popping out—''

"No—"

"—there while they're really *ready* for me?''

"That's the point. Which I am probably not going to make a hundred percent. 'Ready' is capable of several interpretations, some of which are baleful, if not dire—''

"Why get them all steamed, all fired up, and then fiddle around till they cool it?''

"Fiddle is also—''

"Why not strike while the iron is hot?''

"You refer, I presume, to the metal in zippers—''

"The whole reason I'm here is to give the fellows a little *fun,* a little *pleasure,* and so I can meet them all, the committee members, and financiers, and producers, and all.''

"Yeah. Understood. Let me put it this way, Aralia. Fun is fun, but some of these guys may be *serious.* You put out there, as you pop it . . . wait a minute. You *pop* out there, as you put it, and . . . Well, have you ever seen four hundred drunken bull apes getting ready to monkey around?''

"Of course not. Have you?''

"That's beside the point. Ah . . . let me put it another way.''

She had told me once or twice that I was poetic. Maybe a little vivid imagery would impress her.

"Aralia,'' I said, "imagine that we are in the jungle. Strange spooky sounds hoot and holler from amidst the shrubs and trees. You are Jane. You have just been out there, naked, which unbeknownst to you is what caused all the hollering and hooting. Now you pop out *again,* and what do you see? Four hundred horny Tarzans! Do you get—"

"There's only *one* Tarzan." She smiled. "*You're* the one."

"Yeah, I'm the one, all right." I flapped my hands up and down against my thighs. "Let's try it one more time, O.K.?"

"If you really want to. How many minutes have we got left?"

"Aralia! Goddammit, Aralia! I hope you realize I am rapidly losing my sanity. Will you just shut—will you—" I stopped, snorted, started over. I made my voice sweet, and soothing. "Suppose immediately following the blisteringly stimulating and unbearably provocative appearance of supremely desirable and stunningly *naked* Miss Naked California—"

"Oh, Shell, doll, you're getting poetic again."

"Not *now,* dammit. *Ahhhgg.*"

I uncurled my hand from its death grip on the stopwatch. Couldn't afford to crush it now.

"I will not give up," I said. "I will not give up. Listen. Besides that which I have already said, whatever it was, I ask you to mentally view those four hundred thinly disguised beasts out there. Given their beastly mood and probably soaring intoxication, and further given your, ah, um, ahm, generous nature, though it is perhaps not inevitable, it is at least conceivable that they . . . Well, they might stuprate you."

"Stu—what does that mean?"

"What do you think?"

217

"Does it mean they might do to me what you did to me?"

She had me there. "Yeah," I said glumly. "But—four hundred times?"

1:54 P.M.

I had been thinking back over the morning's events, wondering if there'd been anything in those hours that might have given rise to my increasing sense of unease. It wasn't a panicky kind of concern, but more a queasy little worry.

After completing the necessary preparations here this morning and making a test run of the Aralia image or duplicate, I had driven back to the Spartan Apartment Hotel and the flesh-and-blood Aralia.

Nothing significant thereafter. Talk, a bite to eat, a few last minute cautions and explanations to her. Then together in my Cad to the Doubless Ranch, brief mingling with a few of the early arriving guests, then into the teahouse, where we still were.

The hell with it. Probably it was the mild but now constant apprehension that came from walking around without my Colt .38 clamped in its holster under my coat. That, and coldly logical awareness of the many things that could go wrong in those sixty seconds speedily approaching.

Outside in the crowd there were occasional whoops that rose from the general hubbub, or individual voices that could briefly be heard separate from all the others.

I cocked my head on one side, wondering if I had heard what I thought I'd heard, just as Aralia said, "Isn't this exciting, Shell? I mean, even if I'm not *really* going out there the first time, nobody else will know it *isn't* me."

218

"Hey, Shell!"

That had leaked in from outside somewhere. Not loud in here, but quite audible—and, surely, more than merely audible out there. That was what I thought I'd heard before, but I'd missed whatever followed my name then.

"I just wish I could tell you how it makes me feel, Shell, every time, walking out there nude in front of all those men. I can actually *feel* what they're *thinking,* and I won't pretend I don't like it. I love it! Right now I'm so charged, so hyper, so *up,* I can hardly stand it. I mean, I'm turned *on.*"

"Listen. I'm trying to . . . Turned on? Baby, you better put yourself on tilt, this is no time—*or* place—"

"Hey, Shell—" again.

Something familiar about that voice. Disturbingly familiar.

And another voice. "Shell, sweetheart, a bunch of us already called the fire department *to put out your pants!"*

And that first voice, continuing, blending with part of the other guy's dumb yodel, *"I just spent an hour getting a great big present for you. You getting any for me?"*

"Oh, boy," I groaned. I'd recognized that first voice, the guy with the "present" for me. He was a jolly and fun-loving fellow named Roscoe, who possessed a sense of humor that might at times—times like this, for sure—be considered awesome, if not catastrophic. I didn't know yet who the yodeler might be, but it mattered not; it was enough to know I was in trouble.

"Oh, boy," I groaned again. "That's what's been bugging me, I'll bet a bunch, or at least a banana."

"What's the matter?" Aralia asked.

"I almost had it a little while ago. I was thinking three

219

minutes was cutting it close, barely time enough for me to get where I'm going. What I should have been thinking was that I've been planning to walk out of here *only* three minutes before you make your eagerly awaited appearance.''

"Only?''

"Yeah. At least four hundred of those four hundred howling citizens must be curious to know why I've spent so much time in here with you. We have been in here a long time, you know. A *long* time. And it's already damn close to the moment of your appearance, which has of course been bruited about as an enchanting appearance in the altogether. Which means, at least to those uncouth—''

"Oh . . . I see. You mean I should be taking my clothes off about now. But of course. I wouldn't wait till the last *minute,* would I? So I'm stripping right *now,* getting *ready!* *They* think.''

"Yes. They think. He thinks, they think, everybody thinks. Only *I* do not think.''

"Golly-golly,'' she said. Said excitedly, it seemed to me. At least, not as one totally overcome by waves of shock and cruel embarrassment. "I'll just bet some of them, maybe a *lot* of them, think right this very instant you're . . . stuporizing me?''

"Stuprating. Not that it matters. Oh, boy.''

"Well, Shell, if they *already* think it . . . How much time's left?''

That one went right by me, clean as a whistle.

I peered at my wristwatch *and* the stopwatch. "At the plink, it will be one fifty-five and a half, or exactly one minute and a half to go. Plink.''

"And then there's three *more* minutes, too. Well? Why not? You might as well be hung for a sheep as a lamb, Shell. Or is it hung for a wolf—"

"Hung how? What?"

"You sound like a Chinaman."

"*What?* Where the hell did that come from—"

"You were telling me about *Rich Butterfly* and all, and those names like Hoochie-Coochie and—"

"I get it. Jesus, you scared me. Sure, I get it. Ah, pretty frower, ah-so, me Hung How, queer samurai, right?"

"Samurairite? I never heard of those before—"

"Yesss, Hung How, master of singing sword, not to mention humming daggeroo. Pretty frower, I gonna rove you rike nobody rove you come rain . . . *What are we doing? What the hell has happened here?* Aralia . . . ?"

Not a peep from her when I needed it.

"Leggo, Aralia."

Still no peep.

"Aralia. Let go, please. I had no idea you were serious. For all things there is a time, even a season, but this is nooooooo— "

Then I just stood there, thinking. No, not that. I was thinking several other things. Like:

I'm pretty sure I was all right only a minute ago, but how can I be sure? This had to be one of those 3-D movies, anyway. It couldn't really be happening. Of course not; the idea was ridiculous. This was only a bunch of dots or squiggles on a piece of plastic or something. How could I be here like this, with Miss Naked California, on a partially dismantled movie set, in a teahouse, surrounded by hundreds of giant apes, only a minute before leaving to climb a hill on the wild assumption that I might thus catch a hood who was trying to shoot a picture, and kill it? I couldn't be. There was simply nooooooo . . .

"Well, it's time to split," I said.

"Really?"

"Yeah, gotta go. In thirty seconds, that is. But that'll be over in a minute or two."

"Gee, that's a drag."

"You're really wigged out, aren't you? Have you got everything straight, Aralia? Strike that. Are you sure you know what to do?"

"What do you think?"

"Does it matter?"

I watched the second hand of my stopwatch. "Well, if I leave here, Aralia, and some of those idiots outside decide to come inside, I wash my hands of everything. I can do no more. It will be up to you."

"I can handle it."

"Ah, so. Well . . ."

Tick-tick-tick.

1:57 P.M.

I pushed the switch to "On," and it had begun.

CHAPTER SEVENTEEN

SOMEONE wrote that the best laid plans gang aft aglea, which has been interpreted as meaning they often come totally unglued. This explains why even worse things aft happen to plans not well glued to begin with.

I had actually spent considerable time thinking out my moves and planning ahead, but most of that thinking had been concentrated on one rather nebulous "if." *If* a man, with murder in mind and rifle in hand, accepted this publicized opportunity to draw a bead on Aralia Fields while she stood alone in the sunlight, a perfect target, how should I most efficiently proceed in order to foil him without getting shot myself?

I had parked my Cadillac a hundred yards away on the only road providing access into the ranch and the *Butterfly* set. Two hundred yards farther away a side road led north, rising to the single-lane blacktop road I'd checked this morning. I knew I could drive the half mile from where the Cad

223

now was to a spot near the massed trees north of and above the set, and then trot from there into those trees themselves, in not more than one minute. Leaving two minutes, less the time required for me to reach my car, before the start of Aralia's "appearance" below. Already in my car was a high-powered pair of binoculars; and a Colt .45 automatic was locked in the glove compartment.

My thinking had been focused on what my actions would be *after* I reached the Cad, including the question of whether I should take that fully loaded automatic pistol along when I left the car. Just in case. And maybe shoot, and kill, somebody with it, just in case. Maybe that should have been an easy question to answer; but, for me, it wasn't all that easy.

The gang-aft-aglea part of this was that I automatically assumed I would be in my heap and driving toward that side road in maybe a half minute, or less. I had not for a single negative-thinking moment considered the possibility of my being somewhat delayed before I even got started. But there is much to be said for negative thinking, when it is the positive thing to do. Unfortunately, I did not become positively—and shockingly—aware of this great Truth until moments after I pushed that little switch to "On" and stepped through the teahouse door.

I hadn't even realized there would be a band.

It was only five or six pieces—I didn't count them—including drums and bass and what sounded like a few dozen trumpets and tubas and other brassy things, and what each instrument lacked of beauty and sweet harmony it more than made up for in loudness.

BLAAAAAHH!

I guess it was supposed to be a fanfare—greeting me, the Spartan soldier, as I returned home from the Pubic Wars—but it had all the earmarks of wars themselves, the clashing of axes on shields or an attack on the fort, and it *absolutely* transfixed me.

I had stepped from the teahouse and taken two long, purposeful, there's-a-man-who-knows-where-he's-going strides forward. Then: BLAAAAAHH! And I couldn't have moved another inch if somebody had slipped a hot poker into my shorts.

This, of course, was in plain view of the assembled throng, including the out-of-tune symphonic orchestra on my right near that segment of the Great Wall of Japan which, oddly, was still standing. And this, needless to say, was at least part of what the assembled throng had been awaiting with fiendish anticipation. Their fondest fiendish anticipations were fully realized. Certainly, I must have come to a stop that impressed them as humorous.

It didn't help much that something in that unexpected and unearthly sound sent my head straining toward the sky and pulled my arms up bending angularly at the elbows while the fingers of both hands spread *way* apart, while simultaneously my knees bent and I squatted just a wee bit, for this was a maneuver accomplished not as speedily as my halt, which had been absolutely instantaneous, but with what, especially by contrast, must have appeared to be extraordinarily leisurely fashion.

At some point in time during my spasm, I realized my mouth was open quite wide, with my tongue sticking out of it, so I pulled it back in, and this loosened me up enough to crank my head around and gaze upon the assembled baboons, who were howling and whooping, while a few even beat upon their chests in typical dumb fashion. The hubbub diminished in volume enough that the left-handed musicians could be heard playing their right-handed instruments. One of them wasn't even playing, he was singing a cappella while the band played—something . . . what was it?

The tune was one from way back, an oldie from the thirties or forties, with a cute bounce and ripple. Cute then. I had to hear only two lines to realize that some demented practical joker here had conspired against me, because the first line was sung in a horrid tenor voice by the one musician but the second line—the title, and repeated refrain, of the dumb song—was bellowed energetically by all the baboons together.

Tenor: "Oh . . . kiss me *once,* and kiss me *twice,* and *kiss* me once again. . . ."

Then the baboonery: "IT'S BEEN A LONG, LOOOONG TIME!"

It went on with "Never *felt* like this be*fore* since can't remember when—IT'S BEEN A LONG, *LOOOONG* TIME!" and similar crud, but I had recovered considerable power of movement by then, at least in my mouth.

"Well, you smart-asses—" I growled, but they couldn't hear me. Not when the whole crowd was singing and laughing and falling down like that.

I straightened up, started to walk with as much dignity as I could muster across the grass and away from there. It was only then that I noticed two of the baboons were over on *this* side of the pool, next to the microphone.

One of them was Roscoe, whose voice I'd recognized

when inside the teahouse. Where I wished I still was. The other was a guy named Art Jacobs, a magazine and paperback book wholesaler and distributor, a longtime—at least until now—friend of mine. I was disturbed by the close proximity of those two jokers, particularly considering the enthusiastic way Roscoe seemed to be leading the band, and the crowd, waving his arms wildly and yelling, "LOOOOONG TIME!" Something big and white was flapping from one of his hands as he yelled and waved.

I stepped toward them, started to go past. But both Jacobs and Roscoe, grinning like idiots, grabbed one of my arms while Jacobs yelled for silence and got enough so he could be heard fairly well speaking into the mike.

"Here he *is*, men! Yes! It is he—at last—our clown of the year, whom we have all been waiting—and waiting—and waiting for. In recognition of his many exhausting researches into the subject of female anatomy, which he refers to modestly as 'only a small part of the broad picture,' and 'just doing and doing and *do*ing my thing,' this man is today honored by us, his betters, who have just now named him— SHELL SCOTT!—most deserving of this year's Boobies Prize!"

Whereupon Roscoe, turning to face me, chortled, "And here it—they—is—are. Congratulations, or whatever."

And he handed me the white thing that had been flapping from his hand.

I took it automatically, my mind occupied with the thought that I had to get out of here in a hurry before ten more playful guys grabbed onto me for the hell of it, and either it was an accident or else Roscoe carefully maneuvered the thing so I'd grab it just right.

Whatever the reason, the garment—that's what it was—unfolded like a weathered old flag with weathered old Betsy Ross still in it, and I was holding by the shoulder straps, its convex bulges facing out and away from my chest, what had to be the biggest brassiere ever gazed upon by the stunned eyes of man. It wasn't just large, it was dismaying. Naturally, the cretins in the audience were cracking up.

Art Jacobs said, chuckling, "Well, *say* something, Shell. It's expected of the winner."

"No kidding? Of the what? Well, if I do, will you two clowns let go of me so I don't have to use up a lot of time hitting you?"

They nodded happily, and I looked at Roscoe. "You know Sammy Shapiro, the emcee of this madhouse, don't you?" He smiled, still nodding happily. "Will you make *sure* he introduces Aralia, Miss Fields, at exactly two P.M.? *Not* any later? Or else do it yourself by then? *Exactly* two on the button?"

Grinning, he said he would.

I figured a quick "Thanks, boys" and some junk could get me off and away before half of the other men here decided to join the three of us. So I leaned toward the mike, forced a smile, and said with my voice as deep and rumbling as I could get it, "Well, I never thought *I'd* be lucky enough to win a hippopotamus's jockstrap."

There were whoops and howls—and something flashed, glittered on the hill out there in front of me, above me. High on that hill, at the near edge of the grove of thickly massed eucalyptus trees.

I got a sudden chill, a feeling as if my spine were coated with thin ice, a shiver in the hairs at the back of my neck. I looked up, searching, but there was nothing more. Just that quick flash, which could have been sunlight glancing from moving metal. It sure as hell hadn't been a wiggling leaf, or a rock rolling, not that bright metallic flash. Something— someone—was up there.

I really felt chilled, the skin suddenly cool all over my body, cold sweat oozing out onto my face and beading my upper lip. Only a small part of it was realization that some- one *might* be aiming at *me,* starting to squeeze the trigger, not waiting for Aralia at all.

I leaned toward the mike and wrapped it up fast, speaking briskly and with my voice flat, almost expressionless, but nobody seemed to notice.

Forcing a rigid grin, I went on mechanically. "I just don't know how to thank you, so I won't. Fellas, I may not know much about Roscoe and Art, but I know what I like—and this isn't it. Well, I've got to run now."

And then I ran.

I mean, *ran.* Holding the ballooning bra high and letting it flutter and swoop like a very strange windsock at a breezy Amazonian airport. All I'd wanted was to wrap the bit up and get out fast; but I heard yocks and hoots and boozy laughter fading behind me as I sprinted to the Cad.

The last fifty yards of my run was close to dozens of pepper trees growing on the sloping hillside to my right, and I couldn't be seen from that spot higher on the hill. In the

Cad, jamming my key into the ignition and starting the engine, I took the stopwatch from my coat pocket, checked its sweeping second hand.

Nearly two minutes used up. Too much, not enough time left, not enough. But I was shoving my foot down on the gas pedal, picking up speed, then sliding right and gunning the engine some more.

When I turned into the black-topped one-laner I'd checked this morning, I saw another car a quarter of a mile or less ahead of me. It was a racy blue Jaguar, pulled over onto bumpy earth at the road's right, parked there. I switched off the Cad's ignition as I slid to a stop behind the Jag; nobody was in the car. I checked my stopwatch and then dropped it into my coat pocket—only forty seconds until Aralia's appearance, which didn't leave me any time for cautious creeping around.

Or, rather, forty seconds left before appearance of the *pseudo*-Aralia, and a mere minute of that; after which, for all I knew, the wacky babe might be unable to restrain herself from prancing personally out onto the greensward, waving, waving all over.

I jumped from the Cad, carrying my binoculars, then ran at full speed toward the mass of eucalyptus trees. I was almost to them when I realized I'd jumped from the Cad without taking that loaded Colt .45. I'd been hurrying, hadn't thought of it. Or maybe, unconsciously, I'd wanted to leave it. But it didn't matter now. I went on ahead, and in among the trees.

Ten yards farther on, I stopped.

The curtain of leaves and branches overhead was thick enough that only random shafts of sunlight filtered through to

230

make small patches of brightness on the earth. I didn't see anything around me except smooth trunks of eucalyptus and the occasional rough dark bark of pepper trees among them, their rich green tiny-leafed branches drooping toward the ground. Plus a few low, wiry shrubs, and the splash of colors from wild flowers growing.

I could hear something, not the rustle of movement but a voice—from the *Butterfly* set below, amplified by the PA system. A man's voice; it sounded like Sammy Shapiro. I knew he should be finishing his introduction of Aralia very soon now, but I couldn't make out the words. I moved on, as quietly as I could but fast, bent forward and trying to look in three or four directions at once. The ground underfoot slanted downward more steeply, and there were fewer trees, more open space.

I could feel that familiar tightness starting in me, a pulling, almost a quivering, of nerve and muscle, the not really unpleasant coolness and clenching around my solar plexus. I got a glimpse of color below, figures, parts of the set, green of lawn and glassy stillness of the shallow pool where those carp had died and floated belly-up in the water.

A few more feet ahead, I stopped. Here nothing obstructed my view of the scene two hundred yards away, but I'd not yet taken a good look at what was going on down there, still busy looking around, straining my eyes. Here were a few eucalyptus, a half-dozen pepper trees with their thin heavily leafed branches hanging so low, even trailing on the ground, that they looked like large soft green bushes. But nothing human, no stir of movement, no sound.

I could clearly hear that man's voice, though, the speaker

231

at the mike. The words were carried softly to me, audible enough so I had no difficulty recognizing Sammy Shapiro's voice as he said, ". . . and my next picture is gonna be released come November, in time for being considered when they give out them Oscars."

Jesus, I thought. The clunk may still be up there, selling Doubless stock, when Aralia glides into view. She could glide right on through him, too.

While mentally groaning, I pulled the ticking stopwatch from my pocket. Not *quite* two P.M. yet. Seven seconds to go. Which, of course, was about nine and a half minutes less than would have been adequate. Lindstrom's computer-controlled laser beam had been scanning "nothing" on that little cube filled with a whole universe of holographic wiggles for two minutes and fifty-three seconds, and from here on it was merely a matter of counting the ticks down to zero—like the countdown for a rocket liftoff or those last few moments before the bomb explodes—and then would commence the inevitable, undelayable, bare and beautiful exit of Aralia from the teahouse door.

No way now to avoid fiasco; no way to stop it; no way to shut Sammy's wide-open mouth.

That's what I kept telling myself.

But I was wrong.

He did it, he crammed it all in, he got it said.

I didn't expect him to do it and I'm not quite sure how he did it, or how he managed to time the thing so perfectly; but he did it. To give Sammy Shapiro his due, though, that was very often said about Sammy. After the fact. After he'd done it.

Seven seconds to go—

"But I only threw that in because I'm picking up the tab here—"

Five seconds—

"—so I'm entitled."

Four—

"Now I already told you plenty about what we got in store right now, which is plenty—"

Two—

"—*so here's the livin' doll we all wanna meet*—"

One—

"Aralia Fields, *our hoo-hoo, youbetterbleeve it,* MISS NA-KED CALIFORNIA!"

Zero—

CHAPTER EIGHTEEN

ZERO, that final mental *tick,* smack on target, blastoff— there she was.

Simultaneously, or at most a mere half second after their first eight-hundred-eyed glimpse of Aralia bursting into view and moving from their left to right clad, except for high-heeled shoes, only in cool air and hot sunlight, there was a wildly raucous blast of noise, shouts, whistles, only a small part of it a faint but still horrible *blaaahh* and the rest a crude exhibition of male crudeness, or perhaps more accurately an audible accompaniment to the sudden surging of lust, or desire—or I suppose one might simply have called it instant horniness, for Aralia had been right, they sure did sound horny—and four hundred little men in the toy Japanese village down there rose to their teensy feet, applauding their bitsy hands, giving an enthusiastic standing ovation to—

I grabbed the binoculars slung by their leather strap over my shoulder. I had to have an up-close gander at this.

In the second or two before I got the glasses to my eyes, a series of odd impressions trickled into my thought. First was how different it all looked from up here, above it but only two hundred yards away. The shrubs and rocks in the Japanese garden looked like a kid's playthings; the Great Wall was an obviously warped and paint-daubed strip of cardboard without any apparent width at all; the pool was a thin spill of water, the men wee machines, wound up and programmed to wave, gesticulate, issue little whoops, until they ran down. Illusion, illusion, all illusion, except—

The lovely, naked, shapely, so-bright-she-seemed-burning little doll stepping from the foot-high oriental dollhouse, with sweet sweep of tiny thigh and high thrust of tiny breasts, that was real—no . . . I had it backward, that was the most total, the most perfect, illusion of all.

As I brought the glasses to my eyes, turned the knurled knob to adjust the focus, that last idle thought brought another thought, not idle but startling, disturbing, into my mind. If Aralia had mischievously decided to cancel the film and make a personal appearance in its place, perhaps in order more tangibly to *feel* what all those whooping dreamers were *thinking,* there was no way I could know it—unless she performed some act or spoke some word not in the film itself.

For a moment it really scared me, but then wild surmise faded and died. Aralia was wacky, and generous, and hugely unconventional, and many other things; but she was not totally out of her pretty gourd. I didn't have to worry about her pulling anything as senseless as that, particularly in view of all the work we'd put into production of this moment.

236

Just before placing the glasses to my eyes a miniature Miss Naked California had been walking from my left to right— exactly, of course, as she had in the central room at Lindstrom Labs and again here alone, except for me, this morning— about halfway to the "mark," where she would turn and step toward the microphone.

Sammy, to my great relief, had not even pretended he was about to grab with clutching hands some portion of Aralia's anatomy and wrestle it two falls out of three, but instead had stood by the microphone as Aralia appeared; had bent forward visibly as he eyeballed her; had performed a quiver, much as might a hairy dog after not quite drowning in the lake; and then walked away, heading around the pool toward all the other men. Looking back over his shoulder most of the time, true. But he hadn't touched her; or, rather, had not *tried* to touch her, which was fortunate for all, including Sammy, since that might have caused him to shake somewhat more vigorously than he had the first time.

The blur before my eyes got less fuzzy, and then suddenly sharp and bright—and near—was the face, the form, of Aralia. She was turning, stepping toward the microphone. There she stopped, raised her right arm high, that right breast lifting and then rippling with sun-gilded movement as she waved her hand.

Next would be the left arm, equally enthusiastic wave of left hand. Right I was; there it went, flashing up, bringing both of those prize-winning points or point-winning prizes in her march to the only really authentic beauty-contest title in the land rippling, or also waving, as Aralia fluttered both hands high over her head.

237

Sound soft against my ears made the illusion even more convincing, for Aralia was beginning her little speech.

I watched through the glasses for a few seconds as she began: "*Hi,* men! And thanks, you sweet darlings, for this wonderful welcome!"

When figuring out a few things Aralia might say, all three of us had agreed that this should be a safe-enough opening, since it seemed unlikely her appearance would be greeted with stony silence. We'd allowed a brief pause both before and after her next comment, too, and all of it was working splendidly. So far.

"I can't tell you how wonderful you've made me feel with this great big welcome. Well . . . I *could* . . . but"—then a slight swaying movement closer to the mike, and the softer more intimate voice from—apparently from—those sweetly smiling lips—"I'd better not."

Yeah, good thing we'd left plenty of quiet space there during which the guys could hoo-*hoo* for a while. I lowered the binoculars, let the glasses dangle at the end of their leather strap, having decided it was time I started checking the area again.

I tried to put myself mentally back down there, where Aralia was now, at the moment when I'd caught that quick bright flash of light in my eyes. From down there, looking up, it had come from somewhere along in here but more to my right then. So I started moving left, trying to look ahead while at the same time watching for twigs or small limbs, or even pebbles, on the ground near my feet.

Aralia's recorded voice floated up to me. "I want you to

238

know it's really a pleasure to see *all* of you. I mean, see all of *you*. Oh, golly . . . you-*all*?''

The boys had a lot of fun with that. Even while looking for pebbles and twigs, I wondered how come the dialogue sounded so much steamier than it had the first time or two. Undoubtedly because four hundred guys were listening to it now.

I guessed about half of Aralia's minute was used up, and I was sort of creeping forward, slightly bent over, one foot in the air, when I stopped moving. Just stopped. Foot still in air, then lowered, slowly and carefully down.

I hadn't seen anything, or heard anything. At least, not that I was aware of. Maybe there'd been a sound or movement that hadn't quite registered, a little ripple on some subconscious level . . . but *something* had stopped me, jarred me. I stood very still, moving my eyes from side to side, straining to hear.

"Don't forget, now, next Sunday I'll be competing in the Miss Naked USA *finals*—right here in wonderful sunny California—and I hope *all* you wonderful men will come to see me . . . and the other forty-nine girls.''

Nothing, not up here.

Aralia, the rest of it, filtered in, barely touching awareness. I was aware, without really giving any attention to it, that Aralia was about to speak her final words, because the last part of her minute included the time it took her to turn, and go back into the teahouse the way she'd come out to the mike—exactly the same way, same chalk marks in reverse order, which had been the simplest method for filming the action in the time available to us last night.

I didn't catch all the words—nor could those four hundred

239

steamed-up men have heard them all, either, because building almost ominously was a chorus of phrases flung out from the gang down there, and a rumble of just plain indecipherable sound, because they very likely knew Aralia was ending her talk, about to leave, and they didn't want her to leave, and I didn't blame them.

Immediately in front of me, only a couple of feet away, the thin but heavily leafed outer branches of a pepper tree drooped to the ground. I could see with unusual clarity the masses of little red pods, but I couldn't see clearly into the center of the tree, couldn't see the earth around its trunk at all. The branches of some of the pepper trees here on the hillside were so thickly bunched, and the small narrow leaves so abundant upon them, that it would have been possible for a horse to stand in the hidden space enclosed by the green barrier without being seen.

So it was, of course, possible that a man could be concealed even beneath the tree I was almost touching. Or one beyond it somewhere. Or the one right behind me.

And I knew *something* had stuck me, made the muscles in the small of my back start to ridge and tighten.

". . . even though, with so *many* of those other absolutely *beautiful* girls competing, I probably don't have even a *chance* to win . . ."

Not according to the sounds arising down there, as of starving savages dancing around the missionary pot, I thought with very little of my attention. During that, I had taken one step forward, reached out to part those thin branches, feeling the softness of the small leaves tickling the backs of my hands. Parted them, bent forward, looked through. Tree trunk, nothing else, except an almost level mass of pepper pods and drying leaves on the ground.

I moved ahead, circling to get around the tree, continued past it and toward another, equally full and bushy, five yards farther on. I was moving faster now, because if a man was anywhere up here—and I was again beginning to doubt it somewhat, since Aralia had been clearly, very clearly, in view for most of those sixty seconds already—his attention almost surely would be concentrated *on* Aralia, and the activity below.

"So thank you all again, darlings. I've had *fun* being here with you, I really do mean it. And I can't think of anything more to say . . . or do . . . except maybe to . . . blow you all a little bitty kiss! Just to say thanks, from me to you—"

Then a sort of *mwaa,* accompanied by a nice little smacky sound.

I wasn't looking, but I knew this was where Aralia pressed both hands to her luscious lips and then threw that "little bitty" great big juicy almost alive-and-kicking kiss at them, as might twin Davids sling flaming boulders at outnumbered Goliaths, then waved a last time and turned, one hundred and eighty degrees, to leave, which would also present a quite memorable view to the throng.

Yes, she was about to leave, all right, because I heard again that *blaaaaahh,* faint but distinctly virulent even from this safer distance, as the band gave briefly posing and then lingeringly departing Aralia what I assumed was their best fannyfare.

That's when the first shot was fired.

The solid crack of the gun came from ahead of me,

nearby, not from the tree I'd been moving toward but somewhere beyond it. I sprinted ahead, digging my feet into the soft earth, saw nothing but kept going.

Tree, monster pepper, straight ahead, thickest and greenest so far, and—from it, from somewhere within that tangled mass of green I was sure—the rifle cracked sharply again.

And this time, though still moving forward, I snapped my head right, stared toward the movement below. Even slowed, to make sure I found her with my eyes. She was still walking away, about to make a sharp left turn at her "mark" and step from my right to left, toward the teahouse.

That was enough of a look for me, and I simply plowed ahead with the determination in mind that I was going to hit the outer branches of that pepper tree and go through them like a bulldozer and grab whoever was triggering the rifle and trying to kill Aralia. . . .

I slowed down a little more.

Why all the hurry, and uprooting of harmless trees, this snarling and gnashing of teeth on the way? *She* was all right. The bastard, whoever he was, had not been shooting at her, but merely poking little unseen holes in a laser-and-holograph-fashioned, electronically vitalized, computer-controlled light sculpture *picture* of Aralia.

As, right then—just before I reached him—with two quick sharp one-right-after-the-other blasts, he poked two more holes into her sweet and airy flesh.

Even for me, now, the real kept slipping into the unreal, because despite acquaintance and even familiarity, it was difficult to keep firm grasp on the slippery concept of pictures that were people until you shook their hands or touched them, or maybe—as surely had occurred to numerous fellows in the last minute—tried to kiss them, or, of course, tried to shoot them. Especially when you had no idea there *were* any such "pictures."

And that thought is really what prepared me for the guy with the rifle. Prepared me for him, if not him for me, and perhaps helped me to understand his mental condition much more quickly than if that thought had not been in my mind.

I slowed enough so thumping footsteps wouldn't tip him of my approach—not that it would have made much difference— then parted branches, saw him flat on his stomach beyond the rough brown trunk with the soles of his shoes a foot from it, in the rifleman's prone position with leather strap around his upper arm, eye behind the mounted scope atop the gleaming barrel.

But he wasn't aiming when I spotted him. The rifle slipped over sideways as his grip loosened, and he turned his head to look at it strangely.

I bent low, stepped toward him, brushing against the brown bark and ready to kick his head off. I wasn't trying to make a lot of noise, but I wasn't tiptoeing either, and he must have heard *some* of my crashing about.

But he did not seem to be aware of anything unusual occurring.

"What the sonofabitch?" I heard him say. "Did you see that?"

He wasn't looking at me. The unlikely impression I got was that he was talking to his rifle.

Yeah, he was.

With his left hand he shook the thing sharply and said, "Well, you dumb crapper, do *you* believe it?"

CHAPTER NINETEEN

IT was a queer sensation. For me, I mean.

I'd come galloping at high speed over the landscape, all fired up; then slowed to a lope on the way, realizing the rifleman wasn't really *doing* anything, only *trying* to do something; then, fully prepared to crash through branches and tear the killer limb from limbs, I had slowed down some more; and now if I got much slower, I'd be going backward.

Still, I had it in mind to hit this guy hard enough to knock his face off, so I continued approaching him, but not very fast.

I got down on one knee by him and raised my right arm over my head, fist all bunched up like a terrible hammer, and was just *that* far away from crashing it down on the sad-looking little old guy, who I guess was close to sixty, with thin gray hair, pale grayish eyes, quite glazed and glassily staring eyes they were, and shiny grayish skin—yes, I was going to crash it down on the old boy anyway—when he turned his head and looked up at me there looming over him and just *that* far from popping him.

"You know, Tom," he said dully, looking straight at me, "I think I'm through."

That's what he said; there wasn't any question about it.

One can never say for sure, in advance, how one will react to an unusual situation, right? If you were driving along in your car, say, and two or three little bugs hit your windshield, and then a cow hit it, who is to say for sure what your reaction would be? Who is to determine that it was not the most natural thing under the given circumstances?

Well, anyhow . . . I unclenched my fist, waggled the fingers, then rested my weight on one hip as the guy slowly rolled over and sat up, wearily and with a pained expression, as though all his creaky bones were being chewed by little dogs.

I looked at the old boy sympathetically. "Through?" I asked.

"Yeah, I've had it. That's for sure. And I was the best, Tom. Ha—was. *Was!*"

"Was?"

"That's it—was. Thirty years at the top. You want anybody killed, you just get ahold of old One-Shot. Yeah, old . . . they'll be callin' me Melvin now. They always said, old One-Shot never misses. Satisfaction guaranteed. Never misses—*never* misses—never *misses*—NEVER—"

"I guess you missed, huh?"

He cocked his frail head on one side, staring at my ear with those glazed and glassy eyes. "Well . . . yes. And . . . no. I did . . . and I didn't."

246

"What do you mean—Melvis? Or Elvin? Albert? What was your name again?"

"Don't you know me, Tom?"

"Sure, Old Timer. Go on. You were saying yes and no and did and didn't."

"Yeah, that's as close as we'll get. She's out there, see. Practically asking for it. In numerous ways. Now, that first one, I put it smack into her, dead center, prettiest thing you ever did see. Had her right in the crossed hairs. Bang. Drilled her kerplunk perfect between the tits and they didn't even wriggle. She didn't even wriggle. Nothing happened. *Nothing* happened. She just stands there with her arms out, tits out, legs out, everything out. *Nothing* happened."

"Must have made you feel funny, huh?"

"Funny? I'm lying on my face here, and I like to took a crap straight up in the air. Oh, it was bad, Tom, bad. Oh, Tom—Tom— Tom—"

"I'm still here, Old Tomer. Timer."

"—Tom . . . I couldn't comperhend it. I am so spooked I don't react with my usual speed. No, that ain't right. I never had to react before. Old One-Shot never misses. Not till *this* broad. Well, she's turning around afore I can get absolute control of my bowels once again, so I get her lined up and *bingy,* I get her in the head this time. You guessed it."

"Just like before, huh? Nothing happened?"

"I don't know how, but you figured it out. All I will ever have to say about this after this, it is a very good thing I ain't had much to eat for a couple days. She's walking away now. And I am staring at her, saying, Die! Die! Fall down! Or at least bend over a little, you dumb broad. Still she's walking

247

away. It was just instink kept me going. I acted like a
automatic robot, got her in the scope, and thinking maybe to
change my luck I shoots her in the ass, *bingy-bangy*—twice.
First in the left ass and second in the right ass. Well, I give
up then.''

"No wonder."

"What hurts most, Mom must be overturning her grave,
rest her soul. I always lived by what she told me from a boy,
and she made me what I am today. All I am or ever hoped to
be, I owe to my darling—"

"What the hell did she tell you?"

"Many basic maxioms. If a thing's worth doing, it's worth
doing well. Find a need and fill it. A good day's work
deserves a good day's pay. Practice makes perfect. Mom
ought to have knowed, she run her own whorehouse for
twenty years." He sighed. "All them maxioms, they stood
me in good stand till today, and helped me shoot to the top of
my profession, but—where are they now? And them self-
starters was always what kept me going, Tom. Till now. I
got *nothing* to keep me keeping on now—that's another one,
Keep on keeping on—"

"How about," I offered helpfully, "if at first you don't
succeed, try, try again?"

"It don't work."

"Yeah, I guess that was a dumb question to ask. Ask
you."

"It sure was." He shook his head again. "No, I'm through,
Tom."

"You sure are. By the way, who's Tom?"

"Huh. Boy, you're worse off than I am, ain't you, Tom? 'Who's Tom?' Tom says. Why, *you're* To . . . Oh, oh.''

As I drove back to Hollywood with Aralia snuggled up against my right arm, she said to me, "One last time, Shell, thanks. For everything. And especially for introducing me to Harry Feldspen.''

"Well, to be honest as the day is long, I never did get around to looking him up and arranging everything just so. After your little talk, and all, Harry found me first, you see, and insisted—asked if I'd be good enough to bring you two together . . . ah, arrange an introduction. In fact, he threatened—"

"That's nice. He really did seem interested, didn't he?''

"I guess you could say that.''

"Do you think I'll really have a part in his next movie?''

"I think you'll have all your parts in his next movie. If Harry said he'd do it, and he said it, he'll do it. I have a feeling you're going to go a long, long way, Aralia. If you can just stay alive while you're going.''

"About that, Shell. Isn't it strange that *nobody* knew anyone shot at me?''

"Not really, now I've thought it over. Even up where I was, the howling of all those guys was loud enough, and anybody close to that yelling, or doing some of it, would not likely have heard anything else less impressive than a ten-minute replay of World War Two. Besides, when people are shot over and over again, they are expected to react in some noticeable way. There *is* evidence—some holes in the Great Wall of Japan, for example—but it's possible today's guests

249

would assume they were made by Mitsui's chopsticks. Nobody heard anything, nobody saw anything, nobody felt anything—"

"Why, Shell."

"Aralia, please. But at least I've got an eyewitness. Unfortunately, his testimony is suspect."

"Who's that?"

"The suspect."

"Oh, the fellow you told me about? Was it this One-Shot?"

"It was. I don't remember what he calls himself now."

"What happened to him, anyway? Where did he go?"

"He didn't *go* anyplace. I tied him up with a brassiere— "

"You what? You tied his arms with a brassiere?"

"Arms and legs. I put him in the Cad's trunk. That's where he is now, dear, right behind us."

"In the trunk? He must be awfully uncomfortable in there."

"I think not. It's possible he still isn't aware that he is, or is not, anyplace."

After a few moments she said, "I *see.* You beat him *up,* didn't you? For *me.*"

"No."

"No?"

"Yes. Oh, before I tied him up, I did crash one down on him. But only one. I didn't want to. You may not believe this, but I had begun getting an almost warm feeling for the Old Timer."

"But you did hit him?"

"Boy, did I!"

"Well, if you didn't *want* to, why *did* you?"

"He went wild. Berserk. Maniacal—felt I'd betrayed him."

"I don't understand."

"Well, on top of all the rest, I guess the last straw was when he found out I wasn't Tom." I paused. "Dear, would you mind very much if I didn't even try to explain?"

Four-Shot Melvin Voister sat opposite me, at the other side of the long table in one of the LAPD's "I" or Interrogation rooms. Lieutenant Bill Rawlins lounged against the wall, letting me handle the questioning this time.

"Let's run through it again," I said.

Voister had been looking down at the tabletop. He glanced up at me and his shiny cheeks puffed out as he blew air through his lips.

"O.K. But this is the last, Scott. I don't care what you do to me."

"We aren't going to do anything to you. The lieutenant already told you three times you can have a lawyer—"

"Skip it. The whole thing again?"

"Just a few high spots. Maybe you'll think of something else."

Rawlins jerked his head and stepped outside. I told Voister to sit tight, and joined Bill in the hallway, closing the door behind me.

"If there is anything else, you better get it quick," he said. "I'm damned if I can see any way we can hold this guy. You know how it is. Besides, even from the crazy story *he* tells, he hasn't actually committed any crime. Unless it was discharging a firearm in the county."

"Well, I told you—"

"I know what you told me, and it wasn't enough. Everybody else I've checked with who was at that barbecue today swears nothing happened. One man—one—says he did hear something sort of whistle or snap through the air a time or two. He thinks. But he wouldn't swear to it. Now, how the hell can that check with attempted murder? By one of the coldest, deadliest, professional hit men in the country?''

It was a little ticklish. To charge a man with making a premeditated attempt to murder a victim, there must in fact be a victim upon whom the attempt is actually made—not merely contemplated. And One-Shot had not in truth and in fact shot any living being, or *at* any living being.

Rawlins went on. ''I know you got a tip One-Shot was out here. Did you manage to slip blanks into his gun? Screw up his rifle? Something like that?''

''No, not—not that, Bill.''

''Then what the hell are you leaving out, Shell? *Holding* out on me, I mean. What *else*?''

He was quite displeased with me, which didn't help.

I still hadn't introduced him to Aralia, as promised—though I hadn't ever said exactly *when* I would consummate the introduction—and it did bug Bill somewhat when he learned that I had, at least sort of, introduced her, without a single stitch on, to four hundred other guys in the meantime. I suppose he had a point, but this put a bit of a hitch in our usual buddy-buddy camaraderie.

I didn't really want to tell him what had happened this afternoon, anyway. In fact, I couldn't. Once I started trying to explain—not that I could ever successfully have done it—I would have had to wind up, inevitably, bringing in Gunnar Lindstrom. And Norman Amber. And the Amber Effect. And everything else I'd assured Gunnar I wouldn't spill without his express and prior approval.

So I said, "I've told you, there is more to it, Bill. And you'll get every last bit just as soon as I can fill you in. But I wish you wouldn't push it right now."

He shrugged. "I've got work piling up in the office. Stop by the squad room when you're through with Voister."

"O.K."

He walked down the hall and I went back into the I room.

"One more time," I said when I sat down again, "just the top, and we'll drop it. You were hired to hit Aralia Fields, and the guy who phoned you back in Jersey was Elroy Werzen."

"Yeah. What's it make now, nine times I told you it was Puffer?"

"Ten. You want to bad-mouth me, pal, we can try for twenty."

He didn't say anything. I went on. "When did he call you? And try to pin it down closer."

"It was Thursday night, and like I said nine times, now ten, it was after I had the spaghetti and fish chowder, so it was maybe eight of the P.M. that night. Maybe seven-thirty, maybe eight-thirty, maybe eight forty-two and a half. I don't write it down, Dear diary, tonight Puffer give me a call and requests I hit a broad named Aralia Fields, and his welcome invite come in at eleven minutes after—"

"You took the first flight out and got to L.A. International Friday morning."

"Yeah. Puffer meets me there at the airport and gives me half the ten G's for the job, the rest to come after I do it.

253

When I make the hit, I don't call him, he calls me. I told you where.''

I nodded. That posed a small problem. One-Shot had a room in a local motel, and undoubtedly there had already been several calls made to that room—not, of course, by Puffer Werzen—which One-Shot hadn't been there to answer. And I wanted that line of communication established so a suitable but phony story could be passed back up the line. But Bill Rawlins would help me set that up. I hoped.

"O.K.," I said. "You weren't told anything about *why* they wanted the girl killed, or *who* was paying for the job?"

"Hell, no. All I got was what I told you come from Puffer, and it's enough. Why tell me all that crap? It's got nothing to do with my end.''

"You had a caller last night at your motel, about ten-thirty, and got the word that your mark, Aralia, would be making a personal appearance at the Doubless Ranch today. But you don't know who that man was?''

"Just tells me he's a associate of Puffer's, who has himself been called away.''

"I find it hard to believe he didn't give you a name.''

One-Shot smiled. "No, you don't, Scott.''

He was right. But One-Shot had described his visitor several times while Rawlins was in the Interrogation room with us, and the description was good enough that neither Bill nor I had to do much guessing about the man's identity.

"I'll tell you who it was,'' I said. "Al Hauk. They call him the Clam, or sometimes Clammy. Not because of the way he looks, but because he's got a reputation on the turf of having an iron jaw. Nobody's ever made him puke. He doesn't spill anything to anybody, just clams. That ring any bells?''

"It don't ring nothing. I never heard of him. He give me the other five thou last night, in advance, which is unusual. And explains why I'm to stick around after. First thing was the girl. That's where I concentrate. But I'm to stay put after she was done, in case they hadn't killed you yet. With maybe another ten-G job I ain't about to split without doing the first job, even if I'm already paid up for it—if I was that kind of rip-off, which everybody knows I ain't.''

"So Hauk, your visitor last night, is the only man you had any conversation with about blowing me away?''

"Only one. It don't take more. One, plus ten G's, is a crowd.''

"All right, let's push some more on *how* I'm supposed to be set up. Tomorrow I'm expected to drive out to the Green Mesa Resort for some kind of meeting, and just stand there looking around dopily while several bastards shoot holes in me, and several more watch.''

"That's about it.''

"All these guys—how many again?''

"I ain't sure, but it's at least half of a dozen, and maybe a couple others going to be there. It's part like you put it, but more they ain't about to take *no* chance you pull out alive from this one.''

"Uh-huh. First, what makes those jerks think I'll let myself be set up like the world's prime patsy, and second, how come you know so much about those nice little details, like exactly where I'm to meet whoever it is?''

255

"Dammit, Scott, you asked it the same way last time, and I already told you—"

"Tell me again." I leaned toward him, not feeling—or, I imagine, looking—very happy about this particular point in our conversation. "Since I'm the guy who's supposed to be slaughtered, be sure to add anything you left out before."

"Didn't leave a goddamn *thing* out, I told . . . Well, I know where it's set up to be done and all that, because if I didn't hear nothing from nobody after I'd finished up—with the girl, I mean, after the job today—that's where I'm to meet this guy who told me about it. Meet him and some others."

"And help them do the job on me."

"Wasn't said like that. But I'm told to bring along the tools of my trade, if you know what I mean."

"Don't get cute with me, One-Shot. Now, Hauk mentioned my name. But he didn't show you a picture, or even describe me, right?"

"That's it. Just the handle."

"So, as far as he knows, you don't have any idea what I look like?"

He nodded.

"I don't get it," I said. "All these guys out there waiting for me, and I'm expected to simply stroll in and wait for it?"

"Well, you ain't supposed to know nothing about all the boys going to be there ahead of time, as you could guess without me mentioning it. They wouldn't want to try it with just one or two because you're supposed to be a lucky sonofa—they already missed you a time or two, as I get it. And it's no secret you're supposed to be damn near as good as me with your own little piece, so they don't figure on getting any of themselves killed even by accident.''

"Well, I might not be good enough to beat a whole goddamn convention of hoods, but I'd take a few if Samson hadn't—"

I chopped it off. I had almost, without thinking, mentioned that I'd not been carrying a piece around, that Samson had my Colt .38 right now. Maybe One-Shot wouldn't get a chance to mention that bit of intelligence to anybody, but it would not be wise to let him know about it.

"Samson?" he said, twisting his face up slightly.

"What's the matter?"

"Is that—did the lieutenant make a mention about a Captain Sam while he was in here?"

"He might have. What of it?"

"Well, I think something come to me. Something I'd forgot.''

"Which is why we go over and over the tale, One-Shot. Spit it out.''

"Well . . . it ain't really nothing, not to me. The dude didn't say much, just something to an effect they'd make you think this Samson, a police captain—is it Homicide he works from?''

"He's the captain of Central Division Homicide, same office Rawlins works out of here."

"That's it. All I got, and I'm not even sure, is they figure on making you think it's him wants you out there at Green Mesa.''

"How the hell could they do that?"

His face was squinted up again. He shook his head, saying,

"I wasn't paying much attention, and it was just a tossed-off thing that was said, anyway. Maybe like one of them was going to make a phone call to you tomorrow and say come out."

"You mean imitating his voice, some slob, or maybe even a pretty fair mimic, pretending to be Samson? He'd have to be damn good to make me buy it."

One-Shot shook his head some more. "It was him, I'm near sure the name's right. And you'll get a call in the A.M. sometime. Anything beyond that, I can't tell you nothing. Of course, Scott, you could just wait for the call and see how it's done—or maybe ask them when you get out there."

"I told you not to get cute, One-Shot."

After a few more minutes of talk, without further additions to what he'd already said, I told Voister that wrapped it up. And I was already wondering what the hell we were going to do with him. So far, he hadn't even asked for a lawyer or started demanding his release, but that didn't mean he wouldn't change his mind any minute. And if he did, he would almost automatically be sprung; in an hour he'd hit the streets.

I, and the police of course, desired that none of One-Shot's associates learn anything whatever about what had happened to him today, or that he'd spilled all the info he possessed to the law and me. But ten minutes after One-Shot was sprung, they would know, I had no doubt about that. They would know, and therefore almost certainly change their plans.

When somebody seriously desires to kill you and you know at least part of the where and when and how, you do not want them suddenly changing those intentions and formulating other plans for your violent demise, new plans about which you are totally uninformed.

After a while I said to One-Shot, "This isn't an offer—I can't make an offer, anyway, as a private citizen—but I've got a hypothetical question for you."

"A what?"

"Just call it a question. Suppose I could pull a wire and help get you sprung, on the condition that you return to Jersey in police custody for a day or—"

"Jersey? You nuts? I ain't going back to Jersey."

"Well, I'm just trying to help you get out. Maybe—"

"Man, you don't comperhend it at all, do you? I don't want out. I ain't going *no*wheres." He was silent for several seconds, and I swear I almost felt sorry for him, he looked so sad, and crushed, and woebegone.

Finally, he looked at me from those pale grayish eyes, which still looked a bit glassy, and said quietly, "After this screw-up today—where would I go?"

CHAPTER TWENTY

BEFORE leaving the Police Building, I stopped off in Homicide and took Rawlins out in the corridor.

"Same song," I said, "but Voister remembered one little thing." I passed on the mention of Samson's name, but that was as puzzling to Bill as it was to me.

"Incidentally," I went on, "when I left One-Shot he was still feeling very sorry for himself. Feels he's a failure, pride wounded to the quick, you know. Says he doesn't *want* to be sprung, apparently resigned to taking the fall—but you know how quickly he might brace up and change his mind."

"Yeah. Which wouldn't be so good."

"Especially not for me. I'd take it as a big favor if you can help keep him feeling the jug's the only place for him."

"Do the best we can."

"And get word to me if he springs out onto the streets."

"Can do."

"And one more little favor, Bill."

"I think friends should do friends favors whenever it is within their power, Shell."

I began getting a *little* suspicious of his sweetness.

"Yeah, sure," I said. "Who'd argue with that? The thing is, some hood is bound to be calling One-Shot's room at that motel, and might get shook if there's no answer. It would be of great benefit if an officer—perhaps one with showbiz ambitions, shall we say?—could stake out in the room and answer the phone. He could say, pretending to be One-Shot, that a big white-haired ape with the eyebrows and such almost grabbed him but he got away, after being severely crashed on the head, and immediately has to split for distant places. Which would explain why he isn't able to meet any of his friendly cohorts . . . You do understand, don't you?"

"Perfectly. You say it would be of great benefit?"

"Certainly would, Bill. At least, could be a lot."

"Benefit to whom?"

"Well . . . everybody? Me, of course. Me especially, I suppose."

"All right. It's done."

"You're a brick, Bill, you really—"

"I mean, it's already done. Man's at the motel now. But I will pass on the bit about mentioning your description, hadn't thought of that. He's fleeing from a big ape, ugly-looking, selfish, mean as hell, white hair and those nutty eyebrows should tag you. Might add that his pursuer dresses in hideous loud taste, is a coldly selfish man, one who professes to believe that favors— "

"Bill, I can't stand to see you going downhill like this. I

will introduce you to this charming girl, you know that, don't you?''

"Well, of course I do, buddy. I mean, you're a fair man, Shell. Always have been. Very fair. And when I'm doing so much for you, almost prepared to put the entire Los Angeles police force at your disposal—''

"Sure. Yeah. Well, maybe tomorrow, Bill. Look, I've got a lot of things to do, a lot—''

"I really do have to talk to her, you know. Officially, that is—since I'm in charge of this case, if there is one, whatever it is. It is my duty, you see. I suppose she'll give me the same totally unhelpful jazz you've been giving me, or *not* giving me, but—''

"Yeah, she will. I can guarantee it. But just as soon as we *can* tell you, we *will*—''

"—entirely aside from that, there are other matters that should be discussed, or at least mentioned. Such as the fact that I am an eligible bachelor, considered extraordinarily fetching by all and even gorgeous by some, and that as a police lieutenant it is my sworn duty to interrogate her stupendously—''

"Look, Bill, if you do talk to her, I wish, ah, you wouldn't use words like *interrogate,* especially, ah, along with *stupendously.* This might confuse her, particularly if she thinks it's your *duty*—''

"Where is she now?''

"She? Who . . . ah, hell, I won't even *pretend* I don't know who you mean, Bill, even though her name has not passed our lips. How's that for fair? She's at the Spartan, of course. That's where she lives, you understand.''

263

"Not in her apartment. No answer when the phone rings there. Do you suppose she's dead, Shell?"

"Not . . . exactly."

"Aralia? Hi, this is Shell." I was calling from Samson's office. Rawlins smiled at me while I spoke.

"Will you do me a favor, Aralia? I've got all screwed up, uh, involved with favors here, and . . . well, naturally there are a lot of men who would like to meet you, who would even take advantage of a friendship . . ."

"Well, there's this friend of mine, Aralia. He is a police lieutenant, you see, and he has placed me under arrest— that's a joke. I think. Well, he's been wanting to meet you . . ."

"Aralia, you don't have to be so goddamn eager . . ."

"Well, his name is Bill Rawlins. I casually mentioned to him one day that he should meet you someday, because the two of you have so little in common that it would be different from the usual having-fun kind of . . ."

"Aralia, you don't have to be so goddamn eager . . ."

"Sure, here he is, Aralia."

I handed the phone to Bill.

It would not be worth reporting any of the conversation. I could listen only to Bill's end, anyhow, and you really have to hear both ends of a dialogue to make any sense out of it.

"Well," I said to Aralia, as soon as I closed the door of my apartment behind me, "didn't *he* make an ass of himself."

"Who?"

"Lieutenant Rawlins. The dummy on the phone."

"Oh, you mean Bill."

"*Bill,* is it—?"

"I thought he was sweet. Aren't you going to say hello?"

"Hello."

"Would you like me to make you a drink, Shell?"

"What for?"

"Oh, Shell, you don't have to act so jealous."

"Jealous? Me—jealous—"

"After all, I'm *living* with you, aren't I?"

"Hmm? You're . . . Well, Friday, Saturday, Sunday . . . You're . . . By God, you are at that."

"So let me make you a drink, darling. And I'll have one, too, and sit with you, and we'll talk about today . . . and tonight."

There's no denying it, she did have a way about her.

It was eight P.M., and I was toying with a wild idea—or, another wild idea. I had been thinking for the last half hour of One-Shot Voister, his fuzzy comments about a plan to kill me tomorrow, the mention of Sam's name, other bits of the day, a lot of things.

I knew the place where One-Shot said I was supposed to go tomorrow, like the village idiot, if I was dumb enough to fall for whatever trickery my would-be slaughterers had in mind. Green Mesa Resort was twenty miles away, a pleasant woody rest-and-vacation spot, where I'd spent a few days during a couple of past summers.

Centered around the Green Mesa Lodge—guest rooms, dining room, bar, and such—were about fifty small cabins and a half-dozen larger deluxe units, plus community swimming pool, big barn for dances and come-as-you-are parties. The elevation was high enough so fir trees grew on the property, along with a lot of big oaks and cottonwoods. A stream snaked through the approximate middle of Green Mesa, wiggling brightly past many of the cabins. I'd had fun there, enjoyed the big steaks served with baked beans, and the nightly singalongs in the cleared space around an open campfire.

In that clearing—where, after the big log fire had been nursed from burning to roaring by the Green Mesa "boys," including waiters, busboys, bartenders, anybody working at the place, the whole gang of guests, in festive mood gathered, had sung "Home on the Range" and other good do-it-yourself songs—I was supposed to get shot ten or a dozen times tomorrow.

Right there where I had so lustily sung "Home on the Range." Struck me as pretty dirty. But I had to admit it was a splendid spot for massacring me if anybody could get me out there. That clearing where the summer-evening fires had burned was only about fifty feet in diameter, and some of the seats were the stumps of trees cut down in order to make even that much space available. The whole rough circle where we'd sat and sung was enclosed by shrubbery and trees thick enough to keep the bears out, if there'd been any bears around, which there weren't.

I could visualize myself standing there tomorrow, though. And I could imagine half a dozen armed bums less than fifty feet away but totally hidden from my sight. And then—bingy-bangy—I'll shoot you *once,* and shoot you *twice,* and *shoot* you once again. . . .

It had been that kind of half hour. All sorts of things crowding my mind, slipping in and sliding out, some sticking, images and pictures and illusions and ideas, with memory of Norman Amber's dead body blending with vivid recall of Aralia's live one. And, somehow, while I just sat and let all those things flow like that little Green Mesa stream through my brain, I had a hunch I might actually be going out there tomorrow sometime. *Might* be going. I'd make up my mind after I got the A.M. phone call, if there was any.

But it was clear that *if* it happened that I buzzed out to the resort, it should be with reasonable understanding of what I might find there and reasonable preparation for coping with whatever I might find.

For one thing, the place would be deserted this year. This September, at least. Only the month before, in August, there had been a fire at Green Mesa, with most of the deluxe cabins and several of the smaller ones damaged, and the big million-dollar main building, the Green Mesa Lodge, completely destroyed. So it would probably be next year before the operation was in full swing again.

But deserted, half-burned, the countryside made green by thousands of trees and a profusion of mountain shrubbery, with only a few isolated privately owned cabins scattered in the area and not another development, or city, for miles around, it was a great place to go if you wanted to disappear. Or make somebody else vanish without a trace. Or, maybe, even for what I was beginning to have hazily in mind. . . .

Another thing I'd thought of a time or two was that one of those privately owned cabins in the area—not at the Green Mesa Resort itself, but only a few miles away—was Samson's. That was where Sam and his wife, Mira, were spending their idyllic and restful two weeks. It was four or five miles from the resort, higher up, built right next to the same stream that wiggled down through Green Mesa and on past the clearing where sang the singalongers.

It was that knowledge, combined with One-Shot's fuzzy report about Sam's name being somehow connected with the plan to get me into the area, that kept nagging me. So when Aralia walked in from the kitchenette, I sighed and stood up.

She was munching an apple again, and said, "Thanks for restocking the frig, Shell. Those are the thickest steaks I *ever* saw."

"Yeah, I thought maybe we could charcoal a couple of those beauties tonight—but I have to leave, sad to say. And I might be pretty late getting back."

"Oh? Where do you have to go?"

"Lindstrom Laboratories again. At least, I must confer once more with Gunnar Lindstrom."

She eyed me silently for some time.

Then she said accusingly, "Shell, are you planning to do something *dumb*?"

I thought about it before answering. And I tried to be honest and fair in my thinking, open and candid in my reply.

"Yes, Aralia," I said finally, "I believe I am."

CHAPTER TWENTY-ONE

THE call came in at ten o'clock Monday morning.

Since my return to the Spartan—less than two hours earlier—I had been napping on the divan in my living room, phone on a small table near my head.

When the phone rang I sat bolt upright, reached automatically for it, then stopped. I shook my head, blinked my eyes rapidly, smacked my lips, shot my tongue out and snapped it back in, and *then* picked up the phone.

"Hello," I said, wide awake.

"Shell? Sam. How about getting your butt up here to the cabin? Couldn't reach you at your office, so I guessed you'd be goofing at home."

"The cabin? What—Sam?"

I hadn't been expecting an invitation to Sam's *cabin,* no matter who might call. That screwed everything up.

Both Gunnar Lindstrom and I had been at that clearing in Green Mesa until after six-thirty this A.M. Assuming I might

269

receive "a call in the A.M. sometime" and would then proceed to Green Mesa, if I went anywhere at all, Gunnar and I had arranged for the climax of our night-long efforts to commence automatically, precisely at eleven-thirty A.M., figuring I could stall until then if the call came much earlier.

But that climax was set for Green Mesa, which added up to a lot of time and effort down the drain if I was supposed to go someplace else.

More, it was Samson's voice in my ear, not somebody mimicking him. I'd have bet my life on it—and very likely was going to do just that.

"Yeah. Or—maybe we'd better meet someplace else, Shell," Sam went on. "I need your help up here, right away. This is important, but I don't want Miranda to know anything about it."

And suddenly there was ice on my spine again, goosebumps visible on my arms. Sam's wife was named Miranda, but I'd never heard him call her anything but Mira. Never.

I almost blew it right there. But then, "For chrissakes, Sam, give me time to wake up. Just taking a nap—had a big night this morning. Now . . ." I yawned into the mouthpiece. "Someplace else, huh? Hell, you name it. But what the devil's going on, what's so important? I thought you were on vacation."

"Still am, but something's come up. I'll explain when you get here, O.K.?"

"O.K. Where you calling from? Your cabin?"

"I thought you knew I don't have a phone here, Shell."

"Yeah, I forgot."

"I'm at a gas station, pay phone. Let's see . . . you know where Green Mesa Resort is, don't you?"

So here it came.

"Sure," I said. "I've had a lot of fun there."

He told me where to meet him. All on the button, right down the line. That little clearing, where they had the campfires in summer.

But as he spoke I was giving his words only half of my attention. Someone else almost *had* to be listening to our conversation, at least to Samson's end of it. And I knew Sam; he might, under certain very limited circumstances, go along with inviting me to a spot where my head could be blown off, but only if he felt sure I realized what he was doing, that the invitation was a phony.

He'd tipped me, sure, and knew if I had a brain in my head I'd picked up on it. But he couldn't be aware of what One-Shot Voister had told me. And, if I didn't let *Sam* know I was wise, he would sure as hell try to tip me again—and, next time, it might be more obvious.

So when he finished telling me where we were to meet, I said, "Good enough, Sam. Some restful vacation for you this is. You can fill me in later, but what pulled you away from your hammock? Must be police business, right?"

He hesitated only briefly. "You guessed it. That's why I need you. I've bugged you plenty about how you operate, Shell, but I've got to admit, your way does have its peculiar advantages at times. Now me, I've got to go strictly by the book, the law is the law—"

"Is the law, yeah. I've tried to tell you, Sam, there's no *imagination* in the book. Well, if it's police biz, I guess I'd better come armed to the teeth. Or at least bring along my never-miss Colt Special."

271

I actually heard his small sigh. "Might as well," he said. "You won't need it, it's not that kind of a job, but I know you don't even go to the can without that popgun. See you here, then—oh, when do you think you'll make it?"

"Give me a chance to do a couple things, like putting my pants on. Let's see . . . eleven-thirty be O.K.?"

"Sure, anytime."

"Look, just anytime won't do, pal. I'm not about to stand around waiting for you to get through catching a fish. Eleven-thirty sharp, right?"

"Right," he said quietly.

"See you, Sam. Give my love to Miranda."

"I—" He got a little bump in his voice there. "I will."

I hung up.

Two seconds later I dialed the LAPD, got Homicide, asked for Lieutenant Rawlins. When he came on I said, "This is Shell. I'm home. Get over here fast, and come alone. I'll explain when I see you—and I haven't got much time. So *jump,* pal."

Then I hung up and waited. For him. And for eleven-thirty sharp.

They started moving in right after eleven A.M.

I was in a tree.

It was damned uncomfortable up in this tree. Especially since I'd been cramped between its trunk and a big lumpy branch for a good twenty minutes, which was longer than it had taken me to drive—a bit recklessly, let it be admitted—the twenty miles from the Spartan to Green Mesa. Or, rather, to half a mile from Green Mesa.

272

I had approached the clearing, which was entirely visible down there below me from my perch twenty feet in the air, through the trees and thick brush with some care. But there'd been no interruption, no difficulty. Not then.

But now I could see the boys coming. Six—no, seven of them. The man trailing, several feet behind the rest, looking as if he'd just come from appointments with both his tailor and hair stylist, was short, husky Vincent Ragan. I'd expected he might be out there somewhere, but had assumed he wouldn't be among the members of my welcoming party. But why not? Logical enough, now that I thought of it—or, rather, now that I saw him here. He was the prime mover behind all of this, the brains and cold-blooded planner. It made sense that he'd want to be in at the kill.

The rest were moving, roughly two abreast, along a narrow dirt path that led from what was left of the Green Mesa Lodge, only a hundred yards away but not visible from here, to the clearing below me. I'd walked along there myself with a friendly lass or two, our feet silent on the inch-thick cushion of pine needles covering the path.

In front, on my right, was Al Hauk. Impressively tall but sort of slumping along, head bent forward, long legs swinging and heels dragging over the top of those pine needles. Next to him a man even taller than Al the Clam, which made him not less than six-five, and about two hundred and fifty or sixty pounds that looked appallingly solid. Virgil. Ex-pro football tackle. The mean cat I'd seen only in his mug shots. Virgil Kovick, heavyman, conk-crusher, two-time loser. A bad one, not quite all there upstairs, capable of going wild or running amok.

273

Behind those two, James M. Collett, pudgy, mild-looking, thick in the middle, the man in whose duplex apartment I'd shot Puffer Werzen. Near Collett was a little man, only three or four inches over five feet, thin, face like a sparrow's, wearing steel-rimmed glasses. I'd seen his mug shot, too, four nights ago in the Police Building: Charles E. Ellisohn. Engraver and convicted forger, among other things.

The other two men I didn't know. Not yet. One of them was of medium height, with a heavy dark mustache, totally bald. The last man was about thirty, tall and soft-looking, with very long girlish hair and a bushy brown beard hiding his face.

Those six, and Ragan a few paces behind them.

They all gathered down there, maybe twenty feet from the base of the tree I was perched in, and Ragan spoke to them in a voice so soft I couldn't hear the words. But he was apparently giving them instructions, where to conceal themselves, and who was to do what. Like who was to shoot me. Or who was to shoot me first. Maybe where they should stand in order not to shoot each other. I was imagining a lot of shooting. But, then, I was nervous.

I watched them take up their positions.

Two directly across from me—the long-haired lad and Baldy—out of sight behind a thick wall of green shrubbery. Ragan back somewhere even farther, behind them. Collett hidden behind a tree on my right but well away from the spot where the path entered the clearing. He was alone.

The others, all three of them, were barely concealed behind a couple of tree trunks and a low bush below me and to my left, all three where they could look straight ahead at the spot where that pine-needle-cushioned path ended. Or, where anyone might normally be expected to come a-walking, blithely into the clearing.

In front, closest to the edge of the clearing, was Al Hauk; on his right, crouched down behind the bush, the little guy, birdlike, wearing glasses; on Hauk's left the large mean cat, Virgil Kovick.

When they were all in place, it got very still out there. A few times there was the sweet sound of a bird singing, and once a quick soft rustling as a squirrel or other little animal ran over dry leaves. After that came the worst part. What is always the worst part. Waiting.

Then it was close on eleven-thirty A.M. Just a few seconds to go now. As I had done once before, yesterday, I mentally counted down, five, four, three, two, one, *zero!*

Nothing.

Of course, I didn't have the stopwatch this time; my own watch could be off a few—

Ah, there he was. *Now* it was *zero,* and the play had begun.

Well, maybe not the play, not even the whole first act. But the first scene of the play had begun.

There, already well into the clearing and with the end of the path six feet behind him, there *very* speedily, appearing *very* suddenly, but standing like a lump, looking around dopily, scratching himself dopily, waiting dopily for Captain Samson—and, unquestionably, just plain asking for it—was Shell Scott.

275

CHAPTER TWENTY-TWO

IT was him, all right.

No doubt about it—big husky guy, deep tan emphasizing the standup white hair and angular white eyebrows, dressed to blend harmoniously with a drunken artist's palette, perhaps not handsome but with a certain *something*. I'd have known him anyplace.

And was I glad to see that big ex-Marine bastard!

During those final few seconds between *zero* and *zero* I had, well, aged. A whole avalanche of doubts had rolled over me. I'd started wondering why I had gotten so far out of my cotton-headed mind that I would even have considered embarking upon an enterprise so obviously nuts, so inevitably doomed to failure; and for those seconds I no longer asked myself what might happen, because I knew what was bound to happen, I was going to get *killed,* that's what would happen.

But when I saw Shell Scott standing there—looking about

dopily, but so obviously filled with a kind of unconscious confidence, scratching his butt with what impressed me as devil-may-care nonchalance—in that instant I started thinking, even believing, everything might somehow work out all right after all. And I quickly got younger. Which was a good thing, because very soon I was going to have to shinny rapidly down a tree, which isn't too easy for real old guys.

I was not the only individual here who was pleased to see me.

Al Hauk—I had figured he'd be the one—strode forward into the clearing, heavy automatic pistol in his right hand, seeming not to hear the questioning voice from the birdlike character behind him and on his right, cheeping, "How the hell did he do that? I was looking right at where he was to come out. How the *hell* did he do that?"

"Just hold it there, Scott," Hauk said menacingly. "Don't move a goddamn muscle, baby."

Shell stood there, heedless of Al. Looking about brightly. Or, perhaps not very brightly. But bravely.

"O.K., baby."

Hauk moved his gun hand a little higher, took steady aim, and I saw his lips tighten over his teeth.

Knowing nobody would be looking over here now, certainly not up into the overhead limbs and branches, I started sliding down my tree trunk. But even while I slid I was wondering if Gunnar and I might have miscalculated the timing of this operation.

Last night, I had recalled his mentioning to me that he possessed "half a dozen" more of the laser-and-cube projector combinations, and I had therefore suggested that we

278

might profitably employ not merely one but several or even all of those units in concocting our invention. He agreed with almost fiendish enthusiasm, made a few suggestions of his own, and later we'd discussed the timing of it all.

I had then decided that fifteen seconds should elapse before commencement of the second scene, so to speak; after which Gunnar and I settled upon the nature and timing of the action to follow. But I feared now that fifteen seconds, which last night had seemed just right, today was about ten seconds too much.

But there was nothing I could do about that now. From here on, it was all automatic.

Under my belt was the loaded Colt .45 that had been in the Cad's glove compartment, and in my coat pocket was a heavy lead-weighted and spring-loaded sap. As my feet hit the ground I left the gun where it was, for the moment, but pulled the sap from my pocket, gripped it firmly in my right hand, started moving left toward the spot where Hauk had just been. Where those two other guys still were.

And right then I heard the ear-banging *BLAM* of the Colt .45 in Hauk's hand. I took two more quick steps forward, leaned around a tree for an almost-clear view of the scene.

Shell still stood there, glancing about, not only unharmed and apparently unconcerned, but obviously deaf.

From Alvin Hauk, "Wha-aa-at?"

I couldn't see his face, but even the back of his head appeared to be wearing an expression of considerable perplexity. All I took was a quick glance, then moved on, still trying to be silent. The moment when I would move more rapidly—in fact as rapidly as I could, and without worrying about noise or even being seen—was not here yet, not quite here.

I saw one of those other men—the little guy, Ellisohn, standing erect, one hand holding the side of his steel-rimmed glasses—and moved farther left to get behind him just as:

Blam! "What the *crud*—shee-*it*—*what* the crud . . . gahdamn . . . *shee* . . ."

Blam! Blam!

Then, finally, those long, dragging fifteen seconds were over and help arrived. The ex-Marines—or, singular, ex-Marine—came a-charging out of the trees ten yards away on my left to rescue his buddy, and to hell with the danger, the flying bullets, the overwhelming force and firepower of the enemy, for he knew that one goddamn U.S. Marine was the equal of . . . however it goes.

Into the clearing fast, bent low, the man—Shell Scott, an identical twin of that first one—charged, Colt .45 in his right hand and a bunch of dirty words in his mouth, both gun and mouth firing: "You dirty rats—" *Blam-blam-blam.* "Try to kill my pal, will you? Try to kill *Shell Scott,* will you? Take that— " *Blam!* "—and that—" *Blam!*

All I saw of Al Hauk was a brief glimpse of his head swinging left toward the new problem, then snapping right, snapping left, while his right arm, as though unable to hold up the gun in his hand, sank slowly downward.

That was all, because by then I was close to the little fellow, who heard me coming up behind him. Heard me, surely, well before he turned his head to look, for when he did turn his head it was as though with extreme reluctance, his eyes magnetized by what he was pulling them away from.

I was smack behind him—and smack is the right word—when with his head only halfway turned he rolled his eyes right until he got me in them, at which point he appeared not to want me in them or even anywhere near them. Perhaps there is no expression in the eyes themselves, that is, in the eyeballs. Many have said that it is only the surrounding elements—brows, lids, ridge of forehead, crinkle of nose and such—that register emotions. Such as, for example, horrified stupefaction.

Don't you believe it.

I was looking into those rolled-around and, I would have sworn, still rolling-around eyes from only a foot or two away and there was *plenty* of expression in them. In the *eyeballs*. So there goes another myth. You can forget that nose and brows and lids stuff.

He saw me clearly, no doubt about it. He knew I was there, threateningly elevating a spring-loaded sap and obviously for the purpose of administering it rapidly to his head. But it did not matter.

He rolled his eyes away from me, back to the clearing, which probably made sense to him at the time, for out there were *two* and here was only *one,* or maybe he was not thinking at all, but it made no difference, because *smack* and *then* he was not thinking at all, and no maybe about it.

I heard grunting and snorting noises. Only three or four feet away, just past that little bush. One quick hop and I was looking over it. And down. There was great big Virgil Kovick, maybe two hundred and sixty pounds of him, in a most puzzling position. Feet dug into the dirt, legs bent like monster springs, holding himself up with left hand pressed against the ground, left arm almost straight, right arm bent and hand balled into a fist the size of a melon, grunting and snorting. It was very much like the position those big burly professional linemen get into before the football is snapped. . . .

Why, the idiot was all cranked up to charge through the line and tackle somebody. Maybe he thought he was back with the Rams in those, his golden, years. Maybe . . .

Yeah, he was looking squarely at old Shell out there.

No, I thought. No . . . But, on an impulse, while he was still snorting and grunting, I said, "Twenty-nine, *hut—*"

Man, he took off like a shot, one instant he was there and the next instant he was halfway into the clearing, head down, enormous arms spread out, charging—

Shell—the first one; the later arrival was reloading his automatic, shoving a fresh clip into its grip—had moved back a little. He stood near the edge of the clearing, and it so happened that directly behind him and about three, maybe four feet distant, was one of the largest, sturdiest trees within perhaps a dozen miles.

And, toward Shell—he sincerely believed—charged this speedy former all-pro tackle of the justly famous Rams. Really moving, too, going faster and faster even as I looked in wonderment at him.

I am not a really *bad* person. I couldn't just stand around doing nothing while Virgil killed himself. And probably ruined one of the really prize trees within a dozen miles.

"No!" I yelled. *"Virgil, don't—"*

Crrruncck!

Actually, that's not what it sounded like. There is no way even to hint at what it sounded like. Forget it.

As a sort of bonus, on his lunging charge to tackle Shell and throw him for a loss clear back behind the stadium, Virgil, who in those good years before he ran head-on into too many really big fellows was accustomed to bumping into or bouncing off of two, three, maybe four different guys before reaching the one with the ball, brushed gently against Al Hauk, as Al stood there with his gun arm hanging down loosely, and knocked him at least eleven feet away.

I didn't know how they'd gotten there, but in the clearing now were Jim Collett and the top man himself, Vincent Ragan, both with guns in their hands. Collett took aim and fired at the Shell Scott who had just finished getting his Colt loaded and was raising his arm to shoot at somebody who, judging by Shell's expression, was a dangerous crook if ever there was one.

Ragan, though, was yelling—at the top of his lungs, but without making any visible impression on anyone else—"Don't shoot at those goddamn things anymore! It's a trick, it's a *trick*!"

Sure. He'd be the man, possibly the only man here, who would know where those two Shell Scotts must have come from.

Collett, obviously, didn't know. Because he sort of flipped both hands into the air, almost losing his hold on the gun, and yelled, "Some trick!"

That was the moment when Shell number three appeared, booming shotgun in one hand, chattering submachine-gun in the other. And that's when it happened. To me.

That's when the charge reared up and went through me and fired my blood and turned on my corpuscles, and for a while

283

I stopped worrying about getting killed even by accident. Because there were now *three* other Shell Scotts out there in the clearing, and at least three of them were invulnerable if not immortal, and if I joined them and anybody shot Shell Scott, there was only one chance out of four that I'd be the one hit. And, except for cowards like Old-West villains who wouldn't kill a man unless they could shoot him in the back, who would want better odds than that?

Not me. Not any of us. So I simply plowed through the bushes and into the clearing whooping and hollering like a scalped Indian and waving my sap overhead like a blunt tomahawk, and immediately regretted my impetuous and perhaps not fully thought out decision.

Because as I came a-running and a-waving and a-whooping along, Jim Collett spun around and saw me and yanked his gun up, and it was clear he was going to start a-shooting and kill himself an Indian.

Well, sometimes you don't plan every little move, every action or reaction. There's got to be something in us that keeps us alive from the crib through the next thirty years, or into middle age, or even old age, which I very much hoped sometime to visit, because we all do so many dumb things in a lifetime that none of us would arrive at age nine unless that "something" gently shoved and pushed us with little nudges from time to time.

Or, maybe not. I am no philosopher.

All I know is that without the faintest ripple of rational thought in my brain I slid to a stop six feet from Collett and his huge gun—a Colt .45 that to my eyes then simply had to be a custom job machined to twice normal measurements—

and pointed my sap at his gut yelling, "Bang—BANG—bingy-bangy, I got you, by dangy," and then looked left waiting for the slug in my jaw and hooted, "Hey, SHELL, baby, get a load of *this* one."

When I looked at Collett again he'd snapped his head around and was staring at the pair of Shells I'd hooted at, one of them leaping and bounding back and forth from one spot to another, but from and to very peculiar spots, for I noted with some concern that his big leaping feet never *quite* got back down onto the ground but rather descended to a half-dozen inches above it and then sprang vigorously sideways again, as with each spring he yelled as though in terrible pain, "Shell—*Halp!*—these sonsofbitches are *killing* me!" This while the other one swept his chattering submachine-gun in a long left-to-right arc, shooting everybody around, including his old pals, all of it together, needless to say, making an enormous amount of noise.

A really serious expression was growing on Collett's face, growing by leaps and bounds. He aimed the Colt at that jumping and yelling Shell Scott, hesitated, and he then either started to shake his head back and forth or it started to shake all by itself and sent a wiggle or two down into the rest of him, because when he pulled the gun back around to aim it at me once more, even the big Colt was waggling and bobbing in his hand.

"Bingy-*bangy*, baby," I called to him softly, taking one step toward him, then another. "Or, if you prefer, bangy-*bingy*, because either way, you sonofabitch, you're all caught up."

His eyes rolled around the clearing, at Shell—Shell—Shell—

back at me—Shell—and there was stamped as though forever
fixed on his face a picture of such total, unrelieved, absolutely hopeless and apparently indelible bewilderment that I
knew it would be a most unkind and even dirty thing to
crunch it with my sap. But, it seemed to me, if ever there
was a time when I could be excused for a little unkindness
and dirtiness, surely this was it. I really crunched him a good
one, too.

Ragan had been so busy yelling and waving at guys I
couldn't see that either he hadn't noticed me when I charged
into the clearing or else he became aware of my presence—my
real and solid presence—only when I sapped Collett.

For Ragan, of course, knew that the only one of us dancing around here who could fire a gun that *really* worked—or
swing a sap that *really* worked—would be the *real* Shell
Scott.

He knew which was the real one now, though. Knew he
had me. There wouldn't have been time for me to grab the
automatic under my belt if I'd thought of it. Ragan had
already swung to his left, so he was facing me, and his gun
was aimed at my gut, and he fired, fired twice in fact, and
missed by at least a foot and it could even have been a yard
or a yard and a half.

Because just as he swung to his left, from his right came,
"Over here, Shell!" in the clear, strong voice of Gunnar
Lindstrom, and from *very* close on Ragan's left, "*Hi*, men!
And thanks, you sweet darlings, for this wonderful welcome!"

Even for Vincent Ragan, who knew all about 3-D pix and
Lindstrom and the Amber Effect, these new sounds—and
new sights—were too much. I just sort of strolled over to him

and banged him on the skull. And, you may believe it or not, I just kept on strolling around, finding guys, and stunning them severely.

Actually, after Ragan went down, there were only two left, the long-haired lad with the bush growing on his face and the totally bald chap, both of whom were unarmed, not that it would have made any difference. And, if you really want the truth, when I heard the last bonk on that last guy's skull—Baldy, it was—I was almost sorry there weren't two, maybe three, more of them.

As it happened, Gunnar Lindstrom's own suggestion when he got into the swing of things—which had then struck me as a marvelous we've-got-to-do-it kind of idea—turned out to be wasted, not needed, after all. So the great *huge* Shell Scott—twenty feet tall and carrying a World War II bazooka—merely crashed through the woods and into and through the clearing, feet only a *little* below the surface of the clearing, with a sound like an elephant walking over petrified dinosaur eggs, an effect produced by Gunnar's jumping on wooden boxes and turning over tables and hitting all sorts of things.

The little fellows, too, it appeared, had no conscious audience except me. Four of them there were—the images more grainy, less perfect because they were the result of a double, or rather quadruple, exposure—but still quite effective because they were so impossibly small.

To me, they looked very much as had the individuals in that audience of four hundred when I'd gazed down upon them from the hillside yesterday afternoon. Yes, I thought, they looked rather cute as they came pitter-pattering into the clearing together, prancing on tiny feet and shooting teensy guns held in their wee little hands, like elfin quadruplets trying to massacre the Seven Dwarfs. Four little Shell Scott dolls, racing about and shooting and yelling, screeching all together in faint high tinny voices, "You'rrre underrr arrresst!"

And all for me, alone. But no matter. The job was done.

Finally, *"mwaa,"* and a nice little smacky sound.

Then, silence, utter silence, and emptiness, so still I felt it like a weight upon me. It was like being on the busy, crashing, rattle-de-bang street of a rushing city on earth, then blinking your eyes and finding yourself alone on the moon.

I just stood there for a while. I don't know how long. Not very long, another minute or two.

Then I heard them coming.

Cops, including Bill Rawlins. And they were getting here just about when they were supposed to. After Samson's call to me—not merely the fact that he *did* make that call, all of it right down the line with what we'd heard from One-Shot Voister, but the way he made it, a couple of things he'd said—indicated clearly that the police had more important jobs to do while I kept some of the lads occupied.

Sam's comment about Miranda, for one thing. It might have been merely to top me; but he could have used a dozen other phrases that would have done the job as well. Add to it the bump in his reply when I'd told him to "give Miranda my love." And, the most important tipoff of all. Know Samson as well as I do, then ask yourself what would make him call me and try to get me to an isolated spot where I could be killed.

Not a hood holding a gun to his head and saying, "Go ahead, call him, or I'll blow your head off." Samson—you

288

can take my word for it, friends—would have said, "So blow."

I waited as they came closer, moving fast.

Rawlins was first. But close behind him, to my vast relief—and surprise—was older, heavier, but damned speedily moving Phil Samson. And then a considerable number of cops. You wouldn't believe how much fuzz was suddenly there, in and around the clearing, and maybe out among the trees as well.

There was a lot of fast, and somewhat disjointed, conversation where Sam, Bill, and I stood together, but much was made clear. And after a bit Rawlins said to me, "They had Mrs. Samson, all right. In one of the big guest cabins here. One guy there with her, we've got him. She's O.K."

And Samson put his big horny hand on my shoulder and said, "Shell, thank God you knew what I meant—and let me know you did. I swear, if I hadn't been sure, I'd have popped out with something else to *make* sure, no matter what—"

"I know, Sam. Don't be so goddamn nice, O.K.? I get very uncomfortable around you when you're not obnoxious. Mira's all right, huh?"

"Yes, you exasperating sonofabitch, she's fine. Way it was, I never did see any of the bastards, haven't yet except the one who was with her in the cabin here. They grabbed her while I was out, and everything after that—with me, anyhow—was, first, by a note left in my cabin for me, and then conversations on a pay phone I was sent to. Mira didn't see any of them, either. Masks on, kept her looking away from them. Christ, I never thought there'd be a try for *me*, or *my* wife.'' He shook his head. ''They're getting wilder, crazier, these days.''

''Yeah. Takes strenuous methods sometimes to counterattack and confound the bad guys. Well, even if you haven't seen any of them, I'm sure they're around here somewhere.''

I pointed at a couple of them, lying still and prone.

Sam stalked around for a few seconds. Then he waved an arm at the police officers, both uniformed and in plainclothes, and roared, ''Back! Clear the—the clearing. Move!''

In seconds the immediate area was empty, except for Sam and Rawlins and me, and a lot of lumps on the ground. Samson looked at the large number and variety of lumps.

Then he faced me directly, looked at me sternly, and said with unusual solemnity, ''Shell, I want you to understand that—no matter what you've done—I will be indebted to you, as long as I live, for . . . what you've done.''

''Sam—''

''Don't interrupt. You know how it is with Mira and me, we won't go into that. And because she's all right, safe, you can from now on ask almost anything of me and I will do my utmost to see that you get it. *Almost* anything. But this time''—he swept a big hand around loosely—''you have gone too far.''

''Sam—''

''Don't interrupt. This is difficult for me, old friend. Difficult, but I've got to do it. When you gave me your word you wouldn't shoot anybody, wouldn't even shoot *at* anybody, I thought I could believe you. I never doubted it for a second. It never entered my *mind* that you would—''

''Sam—''

"—even plink with a twenty-two, much less perpetrate the kind of mayhem we witness horrible evidence of here. After this, Shell, how can I ever trust you again?" He looked at the Colt .45 in my belt, shaking his head sadly, then took the gun. "It pains me to do this Shell, you'll never know how much, but I'm afraid I have to place you under arr—what was that?"

"That" was some bubbling and babbling and high keening noises. It was Hauk, sitting up, and mumbling. We could pick out some of the words. ". . . giant, goddamn jolly crappy giant . . . right over me, ho-ho-ho, then . . . *aaaahhh* them little fellers, right under my perishin' nose . . . beebbledebeebbledee . . . bingy-bangy. . . ."

"Who's that?" Sam said.

"Al Hauk," I said.

"What's he babbling?"

"Well, I guess the last bit here wasn't entirely wasted, after all. Hauk must've been conscious, but not really in the spirit of things anymore, and it would seem he was suitably impressed by the show, which was the idea."

"Show? Impressed? Idea?"

"Uh, maybe this isn't the best possible time to attempt an explanation. Besides, I may still have to get permission first."

"Hauk? You mean one of them's still alive?" Sam asked.

"Hell, they're all alive."

"Come now," he said.

"I was trying to tell you, Sam. I didn't kill 'em all—didn't kill anybody. Just knocked them on their heads a bit. Couple of them I didn't even touch. They did themselves in."

291

"Come now. We heard—we all heard—the shooting. Like a revolution, yelling, shooting, and automatic fire, a machine-gun for sure, I know a machine-gun when I hear—"

"Sam, I didn't even fire that forty-five automatic you've got in your mitt. Look at it, smell it. But be careful, it's loaded."

It took a little time to convince him that all seven of the guys were merely unconscious. By then a couple more had started coming to. Cops were putting cuffs on the men; Rawlins and a sergeant were squatted by Hauk, talking to him. After a minute or so, Rawlins came back over next to Samson and me.

Sam was listening, head cocked to one side. "Who's that spilling his guts? Murders, stickups, parking tickets—even this caper here, snatching *my* wife. Who's the blabbermouth?"

"I realize now that wonders never cease," Bill Rawlins said wonderingly. "That blabbermouth is Al the Clam."

Phil Samson, captain of Central Homicide, was silent for a long time.

Then he looked at me and said, "Shell, I do not understand how you have accomplished . . . whatever it is you have accomplished. But—well, is there any little thing I can do for *you*?"

"There is one little thing, Sam."

"You just name it, Shell."

I will not describe his reaction, except to say that I got the distinct impression the captain was not immensely pleased by my reply.

"Well, Sam," I said, "can I have my gun back?"

CHAPTER TWENTY-THREE

"AND, after we put together everything we got from Al Hauk, and some of the other boys," I said to Aralia, "along with what Gunnar Lindstrom told the police, plus a bit from One-Shot Voister and a contribution here and there from me, we had it all."

"But . . . Ma and Peter, did they know I was supposed to get killed? Be murdered?"

"They weren't told that, not in so many words. But they must have suspected, maybe they even knew. But it's not too important now. Look, let me give you the quick nickel tour of the high points, then we'll drop it and finish these martinis, O.K.?"

It was that same Monday, several hours after Ragan—who, among other things, had been present at Norman Amber's murder, since only he knew for sure what to steal—and his cohorts had been hauled off to the can. Night now, dark and velvety outside, warm and softly lighted and kind of velvety inside—inside being again, or still, Apartment 212 in the Spartan Apartment Hotel.

And Aralia was still here with me, though she could go anywhere, anytime, now. And, as I'd told her once, I had a feeling she was going a long, long way.

I hadn't got back to my apartment until after ten P.M., and it was nearly midnight. I'd showered and dressed in marvelous lavender slacks and a long-sleeved long-collared white ''Byron''-type shirt, with white shoes, socks, and belt, and I knew I looked pret-ty wonderful. At least, the outfit did.

Aralia's outfit was great, too. She didn't have anything on. She did have a way about her, but I've said that before, too.

For the last half hour or so we'd been sipping martinis while I told her what had happened out at Green Mesa and in the hours since then. I was unwound finally, deliciously relaxed, with that warm gin-and-vermouth glow in my midsection.

''Wonderful,'' Aralia said, ''this martini of mine has no martini left in it. And that's like no martini at all, isn't it?''

''Good thinking.''

''Leave the olive out this time, will you? I don't eat them, anyway, you know.''

''Yeah. It's just that they're so pretty. . . . Aralia, I wish you wouldn't do things like that.''

She'd picked up the pimiento-stuffed olives from her first two martinis, and was holding one in front of each breast.

''It's an interesting effect, though, isn't it?''

''Well, yeah, I guess interesting—''

''And you just said they were pretty.''

''In the *martinis* they're pretty.''

"Can you finish in two minutes?"

"Finish what?"

"Explaining everything."

"I think maybe I can do it in one." I paused. "Well, your dad went to the jugs—jug, you know that. And apparently he was guilty as charged. I haven't dug into it all yet, but that's how it looks at the moment. The important thing is, he shared a cell in the joint with Buddy Brett, pal of Puffer Werzen and others, all of whom were already involved in a complicated caper with Vincent Ragan—which I needn't now burden your pretty head with."

"That's stealing the inventions and all?"

"Close enough. In a cell, in prison, there's not a great deal to do. Amber talked a lot to Brett—and later to Puffer Werzen—and convinced them he was a scientific genius who'd been working on an invention worth hundreds of millions, maybe billions of bucks, at the time he was arrested. Busted, apparently for appropriating items he needed for his work. And it was clear to those cons that he meant to complete, to perfect, his invention as soon as he was released from prison."

I finished the last of my martini, lit a cigarette. "Puffer and Brett got this word to Vincent Ragan, who checked up on Amber. Your dad's track record was impressive, a lot of important patents, that sort of thing. Ragan got excited about the huge monetary possibilities, but after Amber was released, and completed work on his process, he applied for a patent on his invention before Ragan could get to him, one way or another. Well, with the patent on what Lindstrom calls the Amber Effect granted, Ragan had to go another way if he wanted control of it, and more than anything he'd ever stolen in his miserable life he did want control of the Amber Effect.''

''Is that what got Ma and Peter into this? And me?''

''That's right. Your dad didn't have a will. If he died, his estate—including patents—would, after probate, go to his closest kin. He'd never remarried, had no other issue or close relatives. So closest kin would be his only child.''

''But there were two of us, Peter and me.''

''Yeah, only Norman Amber didn't know that. He really didn't know about you, Aralia.''

''Just like—I didn't know he was alive?''

''Exactly, and for the same reason. Your parents split shortly before you were born. Your mother told her ex-hubby, on the few occasions when they saw each other after the divorce, that you'd died at birth. And he believed that, believed it all his life. Just as you've believed all your life that your father died before you were born.''

''Isn't it wild? Awful, really. How could Ma *do* it?''

''Apparently it wasn't too tough for her. She thought she had a good reason. Which brings us up to now. To make it simple, Ragan figured if he could make a deal with the former Mrs. Amber—since it appeared that her son, Peter, also Norman's only son, would inherit all the goodies if Dad died—for all rights to Amber's patents, he could then kill Norman Amber and wait for those goodies to come to him. It's more complicated than that—a sizable cash payment to Mrs. Fields, a contract signed by both her and Peter, the only copy of which was kept by Ragan, some complex legal maneuvering and so on—but it would have worked, given time. Except for you. And maybe me.''

''Me?''

''Yeah. And maybe me.''

''Me? What did I do?''

''You were alive. You see, your dad believed you'd died at birth, all right. But he knew this second child, if a girl, *was* to have been named Aralia. And he'd wanted a girl. He never really got over the fact of your 'death' we might say. And he talked about this in prison, too, his dead daughter Aralia, if only Aralia this and that, to Brett and Puffer.''

''I don't see what difference . . .''

''Well, first, understand that Ragan has everything set, he's on his way to being a bloody billionaire, he thinks, he's sure—just so no little thing goes wrong. In fact, with everything worked out as far as Mrs. Fields and Peter were concerned, he had actually gone ahead and arranged for his boys to murder Norman Amber. Which they did, in Ragan's presence. Late last Tuesday night. So now we come to a couple of little things, or very big things that appear little, upon which everything else turns, spins, and does conniptions.''

She really looked interested now. ''Is this where I come in?''

''Like a bomb, dear. First little thing: Aralia, the name of Norman Amber's long-dead daughter, is an unusual name. So unusual, at least, that I've never come across it before, and I have done some research in this area. Second little thing—big to you, of course, but in a different sense—you won the Miss Naked California contest.''

She stuck out her tongue, bit it gently, nodding. ''I'm

beginning to *see* now. The stories about me, the publicity, and especially that story and picture in *Frolic* magazine.''

"On the nose, to phrase it loosely. Picture of you, and below it your name, 'Aralia Fields.' The name Aralia circled in red—by Puffer Werzen, it turns out, who'd been staying with James Collett since helping do the job on Norman. The boys weren't supposed to call Ragan at his home except in an emergency, but even to Puffer this had all the earmarks of a crisis, so he got his boss's home number from Information and called Ragan, thus conveying over the wires to dear Vincent an enormous monkey wrench.''

"I don't quite see why it was such a crisis. . . .''

"Well, Puffer and Hauk, of necessity, knew more about what Ragan was up to than any of the other men involved. And, remember, when Puffer lamped your picture—and, more important, your *name*—it was late Wednesday night. Norman Amber was *already* dead by then, murdered. On the page before Puffer's puzzled eyes was that unusual name, Aralia, and coupled right there with it, the last name Fields. And who had Vincent Ragan been dickering and conniving with? Who other than Mrs. Fields? Former wife of genius Norman Amber, the late but still cooling Norman Amber, father of only son, Peter, who was sole and rightful heir to fantastic goodies since Amber's daughter, Aralia, had purportedly died. . . . The hell with it. You can see how it went from there, my sweet.''

"Yes, I can. All the inheritance and everything could get *all* bollixed up if I was alive.''

"Plenty bollixed. You might even have filed a petition to be named executrix of your father's estate, any number of disturbing possibilities. No olive in the martini this time, right?''

"So they hunted me down, tracked me through the city—''

"Not exactly, you'd recently moved into the Spartan here, and your phone had been in only a day or so, thus they merely checked with the operator—''

"And that's why they sent Buddy Brett to *kill* me.''

"You bet it *is*,'' I said. "And, you know, if you hadn't won the title of Miss Naked California—I mean, if you were not so constructed, put together, marvelously fashioned, all that, so you *could* win the title, and *did* win the title—it is possible that horny Buddy would merely have done you in, without piddling around on the way—''

"So, really, in one sense, it's the way I'm *built* that saved my *life,* isn't it?''

"In several senses. Which, when carefully considered, makes a lot of sense.''

"At least that's true about the first time. But *you* saved me the next time, Shell.''

I smiled.

"They really tried to kill *you,* too, didn't they? Because you saved me!''

"Well . . . partly because of that, dear. But they had a *lot* of reasons for wanting to knock me off. To mention merely one, I saw your mother and brother with Vincent Ragan, at his home, on Friday night. This, significantly, after both your father's murder *and* Brett's attempt to kill you. Also significantly, Ragan knew instantly who I was even then, and tried to allay any growing suspicions I might have had by referring to the lady as Mrs. Green. I'd already shot Puffer by then, but it was immediately after this that Ragan sent Hauk and Virgil Kovick out to fill me with double-ought buckshot at the Spartan. Which doesn't make me feel so bad now about Virgil's poor head.''

''Who's Virgil? His head?''

''Really, none of these things is important now. What's important is . . . um, would you quit fiddling around with those olives, Aralia?''

It seemed a long time ago when I'd had that conversation with Aralia Fields. It hadn't been long, really. Only seven days. That had been the last Monday night in September, and now it was Monday again. But, now, it was October.

The first day, and the first Monday, in October. A mere two days after the Saturday on which Aralia Fields won the title of Miss Naked USA. Of *course* she won it. I know; I was there. It was all quite vivid in my mind: Miss Naked Alabama . . . Alaska . . . Arizona . . . Arkansas . . .

And then:

There she was. . . .

The continuing parade, all the representatives of all the rest of the fifty states, and then the crowning of the queen, hubbub, squeals, excitement, photographers, reporters, a rather pleasant pandemonium.

Especially for Miss Naked USA.

I'd known she was going a long, long way.

Already, she was gone.

In the week since that climactic ''Green Mesa'' Monday, there had been other events of some small interest. Gunnar Lindstrom had kept, in trust, all the profits he'd personally made from the "invention conspiracy," and was making efforts to straighten out patent rights, protection, compensation for those deserving of it, that sort of thing. Complicated, yes, and in some instances now impossible; but he would, I was sure, work everything out as well as it could be done. He wouldn't go to prison, I was reasonably certain; there were compensating factors, many of them, and nobody, really, seemed eager to bring severe charges against Gunnar Lindstrom.

He had continued to make that ridiculous offer to me, about paying me a hundred thousand bucks, all sorts of things. I did work him down to ninety thousand, and we finally settled for that. To his displeasure. He really wanted to give me the whole hundred G's. So, to sort of compensate him for his loss, I let him make me a present of one of the complete laser-and-projector things—with the promise of an entire new camera-and-projector unit with which I could easily make my own 3-D movies, when the unit was polished, perfected, ready for marketing—and one of those films we'd made, too. I'll let you guess which of the films it was.

Odds and ends. Talks with several people—Harry Feldspen, for one. Aralia had been with me then, too. The three of us had lunch at the Beverly Hills Hotel. Among other things, Harry was almost in a fit of excitement about Lindstrom's photographic process—what we know, of course, as the Amber Effect—since he was now aware that the real, living, breathing Aralia Fields he'd seen at the Doubless barbecue had been light only, patterns of light, without substance.

I could see the S-curves and straight lines—or dollar signs—in his eyes as he spoke. "Shell, you just don't understand, this is the *biggest* thing to come down the pike. It's bigger than color, bigger than *sound*."

"Pretty big, Harry."

"Bigger than that. Look, those pictures are so real you can *take* pictures of them, right?"

"Sure. Just like taking pix of the real thing. Lindstrom told me—"

"So now get this. We're shooting on the set. I need the Parthenon, that's in Greece, in the shot. We don't go there. Don't build a piece of it, don't even use a process shot. We use the goddamn Parthenon itself, right? All we do is take a picture of it and *project* the damn thing right there on the set. The real thing, no way to tell any difference. Actor could walk right up into the joint—no doors he's got to open, which of course wouldn't work, could even go clear out of sight behind one of the columns. You get it?"

"Yeah, I'm the guy told you—"

"I never had such a great idea in my life. Parthenon—St. Paul's Cathedral—a street in Paris, a dive in Rome—you need a tree, shoot a tree out there. Goddammit, I'm a genius and *nobody's* going to ever tell me any different. The Taj Mahal? Sure, I'll build it right here—for a buck and a half, sweetie. How does that grab you? And just think for a minute what *I* can do with *Miss Fields* here."

"It would take more than a minute, Harry."

"Throw your imagination lines out and lasso this idea. Can you see that bod of hers, which is starring in a film from a script I supervise to give it the Feldspen touch, the class, the *zoom,* released simultaneous in a thousand theaters? You don't build the goddamn theaters, you show the movie outside on the ground, with seats of course, and project a theater around the whole place. How does *that* grab you?''

"You really want me to tell you, Harry?"

"I've already got a great idea in mind. For Miss Fields, I mean. It's all complete, now I turn it over to some writers to sort of polish it up a little. I wrote it down myself in twenty-five words. Here's part of it: This broad gets here from Venus somehow—the writers can stick that in—and she's used to going around naked. How's it so far?''

"Not very original, judging—"

"Original, original, the dumb writers can stick that in, what do I pay 'em for? Listen to this, it's good. She's naked, a *bee-yutiful* broad, and she's twenty feet tall.''

"Harry, if I hadn't told you about the twenty-foot-tall Jolly Bronzed Giant—"

"She's *thirty* feet tall, O.K.? Now, shut up—"

"How about two hundred and fifty? Hair like tangled mangrove roots in the Okefenokee Swamp, that's in Florida—"

"—now we get to the twist. You got to have a twist, right?''

"Or a broad."

"Where she comes from—she's considered *ugly*. Yeah? Well, all of a sudden she's adored, a goddess, everybody wants to get in her pants. Which she don't have any of, of course. But there's an obstacle.''

"No kidding."

"She falls in love with the hero, vice versa, and he's only five feet nine. No . . . for our audience here—"

"You aren't planning to release it on Venus, are you?''

"He's got to be somebody like Kerry Wilder, he's six-

303

three, no difference. And there they are, madly in love, crazy about each other. How do you like it?''

"How do they overcome this obstacle or discrepancy, this problem, of him six-three and her thirty feet?''

"Well, you dumb—''

"Got it. The writers can stick it in.''

"How do you like it? Really?''

"I think it stinks, Harry.''

He looked at Aralia then. He hadn't been paying much attention to her until that point.

"How do *you* like it, doll?''

"I love it, Harry. Or . . . Mr. Feldspen. I *really* do.''

"Call me Harry.''

That was pretty much how it had gone for those seven days. Scenes like that. Little things here and there. Wrapping up the loose ends.

But now I was sort of at loose ends myself. A little uptight, even. I didn't quite know what to do with myself. It was that in-limbo kind of feeling that comes along once in a while, to everybody. I suppose to everybody.

I was thinking of the last time I'd seen Aralia, though it had only been yesterday, Sunday—last time for a while, anyhow. She'd signed with Feldspen, but her contract allowed her to make "outside" appearances, pick up a little change here and there. We'd been in the front room of my apartment then, too, and she was dressed, packed, leaving for a soon-to-begin national tour—one result of her winning the Miss Naked USA title.

We shook hands. Yeah, shook hands.

"It's been wonderful, Shell," she said. "Really *wonderful.*"

"Wasn't half bad," I said, still holding her hand.

"We'll see each other again. Lots."

"Sure. Can I give you a lift or—"

"Oh, I forgot to mention it, somebody's picking me up."

"Oh? Who—no. Forget it."

"You're an awfully nice guy, Shell. Really. I really, *really* mean it. My sweet Prince Charming Hung How—"

"Yesss, master of *sayonara,* now student of seppuku—"

"Golly, is it *that* late? 'Bye, darling. See you."

Quick peck on cheek. Out the door. I didn't see her out, or down the Spartan's stairs. I was just—just standing there in the middle of the empty room. It was as if something very much alive, wondrously warm, an essential thing, had left and the room wasn't quite right anymore.

And I was standing now, this first Monday in October, almost exactly where I'd stood then, yesterday. Which didn't strike me as a whole lot of progress, not for one of those man-on-the-move type guys.

Couldn't call Aralia. But she wasn't the only babe in the world. Ten minutes later I hung up the phone for the third time and said the hell with it. Mavis had been wonderfully bubbly and friendly, but this was just a bad time. She didn't say exactly why.

Another delighted lovely was packing for a flight to New York, a modeling job there. The last babe I checked on was the worst case of the bunch. She'd gotten married.

It all gave me a kind of chill. A bringdown, that loose ends *blaaah* feeling, a cool wind sighing through the core of my bones.

305

And this wouldn't do; it would not do.

It's splendid to be always optimistic, magnificently positive, right up there on top of the world every minute of every day; it's also impossible. But if you've got a lock on the world, when you know the bruise in the blood or dull ache in your gut is a temporary thing if only you can con yourself into believing it is, nine times out of ten you can tighten those loose ends and warm the chill wind sighing inside, turn the snake of sadness around until it bites its tail and things start spinning, livening up, getting right again.

So I went downtown, into L.A., to the Hamilton Building, and up the stairs to my office. Fed the fish, watched them a while, marveled—for many reasons—at the industrious scavenging of my little *Corydoras paleatus.* Then I hastened downstairs, and into Pete's bar, conveniently next door to the Hamilton Building. It was early; the place was empty.

He nodded, reached for my usual bourbon.

"Give me something else, Pete. Something I've never had before."

He moved a few feet away behind the bar, cocked his head, started picking up bottles. No comment; we'd known each other a long time.

When he placed before me a murky, suitably dangerous-looking concoction in a tall glass, I heard the front door open, then *shoosh* closed. I took a sip of my drink, glancing around to see who'd come inside.

A woman. Tall, dark-haired, young. She'd come in out of the night, and in a strange way it was as if she'd brought part of the night, or dark, inside with her. She sat at the far end of the room, around the curve of the bar, in shadow. It could even have been someone I knew, but the light wasn't bright enough so I could be sure.

Soon she slid from her stool, walked around the curve of the bar and up to me. Tall indeed, and very lovely in an odd, "foreign" way. Full-formed woman's body, simple expensive-looking dress, dark, smooth, smart.

"Do you know me?" she asked. "You were looking at me so . . ."

Well, what the hell, I thought. Nothing ventured—

"Sure," I said. "Don't you remember? We met that glorious weekend in Acapulco. I was diving off a rock—"

"Oh, way up high there, at La Perla?"

"No, it was just this rock. Well, how has it been Madelyn? I mean, of course, how have *you* been?"

"Wonderful."

"I knew it!"

"But my name isn't Madelyn."

"Boy, you don't remember any of it, do you?"

It was a slow smile. Until then she'd been quite sober, serious.

I said, "Why don't we move to a booth? I'll have Pete bring us booze in champagne glasses. Doesn't that sound fun?"

"No. No, it really doesn't. But I think I'd like to, anyway."

"You're starting to remember. Maybe if I describe this rock— "

"You see, perhaps you can help me. I came here, to Pete's, because a friend of mine told me there's a detective who gets bombed here some nights. But he's supposed to be quite good, even if he drinks and all."

307

"What do you mean, and all?"

"My friend said this fellow's name is Shell Scott, but I don't know anything about him. I thought maybe you could help me find him?"

"There's no maybe about it. Lately, there have been several of them around. But, ah, it happens I have some small talent in this detecting business myself—though you would never know it to look at me, would you?"

"Goodness, no!"

"You're not supposed to say that." I stood up. "Come with me."

I led her to a booth, waved at Pete, ordered drinks, waited until they were before us. Then I propped an elbow atop the table, propped my chin against my fist, and, comfortable enough to last through even a long story, looked with interest at her interesting face. And briefly at what is lifelessly called "cleavage," which I haven't mentioned because you wouldn't believe it.

"What would you do with a detective, Madelyn," I asked her, "if you had one?"

She told me.

And perhaps I'll tell you one of these days soon. It was a fantastic story. Almost incredible. You may not believe it. But I think you ought to try—for your own good, of course. *I* didn't doubt what she told me for a minute.

Maybe you remember: If you don't *believe* good things are going to happen . . .